Praise for *Ghosts of Manhattan*

"Mix together Charles Dickens, Theodore Dreiser and Tom Wolfe and you get novelist Doug Brunt and his modern day financier character, Nick Farmer. Faust would have a feast with so many of the people populating Farmer's world—and you will have a literary feast devouring this book."

—Steve Forbes

"After the mortgage bubble burst, if you ever wondered 'What were they thinking?' *Ghosts of Manhattan* provides a thoughtful and thrilling portrait of what they were doing instead of thinking."

—John Stossel

"Awesomeness."

—Kid Rock

"Douglas Brunt . . . is a persuasive storyteller. . . . Reading *Ghosts of Manhattan*, it is easy to understand how the worst of Wall Street came apart. But in Nick's determination to escape his own inevitable destruction we are uplifted and find renewed hope for a cleaned-up world without Bear Stearns."

—Forbes.com

"Former Internet exec Brunt offers up a savage, jaded, and comical depiction of freewheeling Wall Street bond traders during their precollapse heyday in this engaging debut. . . . As Nick's life, his marriage, and the U.S. economy edge closer to meltdown, Brunt brings all the pieces together for a satisfying climax to this compulsively readable novel."

—*Publishers Weekly*

"With his noir-ish debut novel, former broker (and spouse of Fox News anchor Megyn Kelly) Brunt delves not just into the mechanics of the financial crash, but also the mindset that created the explosive state of affairs. . . . A smart shot at the absurdity of Wall Street and the long fall that brought us all down."

—*Kirkus*

"While this is very much a story about greed and moral decay, Mr. Brunt does a good job of making it as much about relationships. To my surprise, I end up rooting for Nick; I want to see him succeed in saving his marriage. I want to see him emerge from the black morass he seems so stuck in."

—*Pittsburgh Post-Gazette*

"[I got] a kick out of reading it . . . we all know people like these in this book."

—Rush Limbaugh

GHOSTS

OF

MANHATTAN

DOUGLAS BRUNT

A TOUCHSTONE BOOK
Published by Simon & Schuster
New York London Toronto Sydney New Delhi

Touchstone
A Division of Simon & Schuster, Inc.
1230 Avenue of the Americas
New York, NY 10020

This book is a work of fiction. Any references to historical events, real people, or real
locales are used fictitiously. Other names, characters, places, and incidents are products
of the author's imagination, and any resemblance to actual events or locales or persons,
living or dead, is entirely coincidental.

First Touchstone trade paperback edition July 2013

TOUCHSTONE and colophon are registered trademarks of Simon & Schuster, Inc.

For information about special discounts for bulk purchases, please contact
Simon & Schuster Special Sales at 1-866-506-1949 or
business@simonandschuster.com.

The Simon & Schuster Speakers Bureau can bring authors to your live event. For more
information or to book an event contact the Simon & Schuster Speakers Bureau at
1-866-248-3049 or visit our website at www.simonspeakers.com.

Designed by Renata Di Biase

Manufactured in the United States of America

10 9 8 7 6 5 4 3 2 1

The Library of Congress has cataloged the hardcover edition as follows:

Brunt, Douglas
    Ghosts of Manhattan / Douglas Brunt—1st Touchstone hardcover ed.
        p.   cm.
    "A Touchstone book."
    1. Financial crises—Fiction.   2. Wall Street (New York, N.Y.)—Fiction.   I. Title.
    PS3602.R868G46 2012
    813'.6—dc23   2012004367

ISBN 978-1-4516-7260-2 (pbk)
ISBN 978-1-4516-7261-9 (ebook)

for Megyn

GHOSTS
OF
MANHATTAN

PART I

And those who were seen dancing were thought to be
insane by those who could not hear the music.

—Friedrich Nietzsche

1 | JERRY CAVANAUGH

November 15, 2005

I CAN'T STAND OTHER PEOPLE HALF THE TIME. I'M NOT a cynical person by nature, but sometimes if you look up, you realize everything around you has slowly been turning to crap. Time screws with everything, and thirteen years on the Bear Stearns trading floor selling corporate bonds can change a person.

There are few careers in life that require a person to be a genius. Business and politics are not among them. Selling bonds and bank debt for Bear is certainly not among them, but I've done it for more than a decade and made a lot of money. It's a lifestyle I knew nothing about before I got here, and I try to keep a barrier between this life and all the people who knew me before. As if I were a CIA agent, other people know only my cover and nothing about how I actually live day to day. They know only that I work in finance and get paid very well.

"Farmer!" I ignore the yell. "Farmer!" Jerry Cavanaugh shouts again from over my left shoulder. Jerry runs the trading desk for the fixed income products we buy and sell every day. Bond

issuances for casinos, airlines, shipping and transportation companies. Stuff like that.

"Nick! Farmer!" It's a thuggish, Staten Island accent, incongru-
ous with a dress shirt, tie, and an annual bonus of three million
dollars.

I turn around with hands in the air and an expression as if to
say I heard you the first time.

"Where are we on the Continental bonds? I want to be out of
that position by the end of the day. What level can you get?"

"Ninety and a quarter for most of it. I'm waiting on a call back
from Chappy." We trade mostly distressed stuff. Companies that
raised a lot of money, hit some hard times, and now the market
wonders if they can pay it all back and service the debt. We factor
in the risk that the company will fail to repay by making a market
for the debt at less than the issued value.

Jerry scowls. "What do you mean, 'most of it'?"

"I'm working on it." I watch the scowl deepen. Jerry has a round,
Irish face, red-brown hair, and translucent white skin like the belly
of a fish. He looks younger than his thirty-eight years, though
I suspect that may be because he's so fat. If he stopped adding
weight, his skin might have a chance to wrinkle. I turn back around
and call my client at UBS who has interest in the bonds.

I like Jerry. Not as a real friend, but as far as spending time with
work folks, he's fine. He has a way about him that he likes to argue
and fight, but in a good-natured way as though everyone should
be enjoying the fight along with him.

I run a sales desk and have five guys working for me—all in
their twenties. We work closely with Jerry's team of traders, ex-
ecuting the buy and sell orders from the traders as they change
their positions. They're responsible for allocating Bear Stearns
capital across these positions, what we call "running a book."

None of this is rocket science. You need to be aggressive and confident and develop a drinking or cocaine habit to help with the socializing. Trading is mainly about having the relationships on Wall Street with other sales and trading guys to get the deals done. That's why there are so many former college jocks—it's a fraternity. It's how I first got the job too. I played lacrosse at Cornell, and a player who graduated a few years ahead of me was a trader at Bear. I had never even met the guy, but he took me in like a blood relation. Lacrosse is a particular favorite on Wall Street, and it helps to have the nepotism extended when you're twenty-two years old and looking for a job.

A lot of traders and sales guys like to point out how stupid they are, that they were always the ones struggling at the bottom of the class but are now the ones making all the money and having the last laugh. They like to attribute it to a different kind of smarts, but it's really only a matter of finding a ticket in and having the will to stay.

A person can lose perspective on the value of a dollar here. In almost any other industry I know, for three hundred thousand dollars a year you can hire a smart, experienced guy to come work for you. He'll work hard, take pride in his work, and live a good lifestyle on that money. Wall Street is different. After a few years on Wall Street, that guy's a loser. After ten years at Bear, if you're not making two million, or five million, you're failing. A guy trading bonds for ten years who makes only three or four hundred grand a year doesn't exist. I've never seen anything even close to that.

Jerry pops me on the shoulder as he walks by. A friendly shot to the arm to say, "Hey, brother, you and I are in the trenches together." Jerry is known for jabs to everyone's arms. I watch him trail off to the men's room, newspaper unabashedly under his arm as his enormous backside fills the aisles between the long rows of desks of the hundreds of traders and salesmen on the floor.

It's an enormous ass with lower back fat coming over the belt. He'd been a good Division III football player in college. He started at Bear just before I did and I remember he was thin then. You have to work hard at eating and drinking to accomplish that transformation—blowing up like a tick engorged on blood.

Jerry passes the food concession shops and rounds the corner to the men's room, the profile of his butt the last thing I see. I don't understand how a toilet seat can be one size fits all. It defies the laws of physics. A skinny twelve-year-old kid could fit in Jerry's back pocket. Whatever seat can support Jerry, that kid should fall right through.

Most of our trading takes place in about 120 minutes, usually in the morning, unless the Fed is making an announcement. I have plenty of time the rest of the day to contemplate such things as the physics of that abused toilet seat.

I lift my eyes up to the ceiling, bored. The Bear trading floor was built to be state-of-the-art when we consolidated offices a few years ago. Ceilings are about fourteen feet high. The trading floor is by the elevators, food concessions, and bathrooms, with two-thirds of the floor for traders and one-third for banking support. On the floor are about five hundred overpaid minions all out in the open, seated like rows of corn, with square columns spaced throughout the massive room, each column with mounted televisions. No office doors, just long tables where we sit side by side, each with our own phones and monitors mounted up in front of us. This way we can stand up and yell directly to whoever may be on the other side of a deal with us. The more monitors you have in front of you, the more senior you are. In theory this is because the more senior traders need to follow more markets, but it's also to signal their status.

Around the perimeter of the floor are offices with a window to the outside world. These offices with actual doors are for management. Some people, like me, are mostly out trading on the floor and share an office. I share one with Jerry and neither of us is in it much. We're mostly on the floor, on the phones.

During the 120 minutes when it's actually busy, it is true madness. So much chaos, yelling, and urgency—so many sources of sound, like walking into a storeroom full of televisions all with the volume up loud. It gets easier over time, though. Like learning a new language.

I see Jerry come back around the corner. Surprised, I check my watch and notice that only ten minutes have passed. Normally these trips of his are like weekend excursions. He walks up next to me and half sits, half leans on the table that is my desk as well as the desk of the twenty others in my row. It strains and bows lower under the weight. For a moment, I worry that my monitors will now slide across the decline to the left and crash into monitors from the guy next to me coming down the other decline to the right and collide at the center of gravity that is Jerry's ass.

"Nick, what do you say we get these guys out for some drinks tonight? Take off around four and head over to Moran's."

Prying my nervous eyes from the monitor that is so far holding its position, I have a sudden and jarring sense of déjà vu. Whether it is the familiarity of Jerry coming over to set up a drinking event, or the memories of a guy in college just like Jerry setting up drinking events, or if I have truly lived this life before, I don't know.

I occasionally get these strong bursts of déjà vu. Depending on my mood, I am either very reassured or very alarmed. In the first case, I feel a sense of comfort that I must be on the right path. In the second, I feel it is a disturbing repetition of the same mistakes I have previously made and failed to correct. Lately these moments have me mostly disturbed.

"Sure, sounds good. I'll get William and Ron to come along." I'm still hungover from last night, but this is usually the best fix anyway. This job isn't much different from life in college, except for the 7:30 a.m. start to the day. That's why it's a younger man's game. It's a hard lifestyle on the body. You need to bank as much cash as you can, then get out by fifty. It's a career that lasts just a little longer than pro sports, and at thirty-five I need to start planning ahead.

Jerry is a little up the totem pole from me. Technically we're peers, but there is more prestige on the trading side than on the sales side. While Jerry will make about three million again this year, I'll make about two million. Not bad for leaving at 4 p.m. to go drinking. And we'll expense the drinks back to Bear.

There is one noble thing about crime. It is the only true meritocracy on the planet. No one in the crime industry cares whether you went to Harvard or dropped out of the fifth grade. They don't look at resumes—you eat what you kill.

Trading bonds at Bear has imperfect aspects of this. Sure, it helps to play lacrosse to get in, and, yes, someone ultimately determines your bonus for you. But for the most part, we eat what we kill. The financial markets aren't perfect. We know how to move money around, take small pieces each time, and make a lot of money for Bear. If I make fifty million for Bear in a year, they should pay me well. Who else should get the money? I made it for them. They seem content to pay me.

I'm happy to take the cash but haven't always been happy doing the job. That's the difference between me and Jerry and what makes him so good at what he does. He's the perfect trader. He has an efficiency of thought. There is an elegant purity to his single-mindedness, the same purity a person would admire in a shark. Nothing in his spirit is at conflict with his profession. This is a real gift for a trader.

Jerry has no distractions, hobbies, or intellectual pursuits. No remorse after nights of booze, cocaine, or strippers. Only fond hazy memories to share over coffee while getting the next trade done. In others you can occasionally see the struggle rise to the surface of a facial expression, the way telling a lie to a loved one can cause a flicker of the eye or a rise in pulse rate. But Jerry is unimpeded. Nothing but clear air in front of him.

At 3:45 p.m., Jerry is back at my desk. Just to the side and behind him is his junior trader Frank Callahan, a twenty-seven-year-old Irish kid from Staten Island. The nepotism continues. "You guys ready?" he asks with a smile that shows he can already taste the first drink.

"What the hell. Let's go." William and Ron hop up immediately. I wasn't aware they were off the phones and listening, but clearly their twenty-something-year-old bodies and fast recuperation rates are ready for another night of drinking.

Off we go, abandoning our phones and monitors and the seventh floor, armed with the knowledge, at least I think we all are, that what we do isn't all that important even if we can convince the world otherwise. We'll spend enormous amounts on drinks and food, tip the waiter the equivalent of a month of his rent, just to show how grand we are. But really we know we don't run any company or build any product. We just found a seam in the economy and know how to game it. If we don't show up to work tomorrow, some other monkey will make the same trades for us.

I go knowing that 4 p.m. drinks will turn into dinner, more drinks, and cocaine. Dinner, drinks, and cocaine will turn into strippers, more drinks, and more cocaine, and I'll be lucky to make it home by 2 a.m. This on a Tuesday. Trading bonds has been hell for my marriage.

November 15, 2005

THE FIVE OF US LEAVE THE TRADING FLOOR LIKE KIDS let out for recess. With a need to cure my hangover, even I'm a little excited to get out of there and get going. The first couple drinks I always look forward to. It's drinks ten and beyond that get me down.

"Nick, slight change in plan." As we ride down the elevator, Jerry cocks his head like he's about to hand me my Christmas stocking. I raise an eyebrow. Nothing is ever slight with Jerry. "Melon's for some burgers."

"You want to go to the Upper East Side?" I live in the West Village. I lean against the wall of the elevator, a little tired at the thought of a long car ride. It's a posh elevator with leather and real wood and brass fixtures. The kind of elevator you see only in the top law firms and the big banks, the companies that make so much money that even after the huge bonus payouts they don't know where to put it all except expensive lobby art and nice elevators. It's the corporate version of the people who make the too-huge bonuses. You can always tell the people who don't know what to do with all their money if they spend way too much on stupid accessories, like a Burberry umbrella. I can't hang on to an umbrella for more than one or two rains before I leave it behind somewhere. Burberry umbrellas and gorgeous elevators. They're really the same goddamn thing.

"No problem. I called a limo—it's waiting outside for us. We'll be there in no time." Jerry loves limos, the way little girls love ponies. I can smell the leather and the polish on the brass.

"Yeah, okay." I feel like the old man. The twenty-something-year-olds are like bulls about to be released in a rodeo, bucking against the walls of the elevator, ready to get a drink on. They still have that youthful reserve of energy that can be called up whenever they want it, no matter what they did the night before. I'm already at the age that I need to grope around for it.

We stroll outside the lobby of 383 Madison and Jerry immediately spots the driver in his little driver hat holding a white sign that has "Cavanaugh" written in black marker. "Here we go, boys," Jerry says, and opens the door for us before the driver can get there to do it for him.

Frank, Jerry's younger, slimmer image, jumps into the car in a sort of headfirst dive. William and Ron go next with a smoother, scissors-kick-style entry. They both have their new tailor-made suits that I can't stand. The suits are snug as can be and the jackets have three buttons instead of two. This is the way fashionable people are getting suits now.

William and Ron both button the top two buttons and leave the third loose. Every time they stand up from their chairs, even to walk ten feet, they go through this buttoning routine. Jackasses. It's at least two thousand bucks to have a tailor run a tape measure around your body and cut a suit from a bolt of cloth. More, depending on the cloth. Good for them for making a nice paycheck, but they should spend it somewhere else. Or at least get a suit with only two damn buttons on the jacket. They look like a couple of mopes.

The driver says there's construction on a few of the avenues going north and it will be better to go out to the FDR. The highways around the outside of Manhattan are the only roads that move reliably, so we take the limo all the way east and, like children who can barely swim and who run around the edge of the pool to get to where they want to jump in, we ride the perimeter of the island north, then exit the FDR to come into the Upper East Side.

Jerry pours out five glasses of scotch from the limo wet bar and hands them out as though answering our ring of his doorbell on Halloween. Everyone ritualistically sucks down the crappy scotch and talks about the trades that happened earlier in the day and the dopes on the other end of the deals. With the limo for the evening and the drinks at Melon's, we are at a price tag of about two grand and counting for the night. Usually Jerry has a broker from Chapdelaine, which everyone just calls Chappy, or one of the other shops take him out for the more expensive nights. He'll have no problem expensing this back to Bear, though. We could call up the Goldman guys to come meet us to talk about the Continental bonds to add some semblance of legitimacy to it, but why bother?

The limo drops us in front of Melon's on Third Avenue at East Seventy-fourth Street. The place feels like it hasn't changed in a hundred years, including the bartenders. I don't mean just the type, I mean the actual guys. It's no frills here. There are no cute, sexy bartenders and waitresses. Here it is old men bartenders who look like they've been around alcohol their whole lives. If you order a mojito you get a glare that holds like stone until you realize you need to change your order. These guys don't know any

GHOSTS OF MANHATTAN | 13

drink that came into fashion after 1950. For them, it's old-fashioneds, rusty nails, maybe a grasshopper for the ladies. The place is narrow, with old New York relics hanging on the walls, rickety chairs, and simple tables with red-and-white-checkered tablecloths. There is a long, wooden, old-style bar running the length of the left wall with two bartenders who are such curmudgeons you have to love their style. We make directly for them. The place is usually jammed up but we're early enough to find room for five to stand huddled at the bar.

Jerry orders two bloody bulls for himself. A Bloody Mary with beef broth mixed in. He always chugs the first and sips the second. He's made this his thing. He loves playing the part. I get Maker's Mark on the rocks. I usually start with beer to ease in but today want a quicker start. Ron and William both get vodka sodas, with Ketel One. Has to be with Ketel One or they get into a snit. Frank, of course, gets a bloody bull, but only one. Two would be to step out of his subservience and encroach on Jerry's thing.

I look over at the jackets of Ron and William, unbuttoned while seated in the limo, now rebuttoned again, but just the top two. Ron and William are both slim with dark hair and small features. They're sort of normal and nice-looking and both give the appearance that they're good kids, which makes them seem twice as devious when they aren't. The main differences between them are in the way they move and in about six inches of height. Ron is about six three and moves slowly like he's stretching his limbs with each motion. His speech is slow to match. William is five nine and speaks and moves in a blur.

"What is it with these three-button jackets? Can't you two wear a normal goddamn suit to the office?"

Blank looks back at me from both of them. Clearly they like the suits and had thought they were making a favorable impression.

I'm feeling a little tired and grouchy and go further. "You're not in Milan. Go to Brooks Brothers and get a normal goddamn suit and save yourselves some money."

Jerry chuckles. He enjoys humor abuse of anything thin and good-looking. The fat bastard looks like he just stepped out of a JC Penney catalog. Ron and William just look uncomfortable. Because I sign off on their bonuses, they are now in the difficult position of having to come up with a witty retort that shows they aren't defenseless but that doesn't piss me off either. Not exactly a fair fight. I feel a rising knot of shame at behaving like a bully, but knock it back down with another sip of bourbon that makes the ice slide against the front of my teeth.

I almost never give these guys a hard time, and they aren't used to hearing me dig at them with an edge. They laugh softly and uncomfortably and feel around for firm footing to make a stand.

"My fiancée likes the suits," William offers. "I go to a tailor in Midtown that her dad always used. She drags me in there once in a while to get a few suits and shirts made. The shirts are stupidly expensive." He shakes his head.

"All for the ladies," chimes in Jerry. He's finished his bloody bulls and his first beer. He used to drink hard liquor but would pass out in bars and on sidewalks. Now if he sticks with beer through the night, he at least makes it home. He's already got the wound-up look of a big drinking night. Jerry's sobriety is like an unstable chemical compound. Pour in a little liquid and it teeters off to something explosive.

"What's your excuse?" I look at Ron.

Feeling the pressure is diffused a bit, he shrugs. "Hey, I just want to be stylish."

"Stylish? That crap will be in the back of your closet in a few years and you'll be embarrassed you ever wore it. Better to be classic than stylish—it's the difference between Mick Jagger and Huey Lewis."

A moment later comes a heavy exhale through Jerry's nostrils— a sort of half laugh to indicate, Good one.

"Tell me about this fiancée," I return to William. My shame is back and winning. Need another drink. "When are we going to meet this gal?"

"We're having you and Julia over on Sunday for the dinner party, remember?"

"Oh, yeah." Crap, I had forgotten about that.

"I'm not invited?" Ron tries for mock astonishment but seems partly serious.

"It's a dinner party with wives. You don't have a wife, and you can't bring a hooker. Jen'll know."

Ron seems satisfied. It's not the kind of party he likes, anyway. Me either.

William turns back to me. "She's great. She's twenty-four, hot, great body. Likes to go out a lot, doesn't mind me coming home drunk all the time."

"That won't last," Jerry tosses in. "Trust me." I think he's refer- ring just to the last point but could be any of them. Anyway, he's right.

William nods to show that he's considered this, then moves on. "Her guy friends from college are sorta lame. They're like young kids, like they could be my little brothers."

"Aren't you twenty-six?"

"Yeah, but there's something about being just out of college like these guys. They haven't had enough time to grow up in the real world." The real world, I think. You mean the limo ride we took to drinks and coke. "The girls seem my age, though. At least my age, maybe older. Weird."

"She does have a tight little body, but that hasn't slowed down your rub and tug routine." Leaving nothing to chance, Ron makes sure the conversation goes to his comfort zone and gives his buddy a shove.

I play along. "You have a massage spot with a happy ending?"

Ron smiles. "Not a spot. The spot. Beautiful little Asian gals, and they're amazing. They crawl all over you."

Jerry leans forward, a little more interested. Frank has just been listening in this whole time and has nothing to offer. He seems like the kind of guy who has never had any ego tied up in girls. Everyone has a role. Helps to get comfortable with it. He just wants a nice, normal girl so he can settle that part of his life and not compete with other guys on it. He'll probably end up the only one of us with a good marriage.

"Where is this place?" barks Jerry. The image of a caramel-colored, ninety-pound Asian girl draped over his pasty enormous form goes through my brain like a flicker of the lights.

"Tribeca. They have a converted loft. A few makeshift rooms and a few gals there. It's open all day. You can just duck over for lunch."

"Get me that address tomorrow."

"Will do." Ron and William stand a little straighter as though they've just been promoted.

Frank cocks his head the way a dog will when you speak to it and it is trying hard to understand your words. "Do you feel like that's cheating?" This is a courageous question, especially since Jerry already showed interest. Honest, from the heart. Maybe this is how Jerry was too, thirteen years ago. I can't remember. For a moment, I start to like Frank. On the other hand, it is the sort of wet-blanket question no one wants to hear and is a conversation killer. Bad form.

"I've actually thought about that, and the answer is no, for two reasons." Conversation still alive. William continues his CPR. "The first reason is simple. If I scratch an itch and no one's the wiser, then no one gets hurt. It's like the tree falling in the forest. It's not cheating unless both parties are involved and you complete the transaction."

It occurs to me that "simple" to him means that any corner that can be cut will be cut. "But aren't you stuck in a relationship covered with itches?"

"But they're mine, it's my business. If I'm okay, the relationship is okay. It's not cheating."

I don't follow the logic but am amused by it, so I let it pass. I've been to a rub and tug too. It's just been about ten years since and I did it twice in my life. I haven't waved it in a few times a week like a turkey sandwich. "Okay, so what's reason number two?"

"Number two is a little more complicated." Here we go. "You have to switch roles in your head. If my fiancée had an itch and she went to some Asian guy, or gal, therapist who gave her a massage, then fingered her to orgasm to help her relax and feel good, I wouldn't care. I don't feel an ounce of jealousy over that. It just makes her happier and better able to deal with me."

I find myself smiling while listening to this. I haven't yet decided if it is sheer lunacy or if there is some twisted genius in what this kid is saying. Jerry has leaned back, slowly nodding, while Ron has an "amen, brother" look on his face. Frank looks confused. The silence from all of us lasts long enough that William just continues.

"Anyway, it's not cheating. Because, what is cheating? Cheating is an affair with someone you know, a personal relationship. Not a professional relationship. An anonymous hooker or massage gal is not cheating."

He says this with the tone of a philosopher, like he's quoting an important passage. The philosophy of William. A one-woman-and-many-hookers man. I turn and get another drink. Not only did Frank not kill the conversation, but we just brought back a red-light district Frankenstein. I'm still pondering William's theory of personal versus professional cheating, or noncheating. I'm struggling to connect the dots. Good for him if he can get some mileage out of professional noncheating and make it work. I can allow that he is on to something in that there are degrees between the two. I don't think I could handle being on the receiving end of my wife having an affair and actually developing another relationship that had more meaning than just scratching an itch.

From this happy thought I begin to suffer from another bout of the syndrome I have recently begun to call "what am I doing in a bar with a bunch of twenty-five-year-olds when I'm thirty-five." Bourbon always helps amplify my mood, for good or ill. In the last twenty minutes it's been heading down, and fast. This is my career. By day I sell paper from companies whose business I don't fully understand and could never run. By night, this. I've developed no real talents. A few people report to me, but the extent of my management skills is to give them a hard time over cocktails. Every time I think I need to get out and do something else, that thought is followed up with the realization that there is nothing else. What the hell else can I do? This job is all I've done for more than a dozen years and I have no other skill, if you can even call this a skill. At least I'm making some money. At thirty-five is it too late to pull out and switch careers? I think better never than late.

"Guys, I feel like crap. I'm going to pull the rip cord and get home."

"What!" in chorus. "Come on. A couple more drinks and we'll head over to Scores. We're already on the East Side." Jerry attempts the argument of geographic convenience after having dragged us all the way uptown. Home is downtown and farther west, so there isn't any advantage for me. Plus it has gotten hard to expense strip club bills and we'd probably have to come out of pocket. And I really do feel like crap.

"Not tonight, guys. Enjoy the club, I'm out." I bolt for the door before they can mount another argument.

November 15, 2005

I GET IN A CAB AND REST ONE SIDE OF MY FOREHEAD against the glass window. It's about twenty minutes from J. G. Melon to home. I watch a few pedestrians that we pass on the sidewalk, then close my eyes and my mind drifts. I remember my first time at Bear Stearns when I interviewed and got the job. It's the kind of memory people can have that feels like yesterday and also another lifetime. The winter of 1992 is my senior year. I drive to Manhattan in my Explorer that has 190,000 miles on it and is worth less than what I pay the garage to park it for three days in the city.

I have two days of interviews set and I'm planning to sleep on the couch of a Cornell friend who's a first year at Bear.

The interviews themselves are a joke. I've never had a job or done much of anything worth interviewing about. I sit with four different traders each day for two days and I don't think they care anything about what I've done before. I was told ahead of time that the main test I need to pass is whether I'm a guy they could sit next to on a long plane ride without wanting to put a bullet in their head at the end of the flight. I'm at Cornell, so they assume I'm smart enough. I play lacrosse, so they assume I'm a good guy. As long as I don't walk in there like a cocky punk but show I'm humble and willing to pay my dues, it should be fine.

The interviews are breezing by and all about the same. They ask about what classes I'm taking, how the lacrosse team is doing, and some useless stock interview questions like what's the hardest thing I've ever had to do, what's my greatest strength, greatest weakness.

For the last interview of the second day, they take me to an office on a floor I haven't been to before. The office is small and a mess with papers and magazines. The desk and chairs look like cheap discount office furniture and they point me to an uncomfortable-looking chair in front of a desk with nobody behind it, then close the door.

I sit in the chair and the room is so quiet I can hear the second hand of the clock on the wall. I'm happy I'm almost through this process and looking forward to getting back in my Explorer to listen to music on the drive back to school. Ten minutes pass and I'm getting restless but want to look cool, so I pick up a magazine and flip pages. It's *Fortune* or *Forbes* and I'm not reading anything more than the captions under photographs. Twenty more minutes pass and I've flipped through the magazine twice. I could get another but I'm not reading anyway.

Another half hour passes. I've recrossed my legs in every possible way to distribute the soreness. I decide to stand for a bit and look at pictures on the wall. As soon as I'm up, the office door opens and a voice says, "Sit down."

I turn to see a massive guy in a suit filling the door frame. Someone had pointed him out to me the day before on the trading floor. The guy had been a tight end for Penn State and joined

Bear after one year as a scrub in the NFL for the Redskins about ten years ago. He's six foot seven, two hundred and eighty pounds. I take a seat. He walks past me and he reeks of whiskey.

He drops into the chair, which looks outmatched, and I imagine it to be anxious about how long it can support him. He eyes me in a suspicious way but he looks too stupid to be thinking anything other than whether he's doing a good job of looking suspicious.

"You want to come work for Bear?"

"I do." This seems like the obvious answer but it also occurs to me I haven't asked myself the question before, nor has anyone else. Maybe he's brighter than I have given him credit for being.

He finds something amusing in my answer and he smiles and leans back in the chair, which responds with an audible panic. "That a fact."

This doesn't have the tone of a question but I nod anyway.

"I've seen your type before. Plenty of times." He shifts again, swinging a leg around the side and banging a foot on top of the desk. I've never seen a shoe like this before. It looks like a kayak wrapped in black leather and flopped across the desktop. Stores probably don't bother to carry shoes this size. I think of the giant bottles of wine the size of a child that aren't really available but are in nice restaurants just for show. He seems aware of the effect his circus-like shoe can have on people, imagining their necks underneath it.

"I don't know what you mean." I hope my voice sounds even. I think it does. I'm still more amused than nervous.

His smile gets a little bigger. He keeps his foot where it is, reaches into a desk drawer, and comes out with a full liter bottle of Jack Daniels and a short rocks glass. He doesn't seem to be paying much attention to me anymore. He pours a little bit and drinks it down, then repeats this. He pours a third and puts it down on the desk, holding it in place with his sausage fingers.

I think about getting up and leaving, but his eyes come back to me and it seems like he wants to talk again. I wait for him.

"And what if I don't want you to work for Bear?" He seems to be getting crazier by the second.

"Then you'll tell someone I was a bad interview."

His shoe comes down faster than I thought possible. The leverage brings his body forward and his hand launches the whiskey at me. It hits me flush in the chest and the vapors of alcohol are in my nostrils. I haven't moved an inch out of stunned disbelief, and we're just staring at each other.

"You want to take a shot at me?" I think he wants to hear a yes.

"Maybe I'll wait until you finish the rest of that bottle."

He pours more whiskey in the glass. I stand to leave before I'm drenched.

"Nick, hang on a second." He stands with the glass and comes around to me. He looks happy and less crazy than a moment before. He seems even taller standing right next to me. He rests a paw on my shoulder but it doesn't seem threatening anymore.

"We're just having some fun. I like to see how guys do in situations under pressure. You did good. Most guys really crap themselves."

It occurs to me that half this guy's job description is to be the hired goon hazing new guys and telling inside-the-NFL stories.

He's laughing, so I kind of smile but I'm not really happy and I smell like booze.

"Let's get going. We're going to meet some guys for drinks." The goon's name is Mark Sauter and he takes me back to the trading floor, where a few guys are standing or sitting on desks in a huddle. Rather than walk to the group, Mark chooses to start a conversation from the maximum distance. "Dave, we're all set! You guys ready?"

Dave and the group get up and close the distance between us. "Good. Let's go to Lucky Strike."

We take the elevator down and Dave, one other trader, and I get into a hired Town Car. The other guy is Sam Curry. I had an unremarkable interview with him the day before. He is average-looking in almost every respect except that he is older than the rest. Even adjusting for the years of booze, I'd guess he's about fifty. With age usually comes seniority and respect, but I've learned with traders there's a crossover point where age starts to signal weakness. Sam seems too old still to be doing this. It makes him seem desperate and I think he knows it, which makes him seem weaker and a little sad.

The others are off to some party, and Sam, Dave, and I take the car service to Lucky Strike, a restaurant and bar in SoHo. It's not yet 5 p.m. when we get there. The opening room is small, with a bar on the right side and lounge tables on the left. The restaurant part is in a second room through a passage in the back wall and it's a tiny room too. It feels like the kind of place that is somehow in style and a movie star with a baseball hat pulled low might come in at any time for a drink at the end of the bar.

We keep the bartender company while she fixes our drinks and cuts fruit to prep for the night. There's no question she's an aspiring model. Despite her long hair, perfect cheekbones, six-foot and size-two body, and the fact that I imagine her skipping through ankle-deep water on a beach in a bikini, she looks efficient and at home behind the bar. She gets our drinks almost gruffly, then knives through a batch of limes and lemons like a samurai, all of which makes her even hotter.

Dave and Sam are trying to be funny and flirty, and in the face of her aloofness they look like homeless children scrapping for a meal. I'm too bashful to say anything stupid in front of any of the three of them.

After enough punishment, Dave tells her to pick her favorite four appetizers and entrées to bring us. It seems like his way of declaring something about that relationship, and then he turns his attention to me.

"You'll love living in New York. It's a pain in the ass if you don't have any money, but if you have some dough, it's the biggest and best playground in the world. You interviewing at other banks?"

"No. Not yet," I add, to sound a little more sophisticated about the process. I wouldn't be interviewing at any banks at all if a buddy hadn't called me to get down here.

"It comes down to people and culture. You want to be at a place with a good reputation but doesn't take itself too seriously and treats people well. Goldman and Morgan are too uptight. You don't want to surround yourself with a bunch of Harvard MBA jackasses. They were stealing each other's library books back in school and they're still the same douche bags. If they're not trying to outsnob each other, they're stabbing each other in the back. Bear might be a level down in reputation but we're one of the best names on the Street and we have a good time. Plus, at Bear, traders are kings. Most of the money at this firm comes from sales and trading, not banking. And believe me, we make a hell of a lot of money."

I don't know enough about any of this even to ask a smart question. "I liked everyone I met. I even warmed up a little to that last guy, who dumped bourbon on me." This is a white lie.

"Ha. You might have to put up with a little of that in the beginning, but it's all fun. It's all worth it too."

"That's right." To this point I hadn't thought about a salary number or getting rich quick. I was just feeling the stress that comes with not having any plan in my last year of college. Stress is always about not having a plan. All I want is something respectable, but I don't know enough to want anything in particular or even to rule out anything in particular. Bear seems to answer all this plus makes me rich.

More people have come in and are filling the bar area. Dave and Sam are so obviously trying to pick girls up that it's freaking girls out. A lot of invitations to their Hamptons house are made, which buys more conversation but ultimately doesn't seem to be working. Dave turns to the bartender and tells her to do an hour of open bar for everyone on his credit card. Everyone in the bar shouts thank you and downs their drinks.

Someone turns the music way up and it gets hard to hear anyone more than an arm's length away. We have to lean toward people to launch our words.

Sam flags over the bartender and plants his elbow on the bar top to pole-vault his head over the drink well. "I'll give you two hundred dollars to turn down that music."

"What?"

"I said I'll give you two hundred dollars to turn down that music."

She straightens up and smiles, then drops her well-used bar rag by his elbow. "You jerk-offs come in here with your comma comma bonuses and think you run the place. The music stays. You can stay or go." She turns to the next person waving for her.

Sam turns to us and sees Dave laughing. I'm trying to be expressionless. Sam says, "Comma comma bonus. Never heard that before. I like it." He laughs. At first I think he's trying to seem unfazed. Then I think he is unfazed. He flags her back over and orders more shots and she pours them. I think she's unfazed too.

The night with Dave and Sam is easy. They seem like they want to like me and I don't try too hard. I just sit and drink with them. It doesn't occur to me, at twenty-one, that it's odd to be pounding shots at 5 p.m. on a weekday with a forty-five- and fifty-year-old. It seems great. It also doesn't occur to me even to ask if they have a family, and they don't bring it up.

"Hotchkiss have a good lacrosse team?" All we had to cover in the interviews was high school and college.

"Not really."

"How'd you get recruited out of there?"

"I didn't. I walked on at Cornell and made the team."

"Good for you. You ever been with a hooker?"

When I'm sure I've heard the question right, I try to imagine what connection there is that I haven't made. I miss only one beat. "No."

"We're going to arrange a little surprise for you tonight."

I notice Sam is on a pay phone by the end of the bar. "Hookers?"

"Don't worry. They're gorgeous."

I order a shot and drink it. Jesus. Hookers. In a short while I'm going to meet a hooker for the first time. It's like waking up on graduation day or Christmas morning, things that always seem far off but then there are no more nights' sleep of separation. In this stretch of awakeness it will be on me.

The driver has been waiting, double-parked outside Lucky Strike. Dave closes the tab and we're back in the car. On the ride I learn that Dave has been divorced for more than ten years and has a place on the Upper East Side. The driver gets us to Dave's building and is dismissed for the night. A few guys are already upstairs in Dave's place drinking.

The three of us walk in the lobby and a doorman says hello,

sir to Dave, then quick-steps ahead to press the up button for the elevator. Dave tells us his place used to be a two-bedroom, then he bought the two-bedroom next door and knocked down the wall to join them and switched it all around to make a huge three-bedroom.

Dave opens the door and ushers us into a mini foyer and long hallway. "Those are all Warhols on your right."

The hall is lined with big framed faces of Indian chiefs and cowboys. Even then, my budding cynical side knows he isn't into Warhol. He's into saying he's into Warhol. Even if only to say it to himself. He needs something of interest. "Nice."

I hear the Rolling Stones at high volume, and at the end of the hall there's a huge living room and the goon, Mark, at the far end dancing in an awkward way that seems more about flexing his biceps.

"Hey, rookie, get in here!"

I give Mark a wave but don't try to shout over the music. It's definitely a single guy's apartment. I don't know enough to criticize but it feels uncoordinated and underfurnished compared to noncollege dorm rooms I've seen. I imagine Dave just called some store and told them to bring over their two most comfortable sofas and three most comfortable chairs in whatever color was in stock and could arrive next day.

Another trader that I interviewed with is on a sofa with his feet up playing a video game. He hasn't flinched and seems oblivious to the music. He's under a spell cast by the TV.

On the coffee table next to his feet is a mound of coke and a twenty-dollar bill that looks recently rolled tight and is fighting to get back to its original flat shape.

Mark walks over and hands me a glass of bourbon with a few ice cubes. "You don't have to wear this one."

"I appreciate that." I wonder if I'll ever come to like this guy. I take a sip. I've never enjoyed bourbon before but it's starting to taste good.

"You did good today, rookie. Not bad at all." He smacks my shoulder way harder than he needs to. He likes to assert his bigness more than other big guys I know.

"Thanks, it was fun. I had a good time meeting everyone."

"Well, the fun's just getting started." He turns to Dave. "Hey, buddy. We're all set in the back room."

"Excellent, excellent. Nick, come this way." Even the guy playing video games looks over and laughs. Like a used-car salesman, Dave puts an arm around my shoulders and pulls me deeper into the apartment. "Okay, pal. This is a little reward from us for doing so well the last couple days. Enjoy, and I don't expect to see you come out of this room for at least an hour."

We arrive at a door down a hall from the main living room and Dave knocks. "Ready or not, ladies." He opens the door, nudges me in, and closes it behind me.

I plant a foot to stop my forward momentum, turn to see the door click shut, then turn back around to see two beauties in silk robes, one blonde and one brunette. "Hi, Nick," they say together and drop the robes, leaving only strappy high heels and naked bodies. I'm stunned by the abruptness.

I had always imagined hookers as being older, missing a few teeth, and belonging in a frontier saloon. These girls are young and athletic and even wholesome by appearance. They could be any girl I'd see on campus except they're twice as hot and naked.

They make their way over in a practiced, slow, sexy way and start rubbing their hands over me. My ears are simultaneously nibbled and it's clear this is a routine they have performed many times. I'm still grasping for my bearings, and I look around the room. It seems both a place for a friend to crash and a place to store random man memorabilia. It has the required furniture of king bed, matching nightstands, desk, a couple chairs, and bookshelves. This is layered over with autographed footballs and baseballs, picture frames attempting to make meaningful some torn ticket stubs to Super Bowls and World Series games, jerseys and posters on the wall—pathetic for a forty-five-year-old. On the top on one bookshelf are a Jets and a Giants football helmet.

I reach my hands around and grab each of their asses. I need to know if this is real and I can really do this. I can't believe how firm and warm they are. I can fit a round butt cheek in each hand. I get a good handle and raise them up and down a bit.

"That's it, baby," in one ear, and the other ear gets nipped by the brunette's teeth.

I have no idea how this is supposed to go. Do we start having sex or are we supposed to discuss it and choreograph some of this up front? I think with three of us there's a lot more to figure out. I keep palming butt cheeks until I can think a few steps ahead. I'm not even sure I want to have sex with them. Maybe we can just do other stuff. I'd always said I'd never pay for sex, but maybe that wasn't a moral issue, it was just something cool to say. Besides, I'm not paying for this.

"You want to lie down, Nick?" It feels weird to have a stranger say my name. A naked stranger. She's a professional service provider who seems to know I'll find it erotic to hear her say my name.

"Not yet." I squeeze a few times like I'm pumping the ball of a gas line. My hands are sweating a little and I can't get over how good their asses feel.

We keep standing, rubbing and squeezing. I'm at the edge of the high-dive platform without the resolve to take the next step. I'm surprised at my own indecision.

"I have an idea." I'm taking back control. I release their butts, walk to the bookshelf, and pick up the Giants and Jets helmets. They're regulation and heavy. "You play for the Giants." I hand this one to the brunette, and the blonde becomes a Jet. Even when I tighten the chin straps for them, there is still room to wobble the helmets around their heads when I shake the face guard.

I take a step back and smile at the enhanced sexiness. Bright feminine eyes peering out from the face masks, with long hair flowing out the back, and slender shoulders barely wider than the helmet leading down athletic little bodies to four-inch heels, their only other equipment. "Okay, let's run some tackling drills. Line up." I line them up across from each other in the three-point stance of an NFL lineman. I insist on their keeping the heels on, which they manage to do though it forces their butts higher and tips their weight over their hands on the floor.

I've never heard of anything as ridiculous as what I'm doing right now. "All right, ladies. On three. Hut . . . hut . . . hike!"

The girls fall forward with almost no force at all but bump helmets before twisting around each other. They're led around by the heavy helmets and look like two naked babies learning to walk and getting tangled up. There's lots of giggling, also by me.

"Nicely done." I give them a hand up and a pat on the bottom. They give me a pat on the bottom back, then repeatedly pat each other's bottoms, chasing around in a circle.

"What's next, Coach Nick?" The whole thing is getting sort of playful and fun. They're actually pretty nice girls, I think.

"We're ready for something more advanced." As I pick up one of the autographed footballs, there's a short knock at the door and Dave walks in. He had to have been prepared for a scene, but even he is astounded.

"Wow." He looks pleased and close to laughter but has too

much respect for this fantasy. I notice he's holding a tray with a bottle of champagne, three flute glasses, and a pile of coke. He puts the tray down on the desk. "I'll let you get back to it."

He walks out and the music that had been vibrating through the walls stops. I hear hard laughter. In a moment there's another short knock and the door opens. This time it's Dave and Mark.

"Goddamn," says Mark. "I like the way you think, rookie."

"Nick, this isn't the way we normally do things, but this is so excellent we wanted to tell you now that you're hired. You'll get an official letter and phone call, but we've made our decision. We want you at Bear." Dave does a military salute and closes the door.

"Congratulations, Nick!" The girls are genuinely happy for me and give me hugs. They seem so nice that I'm feeling uncomfortable about the helmet charade. I help them off with the chin straps and pour three glasses of champagne.

They separate two lines of coke from the pile and inhale it. I see that they're nice but have also been around the block more times than I have.

The blonde splits off a third line. "Here you go, Nicky!"

I haven't done coke before. I don't want to say no to this as well. Since I haven't had sex, and in fact still have all my clothes on, I feel like saying no is too prudish and I should participate. I take the rolled bill and snort the line. It stings a bit like a blast of freezing air, then the sting goes away and my face feels numb and full of blood. By the end of the glass of champagne, I feel amazing.

Without the helmets in the way, the girls manage to rub, nibble, and pull my clothes off. I lock the door this time and we massage each other and I cross every line except actually having sex. The girls are nice enough not to say anything about this one way or another.

+ + +

The next week back at Cornell I accept the official job offer and a few months after that I show up for my first day at Bear. Mark had already left to work for a broker in Tokyo, but Dave and Sam are there and don't retire for a few more years.

In a four-month period I go from knowing nothing about Bear to making it my career. I don't remember consciously wanting it or choosing it. It chose me, as though the system picked me up and put me on a track and all I had to do was roll downhill. I didn't think about whether I was going any place I wanted to be, because I didn't have to work to get there. It was all passive on my part. I just thought about all the guys going to med school or law school and working hard for less money. It was years before I thought anything more about it than that.

I look out the window of the taxi and notice I'm almost home.

November 15, 2005

THE TAXI DROPS ME IN FRONT OF MY GREENWICH VIL-
lage brick apartment building and I see Charlie in his usual spot
by the door and I smile at having made it home. He's worked the
night shift at that same door longer than the six years that Julia
and I have lived here. With each argument that Julia and I have
had over the years, he and I have become a little closer. He has too
much class ever to say anything about it, but I think he likes me
more than her.

For me, Charlie's been a doorman, a part-time shrink, and a
pretty good friend. He's about my height, a little gray, with intel-
ligent eyes, a kind face, and slow, deliberate speech that is comforting. Picture the 1990s version of Christopher Plummer with a
lingering South Carolina accent.

"How are you, Nick?"

"I'm all right." I lean against the brick of the building and cross
one ankle over the other to settle in for a few minutes of conversation rather than head straight up.

"Better shape than last night." There is amusement without judgment in his voice, which I appreciate. "How's Julia?"

Hearing the name in a southern accent reminds me why I don't even like the name Julia much. It feels like counting to three in French. Three syllables make the rest of the world work too hard to talk to you. There's a built-in presumptuousness. "Okay, I guess. You've probably seen her more this week than I have."

"How's that business a hers doin'?" Julia's interior design business is about two years and three unprofitable clients old, and she's managed to turn our extra bedroom and half of the rest of our apartment upside down setting up a home office. This has had me pulling my hair out, which Charlie knows and uses to playfully press my buttons.

"It's a living," I say, wondering in what sense that could possibly be true. "We've got a few things to work out with it. I'm not sure it's a great idea. It's adding some stress in the household." I shake my head like the old men who sit around in barbershops and talk a lot about sports and nothing all day. "What are you going to do?"

Charlie nods his head slowly back and takes a loud, pensive breath like Yoda. I love this about him. "You know I grew up by the water, outside Charleston." I nod. I know this. "You know how you know which way the wind's blowin'?" I nod the other way. I have no idea. "It's the seagulls." He smiles. "You see, seagulls the world over, they always point their bodies straight into the wind. Like an arrow. So, you out on your boat in the harbor, tryin' to get your bearings, and you got to figure out the winds, you jus look over to a seagull standin' on top of a pylon and he'll let you know just exactly where the wind's comin' from." He smiles again and gently pokes a finger into my chest. "Nick, you got to find yourself a seagull."

Clearly Julia is the typhoon in this metaphor. "Charlie, you're my seagull. Why the hell do you think I'm always leaning against this wall talking to your ugly mug?"

Another loud inhale and a soft laugh as a taxi blares its horn on Sixth Avenue behind me. "Yeah? Things are worse than I thought."

In less than a two-hour span, I'd had crash courses in the philosophy of Charlie and the philosophy of William. These are different schools altogether. What's the closest analogue for this contrast? Lincoln to Caligula? Socrates to Torquemada?

"Well, you South Carolinians have it pretty well figured out. Goddamn seagulls." I find that after talking with Charlie for a while, I sometimes take on aspects of his diction. It's infectious. "Pretty well figured out" is not my usual way of talking.

"Life's a little simpler down there."

"Can't you find a way to bring simple with you wherever you go?"

"Most places, Nick. Not here."

I find myself agreeing in the way a person realizes they've agreed with something all their life but haven't been able to put a finger on it before. From this little Manhattan island, the rest of the country looks roughly the same. There is a difference between Manhattan and everyplace else. To make a real change, a person has to move farther into the wild, like Thoreau. Or farther from the wild, like Tarzan coming to town. Or in my terms, from New York City to anywhere else or from anywhere else to New York City. This city isn't like anything.

I've thought a lot about making that move, but there's nowhere else I can do this job. "Truer words never spoken, Charlie. It's complicated here." I give him a jab in the arm, Jerry-style, only I mean it. Maybe Jerry does too, in his way. "On that note, my friend, I'm off to see the wife."

I walk through the lobby and around the corner and take the elevator to the third floor. We live in a brick prewar building with only six stories. I like the low skyline in Greenwich Village. It's one of the few places in the city where you can see a big sky.

The apartment is dark, so I take a tour to every lamp and wall switch to brighten things. I see the coffee table crippled in the living room. I had gotten home late and drunk last night and taken a stumble into it. One of the legs has splintered off and the top has caved in. It looks as though Julia has swept it into a heap for me to deal with later. Julia decorated the place in a French country theme and we have lots of woods and neutral tones in the rugs and the fabrics of the furniture. She wanted to add accents of color, so the curtains and throw pillows are soft blues and red. It feels like a nice place to be.

I round back to the front door and empty my pockets of keys and phone onto the console table. I notice a voicemail from my mother and check it, telling myself whatever it is, not to let it bother me.

*Nicholas, it's your mother. Doesn't your phone let you know
that a person has called even if they don't leave a message?
In the future, if you see that I've made a call, just assume I'd
like you to call me so that I don't need to speak into these silly
recorders. Good-bye.*

I should have deleted without listening. I put the phone down and move to the living room. I don't feel like sitting in front of the TV, so I decide to start a book, which I'm always telling myself would be a good thing. I walk to the built-in bookcase in the living room to browse the titles. Julia's always reading new books and our shelves fill up with them. I want to find something better than a spy novel but still entertaining. Julia always goes in for that kind and I have the thought that it would be nice if we read the same book and could talk about it.

Half-tucked behind a stack of books on the end of one shelf is an old photograph of my family. I'm about twelve years old and sitting on a stool next to my little sister, Susan. We're both in front of my parents, who are standing in front of a background of trees and sky, only it's obvious the photo was taken indoors. It's one of those corny professional photos and there must be about five hundred thousand other families that were plopped in front of that same fake background.

I focus on my mother's face, concentrating on it as though I'm trying to recognize her. It's a handsome face, but I wouldn't say beautiful. It's too strong for that, and full but with hard angles. She looks like she could have been an English queen. Not the gentle, maternal kind, but the kind that could lead her people into battle and be as tough as any king.

There are the first streaks of gray running through her black hair. This is the face of my mother that I remember when I think of her. It's the face I grew up with before I finished growing up away from home at boarding school. I remember that face the day they sent me to Hotchkiss. It wasn't long after this photograph was taken. My parents had wanted to see some show in the city and so they decided to take Susan to lunch and to see the show. On the way they dropped me at Grand Central so I could get the Metro-North train to Wassaic Station, then a taxi to the Hotchkiss campus, which I'd never seen before.

I was scared half to death and I remember standing on the platform with my bags on the ground under my hands, staring at the three of them, when tears started to fill to the brim of my eyelids, enough that my mother could notice. She looked disappointed and a little rushed to get to her show. She put her hands on her hips and leaned forward and said, "Stop playing the victim, Nicholas. Not attractive." My tears drained back inside like someone pulling the stopper on a sink of water.

My dad stepped forward and shook my hand. "Good luck, son."

I looked at Susan, who was crying, and that made me feel better. I kept looking at only her. I was afraid to look back at my mother or I might start to cry again. Finally my dad took Susan's hand and the three of them left.

I hear Julia's keys in the apartment door and I put back the photo and walk away without a book.

November 15, 2005

JULIA WALKS IN STILL WEARING HER WORKOUT clothes from the gym. She had been a high jumper for the Duke track team and her body is even better now fourteen years later. No kids and the fact that she deals with stress and insecurity by scheduling more personal training sessions at the gym have kept her toned.

"Hiya, babe."

"Hi, Nick. Didn't expect you this early." It's 8 p.m. I can't tell if there's an edge to this. It's a neutral tone. We haven't spoken all day so she wouldn't know whether to expect me early or late, but I know my drunken collapse into bed last night and the wrecked coffee table have her angry. She doesn't eat later than 8 p.m. for fear that the meal turns to fat overnight, so I know she's already taken care of her dinner. This is the norm for weekdays. The default is that we're on our own unless specifically stated otherwise.

"Just took the guys out for a bite and a couple drinks, then wanted to get home." I lean over and plant a kiss on her cheek. It's salty from her exercise.

GHOSTS OF MANHATTAN | 41

GHOSTS OF MANHATTAN | 41

"How are they?" There doesn't seem to be much interest behind this question as she moves into the kitchen to get a bottle of water from the refrigerator. Last night must have been worse than I thought. I'm sure I didn't piss the bed, though. I ruffle her hair to try to break through. This is a thoughtless and desperate reflex as I know she hates when I do that, and I jerk my hand back awkwardly.

"Fred Cook called again," she says.

"Did he leave a message?"

"No, he just said to call him. He's very rude."

"He's not rude, he just doesn't have any social graces. He doesn't know anything but math and software programming. Not a lot of gals. Even on the phone with a woman, he gets the way a little kid who's never had a pet will get around a dog. He doesn't know what to do, so everything gets tight."

"Well, why does he keep calling you at home?"

"He's a conspiracy theorist. His job is to analyze the overall risk of the firm and he thinks what we're doing is too risky. He thinks he's Deep Throat."

"Why does he want to talk to you?"

"I think he wants to speak with someone in trading. We're the ones making the risky bets. Plus I've known him for years."

"Can you get in trouble for talking to him?"

"No, the company pays him for this."

"Then why does he have to call you at home?"

Good question. "I don't know. He's just paranoid, I guess."

"Paranoid about what?"

"Freddie thinks we're taking on too much leverage, making bets with cash we don't actually have." Julia has an aptitude for numbers and she seems genuinely interested. Maybe she thinks the more she knows about my career, the better she'll be able to convince me to leave it. "It's like you want to buy a house for a million dollars. You put down two hundred thousand and the bank loans you eight hundred thousand. You pay the bank eight percent on the loan."

She nods. Along with the rest of America, she understands this much already. I go on. "So the bank holds that loan as an asset making eight percent. We're trading in products called derivatives, sort of like insurance, that basically allow us to sell that asset over again. Maybe we sell it four more times, so now it's the equivalent of five people paying that eight percent for a total of a forty percent return. All of this with just the initial two hundred thousand you put down. That's the leverage." She nods again, allowing that five times eight is forty. "As long as the economy is good and people are making their payments, it works. If the payments are missed, then everything fails, not just the original eight-hundred-thousand-dollar loan, but all five million."

It feels good to be having an actual conversation, even if it is work crap. Her mood feels like it's lightening and we're getting past last night. I'm thankful we're in the kitchen and not by the coffee table. "And what's the chance that happens?"

"Freddie's point is that it will happen. It's just a matter of time."

"What do you think?"

"There are always cycles. Eventually it'll cycle down. I don't know if it'll be the apocalypse for Bear that he's talking about. But Freddie's a brilliant guy. He went to Harvard and has a PhD in math from Princeton."

"What's he doing at Bear?"

"Most of the big firms poach these quant guys to do market risk analysis of the firm's positions. Bear pays better than academia. Not every CEO wants to listen to it, but they all have this kind of department in place now. These guys don't fit into the culture very well, though. They're treated like internal affairs."

"That's why he's acting like it's a big secret?"

"We're a public company. If he publishes this report, even internally, it's on the record and someone has to do something about it or they're on the record as ignoring it. Right now nobody wants to hear about it because we're making too much money. Nobody wants to be on the record for something that might bite them in the ass later, but they don't want to change what they're doing either. Freddie's forcing the issue. People might have to choose."

She nods again and seems finished with this, like she's closing a book and putting it down. She turns her head then. "We should call Oliver and Sybil Bennett and set our dinner date."

Crap. We had been seated next to Oliver and Sybil at a wedding in Long Island a couple weeks earlier and managed to have a civil conversation. Oliver's an investment banker at Bear and I know him in passing. He's a blue-blood little snob, someone I'd expect to be a natural son to my mother. He also reminds me of Julia's father. "Babe, I don't want to go to dinner with those two." I can feel the whine in my voice.

"They seem like nice people. He's one of the few people we've met lately who doesn't have to talk about himself the entire time and spent some percentage of the time, greater than zero, asking questions of me and listening."

"I don't think they seem like nice people at all."

"Well, we've said we'd make a dinner plan in the city with them."

"No one actually meant that, did they?" I truly believed that no one did.

"Of course they did. And we did. At least I did. Nick, I want us to make more friends in the city, especially friends that aren't Neanderthals." This reference needs no clarification. We've had plenty of talks about my job and the sort of people it forced into our lives. "Just please call Oliver and make a plan."

"I'm not calling Oliver. You call Sybil." Damn it. My counter-move has opened a door.

"Fine. I'll call her."

"Jesus Christ. I don't want to do this." I really don't. Not only would dinner be painful but there's something about Oliver that I don't want to invite into our lives even more so than the Neanderthals.

"Look. I'll just make one call and make the offer. If it doesn't go anywhere from there, so be it." She says this in a conciliatory tone as though we've reached a compromise, though we still seem to be entirely on her agenda as best I can tell.

"It's already forgotten. Why mess with that?"

"Nick, we can't be flakes. We'll hold up our end and make an effort at follow-up."

There is a forced and artificial casualness about her approach that is unsettling. She is pinning her determination on social etiquette. Since when has she ever cared about being a flake? She wants this dinner to happen for some reason and I know it isn't the reason she's given. I think of J.P. Morgan's observation that there are two reasons why a person does something—a good reason and the real reason. She holds her stare with me, one eyebrow up, defying me to knock her from the social high ground of good manners, as if to say, "You know I'm right and we have to do this."

I know no such thing, but it's time to get out of bounds. Better to put this into the loss column and not fight. Maybe I can win a few points and get out of my hole from last night. "Christ, okay. Call her."

"Thanks, Nicky." She smiles, trying to be a gracious winner. Instead, I feel mocked.

She stands and I see her tiny workout shorts, the kind that stop right at the seam between the end of the buttocks and the very start of the hamstring. She takes two steps toward me the way a kitten will approach a ball of yarn and slides one of her long, tan legs around behind me. She wraps her arms around me, resting her elbows on top of my shoulders. I lower my hands to cup her butt over the mesh of her shorts, like grabbing two not yet ripe cantaloupes.

My blood is up and I'm angry from our sparring over this dinner with Oliver. As usual, my aggression is channeled into an almost make-believe world where every muscle and nerve can lose control in violence and conquering while still getting and giving pleasure, release, and intimacy. This is a tactic Julia often uses, and one that has always enabled us to bury the awkward moments and stay happy. I'm not complaining.

At five ten and in her very high heels, we're almost eye to eye. I like times like this when she is in her bare feet and I can lean slightly forward over her and pronounce my height advantage. She pulls down on my neck and runs her lips from my chest to my jaw with the touch of a feather. I squeeze her ass, lifting her up and into me, and with her legs around my waist I walk us into the bedroom.

On the way, I pick up a bottle of lotion from the bathroom counter, then pulling her clothes off, I push her lying facedown on the bed and straddle her lower back. I squirt lotion on my hands and into her shoulders. Her hands over her head with palms down as though she's under arrest, I feel the hard muscles under her soft skin. I press down on the sides of her gentle V that leads from her shoulders to her small waist and back out again over her hips. I lower myself to sit over her calves while I spend more time working on the muscles of her butt. The longer I massage her, the shorter I'll last, so I move on to the hamstrings and calves, giving them less attention than they deserve. Sliding my hands back up her legs, over her ass, and around her waist, I lift her hips up off the bed and back to me, her ear still to the mattress as though she's listening for a far-off herd, and her arms stretched straight ahead with her palms pressed down hard and ready to push back.

I enter her from behind. The first, slow entry always feels almost as good as the last will. I clamp my hands to her sides at the bend of her hips, controlling her motion. I'm like a captain at the helm of his ship, navigating the rolling waters onboard the envy of the fleet. She starts massaging herself with one hand.

Why the hell is she so keyed up on this dinner with Oliver Bennett? It has nothing to do with Sybil, who's as dull as a spoon. Julia barely paid any attention to her at that wedding. I'm sure she's interested in some new friends who have something different to offer from Jerry Cavanaugh, but she seems unusually interested here, like she's trying hard to seem uninterested.

I've developed a strong inner monologue living with Julia, especially during sex. I just can't always control the subject of conversation. I increase the pace, pulling back hard on her hips and straining my stomach muscles to throw myself forward in a thud of flesh. Each collision sends a minor tremor up her lean backside and the bounce forward of her body gives an appealing resistance to my next pull back against her hips and we build a rhythm like dribbling a basketball.

Looking down at her back and ass, I can imagine this same form in its college days, clenched and springing over the high bar. This is a visual that has sustained me, even when alone. With enough foreplay, this position can bring Julia to orgasm and sometimes we don't adjust. In a few thrusts, I hear her moans that are our verbal cue that she has come and that I can finish. I've felt on the verge since the beginning and in a few more thrusts I'm done.

I lower forward, stacking my shoulders on top of hers, and we press our hips down flat on the bed and in another moment I'm no longer in her. The sweat between us feels slippery and good and I kiss the back of her neck but neither of us says anything. There's no conversation topic at the ready. I don't want to talk about my workday and I certainly don't want to talk about that god-awful dinner plan. She's already settled her victory there and won't bring it up again. Why force a conversation? I roll off her and enjoy the silence.

We used to wake up late on a Saturday with nothing planned and decide to drive four hours to Maryland just for a crab dinner that night. Or out to the Hamptons to rent a boat so we could spend the day sailing naked, swimming, and sunbathing. It was a standing decision to be together that was binding like a country of citizenship. It was our relationship that we loved. We were committed to it, worked for it, took pride in it, would take up arms to defend it. We each brought energy to the other, and each evening or weekend was a mini adventure with my companion and confidant. We were two kids masquerading as adults.

When we met at twenty-seven, she loved her career working for an interior designer in the city. When we married at twenty-nine, she seemed to care much less about work. She still worked but seemed to want to focus on family and a great marriage. I was already making good money and she knew plenty about the lifestyle of my job, but everyone thinks they can change a person a little. Just enough to suit them. She has tried with me in the years since, less and less over time. The less she tries with me, the more she disappears into her design books or the gym.

I don't believe in fate and I don't believe there's just one person out there for each of us. I also don't believe there are very many. Maybe there are a few hundred in the whole world who can really be the person to find their way to our soul. How many opportunities, chances, encounters are we likely to have in our lifetimes to capture a moment with one of them? Maybe there are only five or six events in our lifetime when we have a glimpse of someone who could be that partner. I know Julia is one. Our chance for each other came early and I worry that we can't sustain our bond as we have grown into adults.

I put her through more headache than she deserves. Not many thirty-five-year-old wives have husbands that routinely flop into bed drunk in the middle of the weekday night as a part of the job. And worse yet, I doubt many wives have husbands who experience the world so privately, not sharing any observations or conclusions or real feelings. She knows I don't like my mother, and when she asks why, I say it's because my mother's a pain in the ass. I'm sure I can be frustrating to speak with.

I look over at her sweet face, eyes closed, lips slightly parted like a child sleeping. I still love her very much. I feel it in a swell, so strong that I discover I suddenly want to exclaim it to her, like a sailor first sighting land after long months at sea.

I reach down and squeeze her hand, hoping I can pass this swell to her in a current, like plugging in Christmas tree lights. She squeezes back. "I love you, Nick." That felt good. Could this be so simple?

"I love you too."

She rolls toward me, laying an arm and a leg across me, and angles her chin on my shoulder. "Your sister called. She needs to move the party back by an hour. Something to do with a soccer game with the kids."

"Okay." I had forgotten about her party and am now looking forward to it. My sister, Susan, is so much like me, only so much better. Mainly we have the same sense of humor. She's two years younger but I always included her with my crowd of friends. Even among my closest friends it was she and I who were in on the silent joke. No one else in the room could speak our language of glances and nods and lips curled in a half smile. Speaking with her is like a window into a healthy me. One who hasn't polluted himself. "It'll be great to see them. Been too long." She and her husband and kids live in Pelham. We rarely make the thirty-minute drive north out of the city to their house.

"She has a home and kids and a normal life." Julia says this with her eyes still closed and the words come out as effortlessly as breathing. This doesn't require deduction. She felt she was just stating the obvious reason why we hadn't seen Susan for so long.

Julia and I haven't talked about kids of our own in years. We've always brushed it aside, saying there's time and we're having too much fun living a city life in Manhattan. Actually I'm terrified I'll be a complete bust as a father. I think she secretly thinks the same. If her comment is an invitation to talk about kids, I'm declining.

I give her hand another squeeze, then release and run my fingers through my hair, stopping with my hands behind my head. Fixing Julia's dissatisfaction with our lifestyle will not be so simple. I realize this, truly realize this, for the first time. Panic is setting in and my eyelids are stretched wide open as though I'm trying to see more of the ceiling. I've always been able to count on at least one part of my life going well. If I was unhappy at work, I could come home to Julia to feel her healing. If Julia and I fought, I could go to work to forget and enjoy mindless therapy. Like the air of a balloon when one end is pressed down, I can escape to the other end. I can't have both work and home turn bad at the same time. I know I'll go to pieces.

"Let's go out." This suddenly seems like the thing to do together.

"What are you talking about?"

"Let's get out, go for a drink somewhere."

"Right now?"

"It's only nine thirty. Someplace casual, just put some jeans on."

Julia and I have never been one of those couples that has to do social things only with other couples. We like when it's just the two of us. I prefer it. We sometimes go out to dinner and I look at other couples sitting in silence, staring at their soup with an unhappy expression, and then I look back at Julia and realize I have a pretty good thing. We have stories and laughter and then some silence that is in appreciation of everything else.

Sometimes we go out and get a little drunk together. Not college, puking drunk, but a few drinks. We've loved going to the Hog Pit for years, and we decide on that for tonight. It's a bar that could be in west Texas. It's got a sort of swinging saloon door, only really it's just a rickety old door barely hanging on to the hinges. The front room has a long bar running along the left wall, lined with bar stools. The rest of the room is little tables and a jukebox with a good amount of country. A hallway in back passes by the bathrooms, then opens to another room with a pool table, foosball, and a few pinball machines.

Most places in Manhattan charge at least eight bucks for a beer. Here it's two for a Pabst Blue Ribbon. We take two bar stools and order two beers. The bar is full of some younger kids out of college who don't yet make enough money to go to nicer places, and some older folks who don't make enough money either.

We take our first sips quietly. I know there is this evolving problem between me and Julia, and like most guys I'm frustrated that fixing it isn't as simple as turning wrenches in the physical world. It'd be nice if I could make a few tweaks to the motor, maybe change a fan belt, then turn it back on, slap it on the side, and say, Yup, this baby's running fine again. It won't be so easy. We're outgrowing the lifestyle my job has created and this tension is a deterrent to us growing in any other way, including having kids.

We're noticing all the off things about the people around us, which is a fun game with Julia in a place like this. All the while I'm searching for my verbal quick fix tools like a klutz.

I should just engage her on it. She's a trusted listener and she needs me to talk about it, but I'm waiting in front of it like a cold swimming pool, trying to work up the nerve to jump in. I start the jumping motion a few times, then step back and tell myself just jump in, once you're in it's fine.

"I'm going to go to the bathroom. I'll be right back."

"Okay."

The bar is filling up and I weave through some people on the way to the men's room and stand in front of the urinal staring at a 1980s poster of a blond bombshell in a Budweiser bikini and a hard hat while I come up with my game plan.

I walk back toward the bar stools and I see Julia raising her voice to a guy sitting on what used to be my stool. I come up behind them and hear her holler, "That is my husband's seat. We're still using it. Please move."

The guy is ignoring her and trying to get the attention of the bartender to order a drink.

I put my hand on his shoulder and give enough of a squeeze to let him know that my hand isn't going to move away. "Hey, buddy. You're in my seat."

I've learned in almost all cases you don't have to fight. You just have to convince the other guy that you really will. Sometimes in a place like New York you run into a crazy person who really will too, and worse yet might have a knife or some other crap. But I'm pretty sure this kid isn't that way. He's just a little geek who's had too many two-dollar beers already.

He spins around to me, keeping flush on the stool. "I don't see your name on it."

I slowly reach up and squeeze the hell out of his nose and hold on to it. "It's written right under your ass. Stand up and I'll show it to you." I've got an excellent grip on his nose. I feel like I could pull it right off his face. I squeeze harder.

"Okay, okay." His voice sounds like he just inhaled a helium balloon. Julia half laughs but I'm still trying to act like a tough guy.

I lead him by the nose to the side and off the stool, then let him go. He reaches for his nose to make sure it isn't bleeding and walks away to a table.

I sit back down, half-turned to keep an eye on him. "I hope he doesn't have a bunch of enormous friends back there playing pool."

"My hero." Julia clinks my bottle, takes a sip, and orders two more beers. I'm still watching after the guy and feeling less tough than I was a minute ago.

"Don't worry. If there was going to be a fight, it would already have happened."

"I guess."

I turn back to the bar and look at Julia in time to see her eyes go over my shoulder and she says, "Uh-oh."

I turn back around expecting to see muscles and a tank top and instead it's an overtanned Italian-looking girl with huge black hair and crazy blue eye shadow. She has on what could be just a bra and leather or plastic pants that look impossible to get in or out of. The guy I removed by the nose is right behind her and looks like he's trying to slow her down, but she gets right to us.

Her accent is just what I expect. Nasal and Staten Island. "Oh, big tough guy, tweaking noses. You loser. What kind of a creep even does that?"

Julia gets off her stool and gets between me and this thing. Her movement is slow and nonthreatening. She just places herself there, which doesn't surprise me at all. Julia always gets my back. She always fights for me first and only later does she ever wonder whether or not I was in the right. I love that about her.

"Your boyfriend took my husband's seat, and he knew it. My husband just taught him some manners."

The thing puts a finger right in Julia's face. "First of all, bitch, he's not my boyfriend. Second of all," and she wags the finger, "why don't you shut your mouth before I smack you?"

Julia doesn't flinch from the finger wag. She doesn't even look at it but keeps eye contact and her expression only gets more calm. It's clear the girl is waiting for a response from Julia and it's clear Julia is about to give one. "Why don't you . . . pluck your eyebrows?"

The conversation pauses like a needle scratch and we all look at the thing's eyebrows. They stand out as pencil thin against her thick head of hair. They look perfectly waxed. Impeccable.

The girl's eyes seem to roll back to get a look and check in on the eyebrows too. Her face looks terrified.

The guy with the tweaked nose lets out a moan and looks at the floor. "Oh, God."

The wagging finger is long since back to her body and playing defense. She turns on a heel and runs back to the girls' room. Two other girls from a table nearby run in after her. The nose guy retreats back to a table and Julia and I are left standing alone, shoulder to shoulder, as though everyone else had just been carried off by a tornado.

"My hero."

She looks at me. "I couldn't have you trading blows with that insane person."

"Should we get out of here before round three?"

We turn back to the bar. It's pay as you go here so we have a small pile of cash on the bar top that has been changed back. I pick up a few bills to figure out a tip, then decide just to put them all back down. We take a last sip of beer and before we can get away from the stools, the women's room door opens and the Italian girl comes out with mascara spread around her eyes and goes directly for the exit, followed by one of her girlfriends. The guy at the table gets up and goes after them. The last girl comes over to us.

"I'm sorry, but I have to know. How did you know to say that? What made you say it? We just looked at her eyebrows in the mirror. They look fine."

Julia shrugs. I guess she isn't going to explain her genius.

"There's nothing else you could have said that would level her like that."

Julia isn't gloating but she isn't saying anything either. I offer, "Is she going to be okay?"

The girl nods, still amazed at the exchange. "I think so." She turns for the exit after her friends.

Julia sits back down. "Another drink?"

"On me, darlin'."

November 20, 2005

WILLIAM LIVES IN MURRAY HILL WITH HIS FIANCÉE, Jen. It's a new high-rise, doorman building on Twenty-ninth Street. Everything is new and nice in those buildings but they have no character, just a set of box-shaped rooms stacked next to each other, and it feels sterile.

He invited us to this dinner party forever ago, so it's hard to avoid. I'm always rude about asking who else is invited to these sorts of things because I like to prepare for how much of a nightmare the evening might be. These nights are always lousy for Julia but relative to other work dinners this shouldn't be too bad. William and Jen are hosting me and Julia, Jerry Cavanaugh and his wife, Alison, and Conrad Bradbury and his wife, Janice.

The night seems like a butt-kissing opportunity for William to advance his career. The title hierarchy at Bear goes associate, senior associate, VP, director, managing director. William's a senior associate, which is normal for a young guy. Jerry and I are managing directors. Conrad is a trader on the foreign exchange desk and is either a VP or director. William is always networking, which is why he's a natural sales guy.

I don't know Conrad Bradbury very well. He's a southern guy and seems to come from money. He likes to wear seersucker around to claim his southern roots. His southern accent is softened and refined by years of living in the North. He's skinny and sort of frail but not in a feminine way and he has blond hair that he's always touching. He never runs his fingers through it, he just smooths it over with his palms.

Conrad and Janice get to the lobby at the same time as we do. He and I are both holding a bottle of wine. Conrad's a good-looking guy and I would have thought that with the money he's making he'd have a hot wife, but Janice is just sort of average.

That's the funny thing about Wall Street wives. There are almost no tens. They all have plenty of money, so they dress well and have expensive handbags. They go to the gym and are usually pretty toned. They compete on looks as best they can, but you almost never see a ten. When someone on Wall Street has a hot wife, it's a big deal and talked about. It's rare enough that people at Bear know which guy at which firm does. Nobody trading at Bear does, though Julia is talked about some. Nobody on the desks at Goldman or Chappy does. There's a guy at Merrill.

Janice is just finishing her cigarette. She takes a final drag, which nearly ignites the filter, then snubs it out in a trash can by the elevator.

"Hey, Conrad. This is my wife, Julia."

"Nice to meet you." He does a quick up and down of her. Poor guy can't help it. "Nick, this is my wife, Janice. Janice, Julia and Nick." Conrad has a deep voice that pronounces the southern drawl.

We all shake hands as the doorman presses the button to call the elevator and tells us William and Jen are in 22C. We ride up in silence and Janice reeks of cigarette smoke. It's in her clothes and I'm sure by the end of the night it will be in mine the way it was going to a bar in the nineties.

We get off on the twenty-second floor and ring the doorbell at C. William answers looking very sophisticated.

"Evening, gents. Ladies." He's wearing a blue blazer with a handkerchief neatly tucked in the breast pocket. He and Jen must be feeling very grown-up that they're hosting a dinner party, like they're a real couple.

We walk in, shake hands, and deliver the wine, and each of our wives gets a kiss on the cheek. Jerry's already in the living room drinking from a bottle of Budweiser. His wife, Alison, is sitting on a two-seat sofa also drinking a beer. I've met her once before, so I go over to say hello and introduce Julia.

It's a two-bedroom, two-bath apartment and the living and dining rooms are combined into a single larger box of a room. William and Jen have put some extra leaves into the dining room table so it stretches across most of the space, and the sofas have been moved up against the wall. Julia and I circle the dining room table to get to Alison.

She's better-looking as a woman than Jerry is as a man. She doesn't have brittle-looking red hair for a start. She has short brown hair and a round face, round eyes, and dimples. She's short and a little chubby but looks like she may have been athletic. Maybe a soccer player. Overall, cute, and nicely done for Jerry. She's very pleasant and seems to have a go-along-with-it kind of attitude. Probably the kind of wife who doesn't like football much but ends up watching it all day Sunday anyway.

As we're talking, Jen walks into the room from the kitchen wearing an apron. "Hello, everyone. We'll be serving dinner in about twenty minutes."

William jumps in, raising his drink. "We ordered from Smith and Wollensky."

I can't imagine Jen planned to keep a secret that she's reheating restaurant dinners from up the street, but she looks a little irritated at William's interruption.

"In the meantime, William can fix you all a drink."

"Yes, what can I get for you all?"

"Ya have any white wine?" Janice asks this in a tone as though she expects the answer to be no.

"We have sauvignon blanc."

"Okay. One of those."

"Julia?"

"That's great for me too. Thanks, William."

"Nick, bourbon?"

"Thanks."

"Conrad?"

"Vodka soda, lime."

Janice chirps up again. "You mind if I smoke?"

William's face says please don't do that in my apartment. "Sure, no problem."

Jen is tugging and restraightening her apron. "Maybe you could just do it by the window. William, will you crack the window and get Janice an ashtray?"

"Sure." William looks around for an ashtray, which they don't have, and ends up coming back with a cereal bowl. The winter air through the window feels good. The living room isn't meant for eight people and was getting stuffy already.

Most of us get to our second or third drink standing around the room. Conrad's on his fourth vodka soda. I don't know why it takes so goddamn long to reheat a dinner from a restaurant. Julia had started out talking with Janice but after suffering a few minutes of smoke had moved on to Alison and stayed there. Janice likes to talk with the cigarette still in her mouth. Her saliva has formed a sort of adhesive on her bottom lip so the cigarette can dangle from there even if the top lip isn't holding it down. When she talks, the cigarette flips up and down so you can't possibly pay attention to a word she's saying, you just watch the cigarette move like you're being put under hypnosis. She's in the habit of starting to talk before the smoke has cleared her lungs, so the first words are accompanied by white vapor and she seems to like the effect. I think she's somewhere between a college girl trying to look cool and true trailer trash.

William finally comes out with the first few platters and he and Jen ask us all to sit anywhere at the table. Jerry, Conrad, and I all instinctively pull back chairs for our wives. We know how to play the part of a gentleman. Wall Street guys may play around with strippers, but we know how to help our wives on with a coat, out of a cab, and into a chair. Maybe when the wives are rationalizing why they stay with us, this gives them something to hang on to.

Julia's great in these situations. She has interesting things to say and she doesn't have to talk too much or too little. If she's next to someone who talks constantly, she doesn't mind saying little. If she's next to a shy person, she can take on more of the load.

Conrad keeps putting away the vodka and has gotten wrapped up in telling us about the year he lived in Tokyo. His voice has gotten so loud that it's the only conversation at the whole table, and he seems to think we're all fascinated.

"Japan is the best. Women are so subservient there. Every day a couple women would come over and clean my place, fold all the towels, lay my clothes out on the bed. In the evenings they'd give me a massage. Whenever they leave or enter a room, they bow to me." He takes a drink and looks thoughtful. "I really developed an attraction for Asian women there. Seriously. Not just to the way they act to me, but physically. I really got to like the look. The funny thing is those Japanese guys love blond American women. Some low-rent blond model here can go make a fortune in a Tokyo strip joint."

Janice looks uncomfortable. Even the guys are squirming. These are the kind of conversations we try to avoid having with our wives in the room. Nobody gives Conrad a prompt to continue the conversation but it doesn't matter.

He seems to have picked up that Janice isn't happy, so he addresses this for the benefit of the table. "Janice doesn't mind. She knows I have an Asian fetish. The best part is, she actually likes my Asian fetish."

I don't know if William is curious or if he's awkwardly trying to help. "Is that right, Janice? It turns you on that Conrad has yellow fever?" William is laughing along with it and misses an angry glare from Jen.

Janice doesn't know how to respond but Conrad answers for her anyway. "Oh, she digs it." He takes another sip of his drink. "Trust me." His voice gets deeper and more southern.

Jerry's wife, Alison, chimes in. "I have a theory about guys with an Asian fetish."

"Oh?" says Conrad.

"The guys who develop an Asian fetish are the guys who can't get laid any other way."

Jerry and I laugh out loud. Conrad isn't laughing but isn't taking offense either. He's thinking over the merits of the theory.

"No," he says. "That's a lot of bull. Some guys just like Asians. It's that simple."

Janice looks fully embarrassed. I don't know if she's embarrassed about this absurd conversation or if she really does dig his fetish and she's embarrassed that we now know about it.

"Jen, where are you and William going for your honeymoon?" Julia tries to get the table talk back under control. I hope it's a trip anywhere in Asia.

"We're thinking about Hawaii or Turks and Caicos."

"Fantastic." Julia tries to keep it going. Jen looks stunned and can't seem to get a thought together to participate further.

"Turks and Caicos." Conrad slaps his hand on the table. His buzz is huge. I don't think it can be cured with food or coffee and we're stuck with it for the night. "What a place."

We all nod, waiting for the story Conrad obviously wants to tell. "Janice and I went last year right after the bonus check came in." He pans around the table, giving each of the guys a look. "It's the last windy I got. The next one will probably be when I get the next bonus check. The only time I ever get a windy is with a big bonus check." Conrad starts laughing like it's part of the joke and should make it funnier for us.

Jen picks the wrong time to get curious. "What's a . . ." She gets the euphemism for fellatio before she finishes the question. "Oh."

I look up at Julia, who has her nose in her wineglass taking a sip. I can tell she's in disbelief that a night like this can be part of her life. I hear a thud from the other end of the table. Janice's fist has hit the table top and her hands are now pressed against her ears.

Conrad puts his hand on her shoulder. "Hey, babe."

She smacks his arm away. It isn't just a leave-me-alone smack. It has real rage. "You're a bastard! A sick bastard."

"What the hell?"

There's about thirty seconds of silence. This is pretty accurate because after a pause I actually start counting and get to twenty.

Then Janice straightens up and composes herself and looks around the table as though she just arrived and is greeting us all for the first time. "Excuse me."

William, Jerry, and I all do a half stand, then sit back down. Like a gentleman, Conrad gets all the way up and helps her with her chair and she goes to the bathroom.

Conrad sits back down and exhales a big breath. "She can get like that."

"I wonder why." Julia looks at me wide-eyed and I realize I said this out loud.

The silence is making everyone fidget and stare at their plates, so Julia tries to break it. "Jen, this is a great apartment. How long have you and William been here?"

"About four months."

"You've done a nice job with it."

"Thanks."

Silence again.

I look at William and give him a nod to get us out of this, which he understands. "Why don't you all take your drinks into the living room while I clear the table and bring out coffee? Also, if you're interested, the elevator can access the roof and there's a great 360-degree view of the city."

Since the living room is also the dining room, I'm tempted to go to the roof but it's too cold out and I'm sure it's windy as hell up there. I stand and take Julia's hand and we walk a couple steps to a sofa and sit down. Jen and William are clearing plates and Alison decides to make herself busy and helps. Jerry comes to join us and Conrad doesn't move from his seat. He seems to be getting into the tired drunk phase, which is better for the rest of us.

Jerry, Julia, and I have a decent conversation about benign things like the subway and tunnel congestion. It's talk for the sake of talk but we all rightly have the attitude that we just need to get through this.

It's probably twenty minutes before Janice is back. William turns on music and serves coffee and port. We might salvage a half-decent hour before the end of the night, but I need a break first and I excuse myself for the bathroom. I don't need to use the toilet, I just want to kill a few minutes, so I wash my hands and splash my face. I'm drying with a hand towel when the door behind me bangs open and Jen steps in. She looks everywhere but at me and she looks determined. Still not looking at me, she steps to the shower and yanks. All the curtain rings screech to a bunch at one end. We both look into the empty shower, then finally at each other.

It's her apartment, but at the moment the bathroom feels like my territory. I dry the last of the water from my face. "What's up?"

She looks hesitant for the first time. "Where's William?"

This is not a question I expect. "He's definitely not hiding in the shower while I go to the bathroom."

"I think someone brought cocaine here tonight."

I can neither confirm nor deny this, so I don't say anything and I hang the hand towel back on the bar.

She looks at me until she's sure I'm not going to say anything, then walks out angrier than before. I close the door, reclaiming the bathroom for a moment of peace. I decide to take a seat on the toilet and count to sixty. I'd count more but I can't abandon Julia that long. Before I'm halfway I hear Jen shouting from the living room. It's time to find Julia and get out of here, so I open the door.

William has his palms up like he's trying to signal oncoming traffic to stop. "Jesus, Jen. I just showed Conrad the roof deck."

"And you stuffed cocaine up your nose while you're at it."

"No!"

"Don't lie to me!"

Conrad looks guilty as hell and is too drunk to hide it. He won't be any help, but he tries. "Hey, Jen. What's the big deal?"

"Shut up, Conrad. You're an ass and I want you out of my home!"

If William hadn't been doing coke on the roof, he would put a stop to that. Instead he raises his eyebrows to Conrad in apology, which is the same as pleading guilty and throwing himself on the mercy of the court.

"William, we need to get going too." I glance at my watch as I say this, which is pointless since I don't even see what time it is. Julia is at my arm instantly. We say quick good-byes, get our coats, and are in the elevator even before Conrad can get kicked out.

If this night were a freak occurrence, we'd both be bent over laughing in the elevator, racing home to retell the evening so we each make sure the other caught all the subtle, sick moments. If we were twenty-two years old it might be okay.

"Nick."

"Yeah."

"I can't have another night like that."

November 23, 2005

THE FOLLOWING WEEK WE'RE OUT TO THE DINNER WITH Oliver and Sybil that puts Julia and me far down the wrong path. Julia had let me know the plan to meet at the 21 Club in Midtown, a favorite with investment bankers for decades. Like all of these places with tradition, the older and uglier the waiters, the nicer the place. When the wealthy bankers aren't out at their clubs in Long Island getting served by the ugly waiters there, they're having cocktails at places like the 21 Club.

The restaurant is an old speakeasy and they still have the trapdoors and secret rooms where Hemingway and others would drink during Prohibition. From the sidewalk we have to go down a few steps to get to the unassuming front door that leads to a restaurant much bigger than you would expect from the outside.

The coat check closet is the first thing you come across. I help Julia off with her coat. She was in a great mood on the way over. If this holds, the night could actually be tolerable.

"There they are." I hand over the coats and turn to see Oliver return Julia's wave. She has the presence of mind to wait until I get the coat check stub rather than strand me there to go make her hellos across the room in the cocktail lounge, which is a bunch of old sofas and chairs next to a club bar. From there a hallway winds around to the actual restaurant in back.

We start over hand in hand to where Oliver and Sybil are seated in the lounge. Oliver has a slight build with pretty, feminine features and small round glasses like Harry Potter. It crosses my mind that his eyes need no prescription and that he just likes the look. He could be as tall as five ten but seems smaller. It's not that he slouches but that his manner gives the impression that he's always sneaking around corners and it shows up in him physically.

Sybil is pleasant enough. She's quite pretty and quite plain. It's as though Oliver picked her out based on a written resume of her appearance. Pretty blond hair, pretty blue eyes, perfect lips, cheek-bones, and a little button nose, with a nice build. Above-average features everywhere, but when you put it all together and animate it, it is inexplicably plain.

Oliver stands to kiss Julia's cheek and shake my hand. We cross-pollinate cheek kisses and handshakes all around. "We just put in a drink order," Oliver tells us. "But they haven't arrived yet. I'll have them send the drinks to the table and we can go sit down."

I resist letting Oliver direct traffic to start the evening. "Don't bother, there's no rush. We'll have a drink here with you first." I abruptly pull a chair to the back of Julia's knees and move to sit down myself. It's a reasonable enough gesture on my part but I can feel it comes from a need to get into a pissing contest. I know Julia sees my pettiness by the way she sits down.

The chairs seem as old as Hemingway too, with worn and fancy fabrics around wood armrests, and wide enough that you have a few spare inches on either side of your hips. They look like the kind of chairs you see in an old Newport mansion. The whole room looks unchanged from when they legalized alcohol.

"Well, I'm so happy this worked out," Sybil says, smiling as she brings a hand down firmly to the top of her knee for exclamation. "I've been telling Oliver what fun it was spending time with you and what good new friends you are. I was so delighted to hear about getting together again."

So delighted to hear about it? Did Julia set this up with Sybil or Oliver? Maybe I misheard or misinterpreted. Maybe it doesn't even matter. She could have called the house and Oliver picked up instead of Sybil. Christ, why am I even thinking of this? We just sat and already I'm down a path.

I order a gin and tonic. The other three each have a glass of sauvignon blanc. I don't know why people stopped drinking chardonnay but it seems to have happened in the last couple years.

"Now, Julia, where are you from?" Sybil seems to be the mistress of civil small talk. This type of person is always useful to have around when you have no interest to engage in anything more meaningful than the time of day, like listening to golf on television while taking a nap.

"Locust Valley."

"Oh, how nice. Oliver grew up on Long Island too. Just near you in Old Westbury. So beautiful out there."

"It is. I miss it. My parents are still there and I try to visit as much as possible." I know this to be patently false. I avoid the pompous Mr. and Mrs. Pembroke like the Black Death, and Julia's not so hot on them either. At most they get half our major holidays each year, and one of our best arguments for having kids of our own is so that we have an excuse to stay at home on some of these holidays and get the number of visits down even further. But Julia is just trying to be friendly to Sybil.

"I love it out there." Oliver smiles knowingly. God, he's smug. "The North Shore is the most beautiful place in the world."

"I'm from New Canaan." Sybil jumps in the middle. "Oh, what about you, Nick?"

"Bryn Mawr. Near Philadelphia." My drink arrives. I manage to block the ice with my upper lip forming a tight seal around the bottom rim of the glass so I can suck down about half the drink in one pull without making a slurping sound.

"Oh, the Main Line. How lovely." I nod. I'm now keyed in on her annoying habit of starting sentences with the word "oh."

I realize I can't get away with just a nod. "Thanks, it was a great place to grow up. A lot like New Canaan, I guess."

"Yes, I suppose." There's a lull now that we've completed the round of city of origin. Julia leans forward and I can tell she's looking for a toehold in the conversation to regain momentum. She knows she can't rely on me.

"Oliver, where did you go to college?" I already know the answer. Oliver somehow finds a way to let people know within five minutes of meeting him, with all the energy and unabashed praise of a proud parent except directed toward himself. Julia has just saved him the conversational maneuvering to get there.

"New Haven."

Christ, here we go. This clown is right out of a Salinger novel. There's nothing worse than people who say New Haven and Cambridge, pretending to be too modest to say Yale and Harvard when all they're really looking to do is draw the whole thing out. The false modesty is irritating and shows a total lack of self-awareness of what an insecure snob he really is. Just say Harvard or Yale and move on. Don't invite additional questions so you have to put on your uncomfortable act when pressed to answer the name of the school. Loser. Hasn't Oliver accomplished anything more in life to be proud of than a high SAT score when he was seventeen?

"New Haven?" asks Julia.

"Yale." Sybil steps in for Oliver with a smile and pats him on the knee, like a routine they've practiced for years. Could she possibly think he's modest? "What about you, Nick? Where did you go to school?" She asks this with such a perfect smile that I can't tell if it is a taunt or polite reciprocity.

"Cornell." I finish the second half of my drink with my second sip. "It's in Ithaca." I look at Oliver with an unconcealed sneer.

Oliver nods. "Good school. You get a great cross section there. I applied there too. I'm encouraging our son to include some schools like that for his applications next year." With this obvious placement of Cornell into the safety school category, he has let me know that he recognizes that we are now sparring. I'm no longer just shadowboxing. I rattle the ice in my glass, wishing the waiter would come back. "Where did you go to school, Julia?"

"I went to Duke."

"Great school!" He responds with more energy than he had for Cornell. "Beautiful campus. I've done some recruiting trips there for Bear Stearns. The chapel and those amazing gardens. So much land."

"I loved my time there. It was magical." I turn to Julia, trying to remember if I've ever heard her use the adjective "magical" before. "What about you, Sybil?" she quickly adds, probably also feeling odd about her word choice.

"Oh, I went to Vassar." Another lull. Another round completed.

"Let's go to the table," I say, slapping the tops of the chair armrests harder than I mean to. It has the desired effect though, as everyone rocks forward with a start like passengers on a train that stopped short, and I carry the momentum by standing right up.

We walk to the back dining room, which is a little dark and feels like a library in an old mansion except for odd trinkets that hang everywhere from the ceiling representing companies and mergers that have happened over the decades. I sit under an airplane with the logo of an acquired airline. Just like the pecking order in a big bank, there is a hierarchy in the dining room. The tables closest to the left wall are for the bigwigs. The farther right you go across the room, the farther you are from power. Oliver made the reservation and seems to take pride in pulling back a chair at our table one row off the tables against the left wall. This placement is probably due more to the maître d' remembering Oliver's father, who had been a top banker at Morgan Stanley, big enough that I remember his name in the *Journal* a few times years ago. Morgan is a more prestigious bank than Bear Stearns. Goldman and Morgan are the two top firms. In broad strokes, Goldman Sachs is where all the Jews work. Morgan is the white-shoe firm where all the WASPs work and act as though J.P. Morgan were still walking the halls anointing them the kings of investment banking. The fact that Oliver is at Bear Stearns, which isn't even in the conversation, especially when it comes to investment banking, has to bother him. And the fact that his dad was a senior guy at Morgan has to be the source of a huge chip on his shoulder.

"A lot of deals hanging from this ceiling," says Oliver. "Represents a lot of wealth moving around. You know I'm working on a big debt restructuring for Qwest, Nick. It should close in a week and should give you sales guys a lot of product to move."

It occurs to me that in the same way a person can have a kindred spirit or soul mate that they seek out, a person can also have a nemesis that they would like to remove from their life, a person to conquer or be conquered by. I know Oliver's been working on Qwest. He's gotten a hero's praise for past fees he brought in from them. "I've heard about it. Good luck." These client discussions are supposed to be confidential, but in the same way that our own salary information gets around, word gets out. I know Oliver made between five and six million dollars last year in bonus. He probably knows the ballpark of my bonus as well. This kind of knowledge creates a defined pecking order.

The thing about working in the money business is that we don't make anything but money. The upside is that we make a lot of it. The downside is that it's the only measurement of success. In a very defined and communicable way, Oliver is up the totem pole from me. The other thing is that the investment banker types look down their noses at sales and trading. We're the grunts who yell into phones and move product around with the sophistication of a short-order cook. The investment bankers are the intellectuals who navigate corporate boardrooms and put deals together. They've convinced themselves that it isn't just money they make but better companies.

There's some truth to it, but I prefer my friends to be the sales type. It's simpler and more honest. Like Jerry, sales guys think in a linear way. The faster you go, the more ground you cover. More calls, more deals, bigger bonus. Investment bankers think in curves and exponential opportunities. They make trade-offs that have winners and casualties and they play cards close to the vest. This is a talent a person has or doesn't have, and if he has it, it permeates everything he does including friendships and social dinners. It takes effort and a little luck to stay out of the way of a person like this.

"Do you and Nick have offices near each other?" Julia asks.

"No, no." Oliver smiles and shakes his head in a grandiose, you-silly-girl kind of way. He leaves it at that though could have added that he is on an entirely different floor in a large office with a sofa and guest chairs and an assistant outside his door while I sit at a long table shared with a bunch of cretins right out of school. He didn't add that, but he seemed to manage to make it known.

Oliver turns back to me, ending the brief exchange with Julia. "How do you think Morgan is going to fare? Jesus, what a show." He seems to be the type who likes to impress the girls but not actually talk to them. He also now seems settled into the top spot on the totem pole and doesn't need to bother sparring anymore.

"After all that publicity with Purcell, Mack seems settled in. He seems popular." I play along.

"Mack! Mack is a sales guy." Just when I thought sparring was over. This overt jab is not lost on anyone. I can either make a joke about being a sales guy or let it pass. I let it pass. "Come on, Nick. What would Mack know about running the business?"

It's not passing. "Purcell was a management consultant. Was he any better?"

"Fair point, but Purcell is incompetent. I'd take a consultant over a sales guy. The problem is all the boards are getting enamored with bringing in former sales guys as the CEO because they're aggressive and charming. They promise to deliver billions in growth and in a bull market they probably can, but pretty soon it's going to be a real mess. I mean look at Fuld. That guy's a moron. What these shops need is to put a banker in charge. Wall Street just isn't run by gentlemen anymore. It hasn't been for more than a generation."

Jackass. He has the haughty air of an authority on the subject and is keeping the undercurrent that a sales guy like me can't be leadership material. "They could get one of the old guard to come back in. Greenhill or that son of a bitch Fogg." I'm trapped for the moment in this conversation.

"No, those guys have moved on. Greenie has his own shop that he won't leave and Fogg spends half the year sailing the world on his yacht these days. You could make a case Fogg deserves it. He's the best M and A guy anywhere in half a century, but he's a little rough around the edges. You know it was Gilbert and Fogg and the old guard that got Mack in there. Mack was so grateful, you know what he did? Nothing. Not a lunch, not a dinner. Not a bottle of wine. You'd think a sales guy would at least get that right. He won't last. He's charming and likable but his lack of intelligence will catch up with him. Of course he did manage to stack Morgan's board with his boys, so God knows where it goes from here. Maybe he's smarter than I gave him credit, of course just smart in the way that a sales guy can be."

Jesus, he's relentless with the sales guy crap.

Oliver takes a sip of his drink and his pinky is off the glass. He continues, "Fogg. They'd never go with him. He's not part of the aristocracy."

"What about Mack? He's as blue-collar as can be for a CEO."

"Exactly the point. Mack accepts it, but Fogg is doing everything he can to join the aristocracy. If they put him in at CEO, it's an admission that he's made it in. With Mack, they can put him in and it still looks like he's a blue-collar puppet and everyone knows it."

He sips again, and again with the pinky. "See, you have to understand something." This could be the most irritating phrase in the language. He pauses to let it sink in and then regales us. "Someone like Fogg can do great on Wall Street, but you can always tell by his clubs where he really stands. He can get into National Golf Links, that's fine. But they'll let even Bloomberg in there. Bloomberg's as bad a new-money as there is, and he's Jewish. But he's got billions and he's working as our mayor for free. So Fogg can get in there and it's a great club and even the best also belong. But something like Seminole? That's aristocracy only. No Foggs allowed. Now you're in Dinny Phipps territory. The last chief at Morgan who was also aristocracy was Parker Gilbert and I don't think there will ever be another. It will never be Fogg anyway. He's from goddamn Ohio."

I doubt Oliver or his dad belongs to Seminole Golf Club either, but I won't risk asking.

"You boys certainly enjoy talking about work," says Sybil. I get the sense she knows I'm not enjoying it at all and is throwing me a lifeline.

I don't grab it fast enough and Oliver continues, "No one likes what we actually do for work. We just like the trappings that come with what we do. Influence with companies and huge amounts of money, fancy dinners on expense accounts, first-class travel. The nightlife can be a draw if you're young and into women and drugs."

I wonder if he already knows Julia and I have friction in this area or if he just assumes.

"You're also paid very well. That doesn't hurt," says Julia.

"It does and it doesn't," he says. "We're paid excessively. It takes strong character to deal with excess of anything. A girl that's too pretty, a guy that's too handsome or smart. It can wreck a person because he doesn't have to strive for anything. And money's the worst. Look at these young kids trading bonds who are suddenly making millions for a bonus. They end up going bananas on the town. Once you cross a threshold of having your basic needs met, there's actually a negative correlation between more money and more happiness. Many people just aren't strong enough to deal with a lot of money."

I'm so prepared to dislike Oliver that I can't give him credit for making sense. Julia is agreeing with him with her whole body, which is also pissing me off. It makes me feel small even to think this, but I hate to see her agree with other men. It plays into all my insecurities that I'm on the wrong track. Julia's never been one to want the biggest house or fancy things. She'd be happy with a normal life in a normal town on a normal salary. I say, "Easy for you to say, making five million bucks a year."

"Well, not being so excessively handsome as you, it was the only way for me to get firsthand knowledge of the issue," Oliver says.

"Why don't you give a few million to charity every year. That should solve your problem."

"I can't. My character isn't strong enough." He laughs and the girls laugh too. Damn.

"Are you boys please going to talk about anything other than work and money?" Sybil breaks in with a laugh that shows she understands work talk is part of the deal and her role is to make sure we don't spend more than fifty percent of our time on it. I also sense that she's trying a second toss of a lifeline, which I appreciate.

"Of course not." This time I seize the opportunity to get away from Oliver's domain. "Sybil, what school did you pick for your kids on the Upper East Side?" Like starting a ball down a steep hill, I'm rewarded with easy listening all the way to the arrival of our entrées.

The way a person with a stutter can be timid in groups, I can feel that I don't want the conversation to come back around to me. "Sure, Kent and St. George's are also good boarding schools," I hear my voice with detachment like a pilot watching the instruments adjust by autopilot. I'm pretty sure my comment is relevant and at the appropriate time.

It isn't that I'm shy or that I can't deliver on pretty words, it's just that I have no content to offer. I can start off a topic but I'm too out of practice to maintain anything. If I were an architect, I could talk about Renaissance versus modernist styles and the Guggenheim renovations and have a civilized dinner conversation. If I were anything other than what I am, I could talk about ordinary current events in a way that people could relate to me. My problem is that my career has consumed my lifestyle. I need to unlearn and relearn human interaction. I could touch on the topics of my last few work dinners. Maybe discuss William's theories on fidelity or that the coke dealer everyone uses just got arrested and where is everyone going to get their blow now? Sybil's jaw would drop in her soup. At this table, I'm like a rifle with no ammunition.

Even worse would be for the conversation to come back around to the earlier type of work talk that doesn't include strippers and hookers and cocaine but is about the actual work, where Oliver has already established the high ground. Like two silverbacks, I can feel that we have had our tussle and I lost and he is now the leader of our table of four. I look across at his pretty features that show no signs of ever forming whiskers, as though made of a smoothed putty, and I curse myself for choosing the type of career where Oliver can be a king. There's a new kind of Darwinism and Oliver has been selected.

"Nick, you play squash, don't you?" Oliver asks this in a louder voice and directly at me the way a teacher would with a liked but wayward student who isn't paying attention in class.

"Sure, I still play sometimes."

"Nicky used to be ranked in the country when he was a teenager." Julia gives me a wink and a push against my shoulder.

"Not too many people played squash in the country back then. Getting ranked wasn't so hard. Just had to play enough tournaments." This is a little bit modest but mostly just true.

"That's great, Nick. Do you keep it up? What rating are you now?"

"I have no idea. I haven't played since I was a kid."

"I'm a B. I'd say a high B. Haven't played much lately, but last week I beat a guy who's a solid B."

I imagine an era ten thousand years ago when, draped in animal skins, I could leap from my chair and club Oliver to death across the skull, then enjoy my victory by eating the food from the table with my bare hands, making loud grunting noises, and dragging off the women for sex.

But not in this century. Not in the 21 Club. Here survival of the fittest is based on a new set of traits and in my industry Oliver has them in spades.

Humans aren't just a few steps out of the jungle. Humans never left the jungle. The jungle just changed around us. There are those who are selected not to survive, but the selection process is no longer so immediately fatal.

Oliver is waiting for some response, but I have no idea what skill is required to be a B player.

Oliver continues, "Anyway, this guy who's a B used to play in high school and is getting back into the game. Grew up playing hardball and needs to get up to speed on softball. Nobody plays hardball anymore. I try to play a few times a week when it's not so busy. I picked the game up about twelve years ago and got addicted to it. Never played in high school. We should play sometime."

"What sports did you play in high school?"

"None. I wasn't that into sports then," he says.

"Maybe that's why you're so into them now." Julia gives me a sharp look that is meant only for me, but she's angry and everyone notices.

She recovers quickly. "Have you been getting squash lessons for the kids?"

"Oh, yes," says Sybil.

I let the talk move away from me like releasing a feather from two fingers and I listen to it swirl around from squash to schools to vacations to nannies and maids until it drifts too far away. I hear voices but not the conversation and it feels remote as if they are sitting at another table, and I continue with my dinner and gin.

From this perspective I can see the conversation move in physical form like colorful tubes of fluid transfer, moving from person to person and getting redirected back and forth across the table. Julia looks radiant, glowing brighter than the rest. She is strikingly beautiful in a complex way so that you can get lost in her all over again. It is one thing to have a beauty that gets attention, and quite another to have a beauty that holds it.

There is something distinctive about her presence that I can see without really looking, see with only a casual glance across a room or at a long distance when she is just the slight movement of a tiny shape among a group of other shapes. I can know it is her the way a parent would know their child playing with other children far across a field. But this hasn't taken years of a mother's care and learned watchful eye. I felt this force within Julia the moment we met. To be up close next to her can still fill me up, as though I'm standing inches from a painting I had before only seen reproduced in books. I still love her.

November 24, 2005

I'M ROPED INTO A DINNER WITH THE GUYS AT CHAPPY who cover our desk. It's Thanksgiving and they are looking for something fun to do, which typically means something without their families. I'm still feeling resentment toward Julia over the dinner with Oliver and Sybil. I can't put my finger on exactly what it is but I feel it. On an intellectual level, I know the healthy thing to do is go tell her I feel resentful and try to address it directly. On an emotional and every other level, I'm repelled at the idea of that kind of conversation with her. It makes me uncomfortable and I'm not sure I even want to admit to her or to myself that a dinner with Oliver can make me feel resentful. Anyway, a Thanksgiving night work event gives me an excuse to do something away from home with Chappy.

When we buy or sell in and out of positions, we often put the trade through Chappy, who will find the other party in the transaction for us, sometimes keeping us or the other party anonymous so the rest of the Street doesn't know our positions. Chappy never takes a risk on a position; they don't actually buy anything themselves, they just broker two parties together and take a piece of the transaction. We put a lot of trades through Chappy, so they like to make sure we're properly entertained and don't take our business to another brokerage shop. We spread it around to a few shops, but it's human nature to give a little back to the guys who just sprung for a nice dinner. And even more so if that dinner is followed by a lap dance and cocaine.

Doing drugs can form a bond between men. The way couples can build on the foundation of the first big laugh shared or the revealing of a secret, when men get high together it is an intimate act, revealing in its own way. The person has shared something with the other, knows something about the other as though they are part of a special club that likely doesn't include even a person's wife, kids, or parents.

We meet at Bistro 18 on Prince Street in SoHo. Jack Wilson runs the desk at Chappy that covers our products. Jack is my age and played baseball at Syracuse. We have a few college friends in common since I know some of the lacrosse players from there. He has black hair with premature gray evenly set around his head instead of just at the temples, and I think he'll be completely white-haired in ten years. He's about five seven, average build, but his face and neck are swollen from alcohol. The way cookie dough flattens when baked, his features have melted down to be almost flat and unrecognizable. There is enough left to see that it had once been a good-looking face but this now just makes him look unnatural and worse.

He's very jolly, always backslapping and laughing too loud, head roving around and eyes active, constantly searching for the next excuse to bark another laugh and slap another back. He brought with him his schlep, Tyler Atwood, who goes by Woody. I have William with me. Woody and William are about the same age and regular abusers of the Chappy expense budget. They make the rounds to the strip clubs and massage parlors together, but in this area there is no one like Jack. He makes no pretense of doing actual office work but delegates it to Woody and others. He focuses entirely on forging that special bond of coke and strippers with as many on Wall Street as possible. The more people that join the Jack Wilson Club, the more money he makes.

He's out to the morning hours four or five times each week. He knows the best coke dealers, and as their best customer, they all know him and give special treatment. They'll meet him anywhere, anytime, with whatever he wants. If Jack's with a group, everyone is taken care of. If he runs out, the dealer will send someone to stand on the corner outside the restaurant to deliver more.

Most strip clubs require that you pay real cash for play cash to give to the girls. Monopoly money that the girls cash back in with management at the end of the night. Keeps them honest, I guess. I heard Jack was recorded as having spent the second-largest amount of money in some club last year. First was some billionaire from Moscow.

"Hey, Jack." His face is looking even puffier and more engorged than when I last saw him. He and Woody are leaning against the bar, vodka drinks in hand.

"Nick, how ya doing, my man? Looking good as always. Haven't seen you in a few. How ya been? Everything good?" Jack has a way of asking multiple questions in his greetings, none of which requires a response.

"Everything's good."

"Good to see you, William!" Jack gives him a push and a laugh.

"Hi, Jack. Good to see you." William is a little starstruck. We're the customers, the Chappy guys have to entertain us, but Jack is a sort of legend. No one goes at it harder, and William and his friends have been repeating Jack Wilson stories for the last few years to the point they've created a demigod for themselves.

"Cocktails on the table, boys." Jack turns to the bar, where six more vodka sodas are already poured. Two to me, two to William, and one more each to Jack and Woody so there isn't a free hand among us. "Michael!" Jack calls to the headwaiter and they exchange nods and we walk to our table in back.

We drop into our seats, go to work on our drinks, and survey the restaurant. For an old New York restaurant known for its steak, this place always has pretty girls, and usually a few doubtful ladies loitering by the bar. "William, I hear you're engaged." Jack shakes his head. "You stupid bastard."

"Yeah, I guess it was time."

"Time for what?"

"Time to get married. She was ready and I'm okay with it. I caved on this one. She's talking about kids, but I'm not caving on that."

"No? Never?"

"No way. Never." William's emphatic.

"So, you just decided to screw the same woman for the rest of your life?"

The table is quiet for a moment, appreciating the question. Jack has a point. "Well, I just didn't want anyone else screwing her."

"Her little sister is just as hot," Woody says. "When are you setting me up?"

"Not a chance. I have enough to deal with right now." Apparently William isn't completely devoid of common sense.

"Yeah, what's up?" I ask. I know it isn't anything from the office monopolizing his time.

"Wedding planning. I'm getting pulled into more of it than I thought I would."

"What kind of stuff?" asks Woody, inquiring about a foreign land.

"You can't imagine how much. The place, the menu, the invitations, the kind of silverware, napkins, and chairs, the centerpieces, even the kind of doily under the drinks. That's just part of it. There's transportation and hotels, photographer, videographer, flowers, minister. All I want to do is the band."

"Are you guys planning this yourselves?"

"No, we have a guy. Flaming guy. We still need to see stuff and make all the decisions. Every time I show a hint that I don't care about something, she gets pissed."

"Let me give you some advice, William," I say. "Don't tell her it doesn't matter to you. They don't care what your opinion is. Only that you have an opinion. Just pick something, then get out of bounds. She'll probably pick something else, but she'll appreciate that you offer an opinion." I don't totally believe this, but I do about fifty percent of the time, and it's safe advice.

"Spoken like the only married man at the table," laughs Jack.

"Only six years, but I've learned some survival techniques." And I realize they were just that. Julia and I have been only surviving.

"William, you should listen to your boss. A wise man." Jack makes a toasting motion with his glass. "Did you act like a gentleman? Did you ask her father's permission to marry her?"

Woody rocks back in his chair, laughing with a hand over his mouth. "William, tell the story. You have to." Apparently Woody has heard the story already and it's a good one.

"I did ask." William looks at the center of the table, smiling. "I'm going to need a bump before I tell this one. Anyone have a white bag?"

"Of course, young man." Jack reaches in his pocket, then slides in plain view across the table a small ziplock cellophane bag the size of a fifty-cent piece, the kind a store would put earrings in. This one is packed with chalky white cocaine.

"Be right back." William puts it in his pocket, pushes back from the table, and walks past the bar to the staircase leading to the men's room upstairs.

Aside from the good food and great-looking women, Bistro 18 is mainly popular for having a perfect cocaine bathroom. Most restaurant bathrooms in New York have a few urinals and a couple toilets and there are people coming in and out of there like Grand Central. There's no privacy in the room and you can't snort a bunch of coke up your beak with that going on. Snorting is a loud, obnoxious sound, even to other coke users and especially to nonusers, and it attracts a lot of attention. The best bathrooms have a single stall and a lock on the door. That way you can make yourself comfortable in private. You don't need to cut up lines the way they do in the movies. You just dip in the tip of an apartment key and lift out a pile, maybe the size of a mini chocolate chip, and wedge it up the nostril.

William is back in less than five minutes. "Okay. Yes, I did go to ask for permission." We're all leaning forward, already small bursts of laughter happening in anticipation of this debacle. "Keep in mind, they live in Arizona, so I don't see them much. We've met only a couple times before this." He takes a drink, enjoying the effect of his pauses. "So we fly out there. Jen knows I'm going to do this, so she goes out shopping with her mom, and her dad and I stay home at their place for some alone time watching college football. We're all set with our beers and the game on, having some nice guy-bonding time, and I can't figure out any smooth transition so I just go right in. I tell him I love Jen, I want to marry her and spend the rest of my life with her." He takes another sip. Woody bursts out laughing, which makes the rest of us laugh wondering where this is going. William is a good storyteller. He'll have a nice career as a salesman.

"Her dad looks stunned, and I think a little alarmed. After at least a full minute of looking right at me, he says, 'Well, I'm concerned about this.'"

"So he has a pulse," says Jack.

"He then proceeds to rake me over the coals with an interview. Keep in mind, he's withholding any sort of 'yes, you have my permission.' He says, and I quote, 'Tell me about yourself.'"

"Jesus, I hope you didn't." Jack is loving this story. Nothing gets him energized like this, like a dog being fed a strip steak, eating it down so fast he's barely chewing.

"So I told him I smoke, I drink too much, I do cocaine, I like strippers, love hookers, I think his other daughter is pretty hot, and I'd kinda like to nail her too."

Silence. We sit looking at William, blinking. Woody snickers, still with his hand over his mouth. I look at William, my face expressionless except my eyebrows are as high as my forehead can pull them, trying to decide if it is possible that he said those words.

"Are you serious?" Jack looks at William with awe. An almost impossible expression for his face.

"No. But I wish I had. The guy was such an ass."

"What did you really say?"

"I just told him where I'm from, where I went to school, I work hard and career is important, I want kids, and family is most important."

"Was he buying it?"

"Not really. He said he's concerned about my drinking and my quote unquote nightlife."

"You're famous in Arizona now?"

"Jen must have told her parents a few things. She's close with her mom. I guess when we argue, she talks to the mom, then the mom talks to the dad."

"So how did it wrap up?"

"Well, I was getting pissed. I didn't count on the third degree. I would tell him it's under control but he kept pushing, so finally I told him, look, this is just a courtesy. I don't appreciate getting grilled."

"Jesus. And you're still getting married."

"At the end he let it go. He said of course they'd support our decision to get married. So then we watched the game in total silence for two hours until Jen and her mom got back."

"You're off to a beautiful start. I'm sure he'll give a lovely toast at the wedding."

Appetizers and more drinks arrive. Jack and Woody make trips to the men's room. Coke doesn't inhibit the drinking but it does knock back the appetite. Probably why Jack's whole body isn't fat, just his face.

William asks, "Hey, Nick, what's the deal with that guy Fred Cook who keeps coming around the office to talk with you? Guy looks like a real douche."

I turn to William. "Watch it, twerp."

"Doesn't he work in the risk group?"

"Yeah."

"He's worried about all the crap you guys are slinging around?" Jack asks. Jack is a drunk but he also has a lot more sophistication about the markets than William or Woody.

"I suppose he is a little."

"He should be. Mortgage market is overheated. Everyone has a story about their dog walker buying a mansion. And the credit default market is just creating more leverage. Getting so there's more insurance on bonds than actual bonds."

"That feels true. I'm mainly doing CDS trades instead of the bonds," says William.

"We're just moving this crap around and around and around. There's no way this paper's as good as where it's priced. If the insurance ever actually gets pulled in, the whole thing is screwed." Jack actually looks a little distressed.

"Careful, Jack, don't put that in an email," I say. "We've been warned about that. Verbally warned. Email is like signing, notarizing, and filing a statement with the SEC."

William seems like he's barely paying attention. "Things always wind up and then unwind, that's just the way it goes." He speaks like a kid who has never had anything catch up with him in his whole life yet.

Jack seems to recognize that he is not playing his usual role as the reckless one. "That's an awfully long view of the world, four years out of college." He takes another drink. "Maybe you're right, though." He seems to want to change the conversation, and so do I.

"That hostess looks good to me," Jack says looking across the room with intent as though trying to read the lettering on a billboard that is just out of range. I hadn't noticed on the way in, and the three of us turn in unison to see a hostess that is decidedly not hot. She's a bit overweight but not so much that she won't wear skintight pants and a tube top that accentuates her potbelly. Her hair is weirdly punked out, her nose is hooked, and she has layered on eye shadow that is one shade more heinous than interstate blue.

"Jack, what are you talking about?" Woody has genuine concern in his voice, like a relative at the bedside of a sick and delusional man.

"What do you mean? You would turn that down?"

"Yes, I would turn that down."

"Come on. She's sexy."

"She has a big ass and an ugly face."

"She has nice shoulders. You can see the muscle definition in her traps. Makes me want to rub them." I've seen this before with Jack. He manages to find a single redeeming feature in an otherwise unattractive woman. It isn't always the shoulders. It could be the chest, legs, or lips. He'll lock on to that feature and want to sleep with the woman. There's some flattery in there for women unaccustomed to it, but when I look at Jack's glare, I know this makes him more greedy than generous.

"You need help, buddy." Woody shakes his head, unable to generate any feeling of sexual attraction for the hostess.

William is also frowning and looking confused. "Jack, let's get out to a strip club after dinner. We'll go up to Scores. We need to recalibrate your settings."

"Man, I got busted by my girlfriend a couple nights ago," says Woody.

"For what?" Clearly it could have been any number of things.

"For going to Scores. She knows I go but she doesn't like it so I usually don't tell her. She thinks I go a couple times a year when I absolutely have to for work. I just tell her I've been out drinking."

"How'd she bust you?" William sees an opportunity to learn from the mistakes of others.

"The stripper glitter."

"Stripper glitter?"

"The what?" Jack and I get this out at the same time. We've been around a while and haven't heard this one.

"You know. The lotion with the sparkles in it that they rub all over themselves. Makes them glitter when they dance around. I got home early enough that night that Beth was still up. I gave her a kiss and when I looked down she was glittering! At the same time she looked up and saw I was glittering. It was all over my face and neck and arms. Jig was up."

Stripper glitter. Jack and I can add that to our vocabulary. A contribution from the next generation of lap dancees. The glitter lotion must be a new thing. I'm getting old.

"Right. That goddamn stripper glitter. It's hard to get off." William purses his lips, trying to solve the riddle.

"Nick, you haven't been, you must be dying." Jack tosses the white bag over the table and it lands on my fork.

"Thanks." I shove it away in my pant pocket and head for the men's room. I climb the spiral staircase feeling the coke like stones in my pocket. Closing the bathroom door behind me and locking in my solitude gives me a fleeting feeling of comfort and safety, until I pull out the bag and put it on the ledge of the sink. I lean over, hands braced on either side of the sink well the way a person does when he might throw up, and I stare down at the little white bag.

Ten years ago I did blow without thinking much about it. Just isolated moments that did no harm. Of course I knew it wasn't great. You just need to hear yourself snorting to know something isn't right. But I didn't have the knowledge then that it isn't an isolated moment, that there is a cumulative effect, that it can spread like a cancer through the rest of your life. I was innocent of that then. A kid having fun who didn't know better, maybe shouldn't know better. Now I do know better. Doing it now means more.

I try to imagine William and Woody with a few years more on their twenty-six. They could be like Jack. Like me. Something better or worse. I'm not just on the outside looking in at them. I'm right in the mix. It occurs to me that during their private minutes in the men's room tonight when the sound of their snorting reached their own ears, they may have had the same thoughts, made similar comparisons to me. I'm not just a spectator holding tickets to the circus. I'm a clown who can't leave his dysfunctional circus family because he can't remember who he was before becoming a clown.

I unlock the cellophane bag, dip in my key, lift it to my nostril, and listen to my violent inhale.

PART II

You can have anything you want but
you better not take it from me.

—Guns N' Roses

December 6, 2005

I AGREE TO MEET FREDDIE COOK AT A STARBUCKS A few blocks from the office. He had called my home again this morning with the hushed and rapid diction of a panicked target in a spy novel. Something serious had happened the night before, he said, and we needed to talk in person right away.

I pull open the door to the Starbucks and see Freddie sitting by himself at a table in the corner drinking a bottle of Pepsi. He's wearing a suit and it seems his mission is to show that a man wearing a suit can look just as unkempt as a man in a T-shirt, shorts, and flip-flops. He's making a statement to Bear that you can make me wear a suit but you can't make me look good. I don't think it's deliberate, he just doesn't know any better.

I pat him on the shoulder as I walk up to him and sit down. Even the pad in the shoulder of his suit is wrinkled and bent. His body looks soft like raw dough and I feel I could push my finger right through him and see it push out against the skin on the other side of him. He has light-brown hair, ruffled like his suit, and it covers his ears with a couple inches not because it is the style he chose but because he hasn't had a haircut in a few months. He's probably thirty-five and still speckled with pimples around his jaw and forehead from all the pizza and soda. Not even beer but just soda, like he's still a nervous teenager.

"Pepsi?"

"I hate coffee."

"Why the hell'd you pick Starbucks?"

"It's a long story. Someone's meeting us later. I need to talk to you first."

"Okay. Who's meeting us?"

"I'll get to that in a minute. Nick, my analysis is pointing to some very strong conclusions. Very strong. People aren't going to want to see it."

"Take it easy, Freddie. You're doing good work. People are going to want to understand your perspective." Freddie takes an apple out of his jacket pocket and rips his teeth into it like a sailor off a ship. He has no manners at all.

"They're not going to want to understand it, because then they're going to have to deal with it. I'm already getting pressure from my boss to put it aside. He's getting less subtle about it. I think he's getting pressure from somewhere farther up."

"You might just be reading into things. Your job is to analyze the risk of the firm."

"But they don't want me to analyze the risk. They don't want me coming back and reporting that our current strategy is dangerously irresponsible. Have you talked about any of this to Joe?"

I report directly to Joe Sansone and Joe reports directly to Dale Brown, the president of Bear who runs all of sales and trading. Joe is inept and insincere and should never be put in charge of another human being. He's a classic example of a very good sales guy who was then promoted to a management position for which he is wholly unequipped. He has the skills and personality to be a pure sales guy and nothing else. "No."

"Good. I don't think you should say anything to him yet."

"I wasn't planning to, but Freddie, don't you think you're making too big a deal of this?"

"There's a lot of money at stake, Nick. I'm getting pushback on this report before people have even seen it. They just know what it might say and they don't want to hear it. We're selling mortgage-backed securities that are grossly inflated in value. In my opinion, fraudulently inflated. This will crash and at that point whoever holds a significant position in these securities will get burned. Right now, it's us getting burned. If they get warned on the record about the risk and they don't do anything about it, they can get burned if things go bad. But I'm not going to be silent. I'm not going to say what they want to hear and hang my own ass out there."

"How bad is it?"

"This isn't like losing a bet and you move on to try to win the next bet. Every bet is linked to a thousand other bets. It's one bet for the whole system. It wouldn't be like a fire that runs out of wood and burns itself out. Nick, this is like a nuclear reactor meltdown and the first small explosion becomes fuel itself for a growing problem that doesn't end but keeps growing and getting worse and that can't be stopped unless you sacrifice everything and shut everything down."

Freddie looks so nervous and frantic that his story seems less credible. He looks like a mad scientist. But since he's the smartest guy at Bear and one of the few whose salary is not directly linked to trading commissions, it's worth hearing what he has to say. "How are you coming up with this?" I ask.

"I wrote a custom software program that takes into account

our position and the risk of the mortgage securities but also the overall context of the market around us, basically what other companies will do. It's the difference between roulette and poker. If you play roulette and put a million dollars on red, it doesn't change anything around you. They still spin the wheel and it doesn't have anything to do with your bet. But if you play poker and take a card, then bet a million bucks, every player around you reacts. They fold, call, or raise and build a strategy based on your action. A lot of models that look at Bear treat it like roulette, but it's really poker. If we make a big move, it will set off a chain of reactions."

Freddie looks down at his watch.

"Everything okay?"

"Yeah, we have a few minutes. The other thing is we're desperate for trading volume. On the mortgage lending side, Fannie Mae and Freddie Mac are pushing out a ton of loans, to anyone. And the government is promoting it. The borrowers are obvious repayment risks, but nobody cares. As long as there is a commission today in making the loan, nobody cares that it will default in a year. Or less."

"We have a few minutes until what, Freddie?"

He looks a little embarrassed as he puts down his apple and resets his focus. "I had a few drinks last night." I didn't know Freddie drank at all. "I started talking about some of this stuff. More than I should have probably."

"Who were you with?"

"She's a friend from college."

"A girlfriend?" I have an attaboy look for Freddie and I hope he doesn't feel I'm making fun of him.

"No, we just took some classes together in undergrad and she's a nice person." He takes another bite of the apple. "It's just that she's in a unique position now."

"What do you mean? Who is she?"

"Look, before she gets here, I have a favor to ask."

I'm annoyed at the stalling, so I just lean back in my chair.

"I have a meeting set with Dale Brown to present my report. I'm getting pressure to soften it, but I'm not going to. This is the big meeting with the president and I'm hoping you might come with me." He looks at me like a geeky high school kid asking a girl to the prom.

"What do you want me there for? I don't know anything about your report."

He shrugs and looks a little sad. "I just think it would help. To have you there." He looks down at his Pepsi and seems to catch a glimpse of how pathetic this appears and he pulls himself together and declares, "You wouldn't have to do anything in the meeting, Nick. You're one of the few people at Bear that's always been kind to me. It would just be a real help." I have a flash of Piggy and Ralph and for a moment I think Freddie isn't a colleague from Bear but an angel who's been sent down to test whether I'm a bully or a hero.

I was bullied for a couple months when I got to boarding school and it's still close to the surface for me. I was so sad when I first got there after leaving my parents in the station that I must have looked like a natural target, that I expected to get picked on. When it happened, I didn't know how to help myself and I felt that any outreach for help would get pounced on and make it worse.

After a while, you change how you act. You stay alone with your thoughts and create a separate world, all around you but just in your mind, so you can get by. And then you make one friend. That's all you need. One generous, unafraid person to show kindness. You have your friend and get a little happier and after a while you realize you aren't a target anymore.

Once you've been through it, it never leaves you. It puts something inside you that lets you feel things that others can't, the way only dogs can hear a certain pitch of sound. Maybe I can help Freddie out the way I found a friend to help me, so I decide to lend a hand.

"Okay." I already regret it. This isn't about a schoolyard shoving match or a couple kids who want to trap Freddie in a gym locker. I should have just said I'll think about it and then found a polite way to bow out, but now I've said okay and I'm stuck with it. Why the hell would I want to sit in a meeting with the president and associate myself with a report that is going to piss him off?

"Thank you, Nick. Really." He seems so relieved I almost feel better about it. "Have you heard of a three-strike loan?"

"No."

"It's happening out there now. Let me try to explain it. Let's say we take a thousand mortgages. Could be yours, my mom's, or any mortgage. We take a thousand and bundle them into one security and sell it. We need to make representations about the security, so we test it by taking a sample. Let's say we test fifty mortgages for the sample and ten come back as bad. These ten mortgages will default. That's twenty percent of our sample, so you should say that we predict that twenty percent of the security is bad."

I nod.

"That's not what people are doing. If twenty percent is bad, that's two hundred bad ones out of the thousand. What people are doing is to take out just the ten bad ones from the sample and then say that the whole rest of the security is good, even though the statistics say that there should be one hundred and ninety more bad ones. It's statistical fraud!"

"This is happening?"

"Yes. And what's worse, the ten bad ones don't get thrown out. They just get put in the next security that we bundle up, even though they already tested bad. If they get pulled in the sample test of the next security, they get put into a third. Only if a mortgage gets pulled three times in the sample tests, which is very improbable, does it get thrown out. That's the three-strike loan. It makes no sense. It's obvious fraud."

"Jesus, Freddie. Is this in the report?"

"It is." He looks up behind me.

The door is over my right shoulder and has opened and closed several times since I've been here, but this time I turn to see and in she walks. The lighting in the room seems to change. Nothing is actually brighter, but it's as though everyone in the Starbucks suddenly realizes we are sitting in seats of a theater and have in this moment located the stage. She seems to be a source of light herself, not blinding or imposing but warm and a subtle draw of attention.

I know her from somewhere.

"She's here, she's here, she's here." Freddie rocks in his chair and whispers this more to himself than to me, as an internal pep rally to get ready for the big game. He stands and makes his way over to her. He has an awkward heel-to-toe gait like he's walking in a ski boot.

He wants to make a gallant greeting but can't calm himself and instead roughly grabs her shoulders with both hands and delivers a kiss to the cheek that is a blow to the face, and I see her head snap to the side as though caught by a left hook. She smiles. This is clearly not the first time she has been greeted by Freddie. She gives him a short-armed but affectionate hug and he pulls her toward me and our table so that she has to skip a few times to catch up and get her heels back underneath her center of gravity.

I stand to shake hands. "Rebecca, this is Nick Farmer. Nick, this is Rebecca James."

Of course I know her. She's a correspondent for CNBC. She's on the TV with the volume down in our office and I see her every day. She has wavy blond hair over the shoulder and wide-set icy-blue eyes that are smiling. Her hair and makeup are done for television, which is a little much for off camera but accentuates her already beautiful skin and the planes of her features.

"Nice to meet you, Nick."

"Yes. It is." Jesus, I have to do better than Freddie. "A pleasure to meet you."

We all sit down. The Starbucks is in the downtown financial district and everyone seems to recognize her, though she would turn heads without recognition too. She seems not to notice it.

"Can I get you a coffee?" I ask.

"No, thank you. Already had one this morning."

"Of course. One a day, et cetera, et cetera." Son of a bitch. I sound like a fool.

We're silent for a moment and Freddie drinks his soda and I drink my coffee as a tribute to her.

"So, Rebecca, I didn't get a chance to catch Nick up on our conversation last night." Oh, no. I'm starting to put it together. Freddie got drunk with an old college friend and spilled beans about confidential Bear information, and the old friend happens to be a reporter for CNBC who is looking for a scoop and now smells blood. I have the urge to excuse myself from the table.

"Freddie and I had a few drinks last night." She laughs. I have an image of Freddie with his shirt off and tie around his head making Indian noises while photocopying his report for her.

"I see."

"Freddie mentioned Bear is taking some aggressive market positions."

"I see."

"I know you're in sales and trading. I'm wondering if you can tell me more about the strategy?"

"Would you excuse us for a minute? Freddie, a word in private." I walk to the far side of the room and wait with my back to him.

Freddie comes around into my view. "Are you out of your mind, Freddie?" He looks ready for scolding. "What did you tell her?"

"Not much. Not everything."

"What?"

"Nick, she's cool."

"She's not cool. She's a reporter. She's looking for a story. The bigger the better."

"She's a friend. She wouldn't screw us."

"So she's here for her health. Or for your health."

"No, it's for information, but she wouldn't abuse it."

"Freddie, you're playing with fire and I don't appreciate you pulling me into this. What did you tell her?"

He pauses. "I don't remember exactly. I think I just told her there's a lot of risky subprime debt out there and Bear is exposed to a lot of it. That's stuff people have said before."

"Maybe an independent mouthpiece. No official representative of a bank has come out and condemned his own bank's positions. Especially not anyone who reports directly to the chief risk officer."

His shoulders are getting lower and closer together in the front, which means he is understanding. "What should we do?"

"End this. Cut it off, right now."

We walk back to the table and sit down. "Sorry to be so rude," I say. I look at Freddie and push him with my eyes.

"Rebecca, I was talking with Nick and I think it's better that we don't get into any of this. I could get in trouble." He looks over at me to see if that was enough, and I redouble my efforts to give a harsh look. "Not because of what the information is, but just because I'd be talking about it at all. Good or bad, it's confidential, and I can't talk about it."

She knew this was coming. "I understand." She turns to me. "Where are you from, Nick?"

"Westchester."

"Have you lived in the city long?"

"Yeah, since college."

"Where in the city?"

"We're in the West Village. My wife and I."

She looks down at my finger. "What a shame."

I'm stunned. She's flirting. Without thinking, I pinch my ring and twist it around a few times until I realize what I'm doing and I stop. I know I would have only something stupid to say, so I don't say anything.

She smiles. "I hate the Village. So many strange and winding streets, I always get lost. It's a shame. Otherwise I like the area." Clever girl.

"It takes a while to get to know it all, but I still get lost sometimes too."

She reaches into her purse and pulls out a business card and flicks the corner so it makes a popping noise. She leans across and brushes close to me and picks up my cup of coffee, then slides her card across the table and puts the cup back down on top of it. She has total control of her motion, as though this is the customary way for everyone to offer a business card. I love the confidence. "Nick." I raise my eyebrows in response. "If you think of anything, you should call me at this number."

She stands and I snap out of the spell. Freddie stands too. "It was good to see you, Freddie."

"Good to see you." He looks even more disheveled.

She walks out of the Starbucks.

"Freddie, I don't know whether to thank you or punch you."

December 6, 2005

MY APPROACH AT WORK HAS ALWAYS BEEN TO KEEP MY head down and sell bonds. I never get political, but now, getting involved with Freddie, I think I've just agreed to start a political game where people tell me they'll just teach me the rules as we play the first round. I wouldn't say I'm worried yet, but I feel uncomfortable and I want to be with someone away from work. I'd like that to be Julia, but she's the source of another stress right now. I call my college roommate, Matt.

I always look forward to seeing my friend Matt because everything I associate with him has nothing to do with anything else. I'm reminded of a time when I had a more rounded profile and could move between different types of people. Matt knew me back when I was still a dependent for tax purposes and before I had let a job define more of me than it should.

Matt's a coffee barista and sometimes actor, and between off-Broadway plays and bit parts on *Law & Order* and other television shows, he's managed to keep on with his craft. And he's happy. It feels good to be with someone who doesn't have the same set of worries and who doesn't think that my worries are life-threatening or even much of a worry at all when put in perspective, and that helps me forget. He sometimes helps me to get away for a moment the way vacationing to a different language and currency can feel exotic.

Matt's already on a bar stool with a beer when I walk into Cedar Tavern. We've been friends since freshman year and our reunions are always familiar and comfortable. I pat him on the shoulder as I sit next to him and see there's a beer already waiting for me.

"Good to see you." He clinks my glass.

"Very good." My load feels lighter already.

Since college we've had a window into each other's lives like following a character in a novel we can only barely find relatable. While most people would be resentful of the life of a Wall Street trader, Matt is fascinated and amused and sometimes stupefied.

"You look like crap, Nick. You look exhausted."

I feel exhausted and in a way that is worse than hungover or tired. I feel almost defeated. "I am. It's been a rough few weeks."

A girl at the end of the bar is looking over at us, probably considering whether or not we're gay. Girls always liked Matt in college and they like him much more now. Like George Clooney, he started out handsome and a little goofy-looking and got a bit less goofy-looking with each year.

He's about my height, which seems too tall for an actor, with a thick beard that can't be completely shaved away and seems to stain his skin dark. His features are broad and friendly with strong bones but nothing too angular.

"I know you don't work too hard, so you've either been drinking too hard or it's something with Julia."

"I've been drinking too hard and it's something with Julia, both."

"I guess that would follow."

I make an uh-huh noise and the girl is still watching us.

"I thought by now you two would have settled into a routine that you've both accepted and made work."

"I think she's been accepting a routine for a while now and is reaching her limit."

"How bad?"

"I don't know, but we're getting older, and the routine has to change somehow. It isn't just her. I want it too."

"What does she want?"

"For me to quit my job, maybe leave New York. Things I can't really even put on the table."

He nods. I notice the girl again but I don't think Matt has. He's a better listener than I am.

"Anyway, the trouble is once you make your mind up that a thing makes you unhappy, you can't stop thinking about it. So now I sit at work obsessing about what a load of crap it is. I just try to get through it and take it day to day." Day to day like a soldier deployed to war, I want to say, but I don't want to sound like an ass.

Now I'm self-conscious about looking at the girl, so I drink my beer and order another round for us.

I ask Matt about his career and he tells me about some auditions for Broadway productions and a pilot he did in L.A. that he hopes gets picked up and some actresses in their twenties that he's dated or slept with. He tells it in a way that shows he's happy with it. He's not trying to convince himself that it's more than it is, nor does he dress it up in a way that is trying to prove something to me. He has a quality that is selfish and uncompromising but is not about harming anyone.

I think about mentioning Oliver Bennett or that I met Rebecca

James but decide not to. He doesn't know them and they shouldn't matter to me.

The conversation comes back around to my work because my misery is like a third person sitting with us whom we've been ignoring and whom we can't ignore any longer.

"What specifically is it about your job that's so bad?" Matt blurts this out without any connection to the conversation, which shows it has still been on his mind the whole time.

I think for a moment, trying to identify the one main thing at the heart of it. The word comes to me and I hate it and so I know that it's right. "The hypocrisy."

Matt seems not to want to press until he knows what I mean. He's listening.

"The difference between what people think about a person like me and what a person like me is really like is bigger than in any other job. People think I have a sharp mind for economics, and the reality is that I'm a sales guy who doesn't know much about economics and I don't really even read financial statements. People think we make a pretty good wage, and the reality is we have twenty-eight-year-old traders making so much they have running jokes about chump CEOs slaving away for one-fifth the salary we make. People think we're sharp-dressed bankers working long hours, and the reality is we're eight to five and the rest of the time the suit is draped over the back of some ratty chair while we get an X-rated massage." I'm reveling in self-loathing, which I also find repulsive.

"Sounds like a dream come true. You don't have to know anything, you get paid enormous money, and you get to screw off most of the time."

"Exactly. You can't blame anyone for doing it. When we have young kids out of college start up in trading, they're shocked. For the first few years they can't believe they get to do this for money. The trouble starts later when that's how you live your life and you're not shocked anymore."

"God, you're miserable, Nick. No wonder Julia's sick of your job."

"I know. I'm spiraling down, and I'm taking her with me. I was one of those kids, and she was duped more than anyone because she couldn't understand the hypocrisy until long after I did."

"Do you want it to work with Julia? Is that important to you?"

"Of course."

"Then get out. Of the job. You obviously hate it. Make a commitment to something else. You must have some money saved up after these years."

With every January bonus I calculate how far we could stretch our savings. "We have some. We've had some lifestyle creep over the years too, but we could cut back. We have savings and a house in Sag Harbor we could sell and try to make the money last. Not long enough, though. I need more years in."

"It won't be the last paycheck you get. Go do something else. Joe Kennedy said he wanted to give his kids enough that they could choose a career based on what they wanted to do, not what they needed to do. You have that much money. Look, there are plenty of people who came out of college and took a job in a ski town or teaching at their high school thinking it would be for only two or three years, and a decade later they're still there. This isn't much different. Part of the problem is you guys on Wall Street are the only people who make two million dollars a year and don't think you're rich."

He's right but only because we're surrounded by other Wall Street guys making ten million or twenty million a year and living lives we can never afford. The bartender steps in front of us. "The lady at the end of the bar bought you a drink." He puts a single beer in front of Matt. Matt shrugs and tips his glass to the girl and says to the bartender, "In a minute please get her another of what she's having."

I think she must go in for the artistic-looking type or maybe just the not-miserable-looking type. Anyway, she seems to have decided we're not gay and I guess that's something.

I have a sense of how uncomplicated his life is and I'm envious. It could be just that the grass is greener but I don't think so. "If you got married at twenty-two, do you think you'd still be married?"

"I don't think I'm the best test for that. I've never even been close to getting married." He seems to be weighing this for a moment, so I know I'll get a real answer and not a snap response. "Probably not. I'm such a different person than I was at twenty-two and I'm motivated by different things than I was then. Big changes that were unpredictable. The chances that the right person back then could change in a compatible way and still be the right person now have to be less than fifty percent." He pauses the way a person will before walking into a strange house. "Are you thinking about having an affair?"

"No." I say this right away and I have the image of Rebecca James walking into Starbucks. "No," I say again, as though the first time wasn't real and I was just trying it on for size. "I'm not."

"Good. People go through unhappy periods and they recover. There are always ups and downs, with everything. You and Julia have a good thing."

December 8, 2005

JULIA ROLLS ON HER SIDE WITH HER BACK TO ME, though I know her eyes are open and staring. Before ten minutes ago, we hadn't had sex in more than a week. This is our canary in a coal mine. It is the first thing to die when there is something poisonous in the air.

I was home when Julia returned from tennis, and I maintain that no one has yet created the outfit for strippers that is as sexy as the tiny white pleated tennis skirt. It was enough to bring us together, like a beacon through lethal clouds. But the sex was flat. It wasn't savored or varied the way that in a good meal the food is interrupted by wine to make the taste, the pace, and the experience even better. This was medicinal and businesslike. We now lie in the uncomfortable effect of a failed physical connection and the unspoken acknowledgment that comes with it.

"I'm sorry I've been working so much lately." I feel I need to say something. I like happy silences but not uncomfortable ones. I'm a child that way.

"What are you talking about? This is the same way you've

worked for six years." Her eyes are still straight ahead away from me.

"Well, there've just been some late nights." Before she can respond that this is also the same way it has been for six years, I add, "And I've missed you."

She still doesn't flinch but I know that this time it is because her mind is working to process my comment.

"You look beautiful, Julia. You're even more beautiful today than the day we met."

This prompts her to roll over and face me, and I'm startled to see that her look is angry. Not a hurt form of angry but an indignant look that says, How dare you? "You wouldn't have it any other way. Nick, you have a phobia of fat people. It's very hard to live with."

I can see this feels good for her to say. But like a slow leak of a great volume of pressure, a tiny leak cannot give real relief. Relief would have to come in another form. "And if you miss me so much, try coming home. Sober. You can send some other drinking buddy to your boondoggles."

The anger rises and the indifference wanes. Her eyebrows knit down farther under the weight of the creases in her brow, and her upper lip rises on one side in the beginnings of a snarl. More anger has lurked in her than I realized.

"It's like you're caught up in the bad crowd of an eighth-grade class. Some of the people you run around with at least actually are almost adolescent. You're thirty-five, Nick. Thirty-five!" She's screaming now. This feels out of nowhere and I wonder what cue I've missed. She takes a breath and hesitates. "You were a better man when we met than you are today. How do you like that? You think I've gotten more beautiful? I think you've gotten more ridiculous."

The anger reaches its peak and is focused right on me like I'm looking up the barrel of a gun. Just as quickly it vanishes and she seems to recognize the transformation of her own features and is ashamed of them and sweeps them away. Julia gets up and walks to the bathroom. I hear the sink run and water splashing. In a moment she walks back into our bedroom, her bathrobe pulled tightly around her. She sits sidesaddle on the edge of the bed to face me. Her expression is wiped clean of emotion.

"I'm so unhappy, Nick." Her tone is flat, as though she is just stating the obvious facts or reading the instructions of a baking recipe. Two eggs, one cup of flour, and I'm very unhappy. "I have been unhappy. For a long time now."

"I know." Those two words are my first real acknowledgment of our condition. An acceptance of responsibility on my part that I need to address. For a moment it feels like it could be the beginning of a way back, of a plan for us. But my words are left hanging in the air like a coin flicked over a well. Julia looks at me, waiting for more. Hoping for more. When nothing comes, my words fall empty. They sound hopeless and resigned. I know I'm closed off, but I can't cure it yet.

"Nick, the way things have become, I feel more like a stranger to you every day. Like we're locking ourselves deeper in separate prisons and I resent you for it. It makes me want to be cruel to you. And I resent that even more."

Her eyes fill with tears but don't actually form one. All I can think to say is I'm sorry, and I don't want to say it because it feels like an insult to her.

"Nick, I love you. I have always loved you. From the very first moment I saw you." She smiles remembering, and I remember too. We were at a birthday party in New York of someone neither of us knew directly. Along with every other man and woman at the party, I noticed her the moment she walked in. She had on a black tank top and perfectly fitting jeans and her hair was long and straight and simple. The first time our eyes met, they locked. First curious and unafraid, then laughing and interested, the head making slight movements and the mouth stretching to a smile, but always the eyes holding the gaze while we came together. By the time we touched and spoke, we already knew.

I wonder how it even happened then. Love at first sight seems like a romantic, silly notion and I know it to be true only because I lived it. Now if a friend had just told me it happened, I would believe he was being dishonest with me, or maybe just not honest with himself. Because I no longer feel any capacity for it.

"I love you too." I hear my own words as sounding weak and merely reciprocating. Julia doesn't seem to mind. She needs to tell me something.

"You're smart and funny and beautiful. You're your own man. That's what I noticed about you first and what I love and respect the most." She pauses and looks more intently at me, the way a person would look through a small porthole, as though her look could physically take hold of me, and I do sit up in bed. "I love the way you handle my father. He's a pompous big shot who's intimidated everyone I've ever known, including me. But he knows he can't intimidate you because you don't need anything back from him and it makes him uncomfortable around you."

"He is an ass." I'm not joking or serious. I'm just glad we're on the same side for a moment and I want it to continue.

"You don't care what other people think about you. That makes you immune to people like my father, and your immunity drives people like my father crazy. Your indifference fills up the room and it's Kryptonite to him." She tightens a grip on my hand and her smile beams, celebrating a triumph of mine. "You're so good for me. In some ways I'm my father's daughter, but you're not Kryptonite for me. He's too far gone, but I can be saved and you save me."

Her memory seems to progress through our years together and I watch the beam in her eyes fade. "Twelve years ago when you were first at your job, that lifestyle seemed okay. You were right out of college and living in the city on your own for the first time, going to bars and staying out late. That you could do it for work and on an expense account even seemed exciting. When we met, I loved you and I thought that part of you was coming to an end. I don't know why I didn't object then and talk to you about it. You'd come home drunk in the middle of the night from a dinner and a strip club, where you were talking about God knows what with your trader friends from the office. But now is worse because I don't have any reserves left. I don't want more reserves to keep this going either. I want it to be different."

"I know."

"I don't think you do. You're too good a person and I don't know why you're stuck in this lifestyle. I don't think you know either. Maybe it's okay when you're twenty-five and single, but you're thirty-five and you have me. This isn't fair to me. You have to grow up."

"It isn't a matter of growing up."

"It is, Nick. You must know you're not an adult."

This one hits home. Direct hit on my front door and I'm silent.

"Maybe you should see someone. It could help you to talk about it."

"That's stupid. I don't need to see anyone." Most of Julia's friends are in some kind of therapy, along with everyone else with money in New York.

"No, it's not stupid, Nick. You don't like your mom. That's

cliché for a reason. Don't you think it could have anything to do with this?" She waits. Apparently this question is not rhetorical.

"My parents have nothing to do with this. I don't need a shrink, I just need to make some changes."

Tears had come down her cheeks, first one making a slow, jagged path, then others following exactly behind so that you couldn't see the tear itself but just another pulse in the trail left by the first one. I brush it from her face. I can't remember the last time I saw her cry.

"Honey, you're right." I say this as softly as I can, almost a whisper. "I'm not happy at work. I don't like the lifestyle out of the office. I don't like the job in the office. It's not what I want anymore. I haven't wanted it for a long time."

"Then leave it, Nick."

"You want me to quit? Just walk out? This is my career, Julia. This is the only career I've ever had."

"Yes. Quit tomorrow. We have some money saved up. My dad has some money if we ever need it. Quit, Nick. We can go somewhere else."

"Quit and do what?" I feel my pulse quicken. "Julia, I've sold bonds for more than thirteen years. Do you know what skills I've acquired in that time? The ability to sell bonds. These are not transferable skills. This is the only way I know how to make money, certainly this amount of money. Do you think I should start painting houses or mowing lawns?"

"I think you can do anything you want to do."

I make a loud, frustrated exhale through my nostrils as though it is a word that can sum things up. An image passes through my head of me standing at the end of a car wash cycle holding a drying towel in one hand and wearing navy coveralls that say "Nick" in cursive on the front. "Julia, quitting is not the answer."

"Then what is?"

"There are some changes I think I can make. I can shift some responsibilities around on the desk and I can make it clear that I'm not going to be involved in the entertainment side of things as much. Or there are some small boutique firms popping up. If I jump to one of them, I'd have a different role. More strategy and management. I could leave Bear for one of them."

I can't tell if she thinks there is merit in this or not, but she stops pushing. I put my arms around her and pull her in close, each of our chins resting on the other's shoulder. "Julia, let's take a trip. Just the two of us, let's fly down to the Bahamas for a week and we'll find a deserted stretch of beach and do nothing but swim, sleep, eat good food, and do crossword puzzles." I feel her head nod against my shoulder. "I'll look into flights tomorrow."

"Okay." The conversation is over and we're still hugging, ear to ear, each of us looking at the wall behind the other, both knowing that we haven't really addressed anything. It feels like a layer of paint over rusted metal.

12 | A SOCIOPATH
COMES TO DINNER

December 15, 2005

NORMALLY I WOULDN'T BE BACK OUT TO DINNER WITH Oliver and Sybil Bennett so soon, if ever. People in New York can go months without catching up with even pretty good friends. I'm trying to work on things with Julia though, and this is something she wants that I can give to her. Also I want Julia to know that I feel no threat. While I don't like Oliver, he isn't significant enough to be meaningful. I can handle another night of boredom.

Inside there is a part of me that wants to see the drama play out, to see everything come to a conclusion, because maybe that would be a better place or it would at least be exciting to get there. It comes from a deep and self-destructive place inside, and in my stomach I can physically feel the obsessive urge the way a person peers over a high-rise balcony and hundreds of feet down, wondering about the sensation of falling, and grips the rail even tighter because he can't know if something inside him might push him over the rail. So I have agreed to another dinner with them. I feel myself climbing over the rail and starting to fall.

I pour myself a few drinks while getting dressed before we meet them at Da Silvano, which seems a natural restaurant selection for Oliver. The restaurant is a scene full of bankers, socialites, and media personalities, and everything is twice as expensive as it should be. We arrive second again and I see Sybil's coat is already hung up and the first thing anyone can notice is her necklace with diamonds the size of teeth. From there my eyes go to her heavily made-up face, then down to her tight and expensive-looking black dress that seems too much for a dinner at a restaurant. This must be her own version of a brave face. Her previous appearance had been understated, as though the last dinner was just a dress-down scrimmage and tonight is the real game. She must share the same suspicions.

We all hug and kiss hello and I hang up Julia's coat, then mine, and we sit at a square table against the wall. Sybil and I sit across from each other. Julia sits next to me looking across at Oliver. I wave the waiter over for drink orders before he has a chance to greet us.

Sybil's manner has changed from our last dinner. Before she had been inquisitive and generous with a smile. Tonight she sits upright and waits for the conversation to come to her. As much as she has stiffened, Oliver has loosened. He leans forward into the table, resting on his elbows, looking happy to be here and willing to initiate conversation.

"We're going to try to get a ski trip in toward the end of the season. Planning to get to Sun Valley next month. It's never the best skiing conditions, but I love the place."

I manage a sound like "unhh" in response while finishing my drink. With both Sybil and me as grudging participants, starting conversation is like trying to light wet wood. Each flare fizzles with a hiss. I pour more gin on my mood. Oliver excuses himself to go to the restroom.

Julia is the only one left who would prefer not to spend the rest of the evening in silence. I wonder if the others are as aware of this as I am. "Sybil, how are the kids?"

This gets a delayed response from Sybil and a smile that is nothing more than civil. "They're fine. College decisions are still the main topic around the home. I'll miss them when they go. It's such a change to the family unit."

Julia nods and Oliver returns. The waiter delivers the entrées and the silence is less obvious for a while as we eat meals that are not as enrapturing as we pretend.

"Were you able to convince that client to do away with that awful painting?" I have no idea what Oliver is asking about, but the question is directed to Julia and this time it is Julia with the delayed response.

"No. Not yet. Looks like I may have to work around it." Julia gives a weak laugh. "God knows the ripple effect that will have on the furniture decisions I'll have to make in the room. It really is an awful painting."

Even through my gin rinse I'm clear enough to recognize that I don't know about any of Julia's clients, let alone particular paintings they have. I never ask and she rarely volunteers. I realize I had been thinking of her career as one notch above a hobby. I feel a pulse of remorse, the way I would if inadvertently cutting off a person in traffic and finding the best I can do is give a meek wave and hope it didn't hurt anyone or wasn't even much noticed. The pulse passes because really I just want to know, When the hell have they been talking? And where?

Oliver is so smooth, he doesn't show a moment of doubt. He

lets off a loud laugh that sounds genuine even to my suspicious ears. He turns to Sybil. "Julia was telling me about a client whose house she's designing, and the client loves a hideous painting and absolutely insists on making it the showpiece of the living room." He turns back to Julia. "Julia, you should consider that there is certain business that you should turn away. You can't compromise your standards." Oliver shows no strain and seems satisfied that his tracks are covered. Sybil looks as sick as I feel. I look at Julia and my face feels expressionless, but I see that she has instantly read my mind. We each know that the other understood what just happened. Julia doesn't look panicked. Maybe just a little sad. Oliver excuses himself for the restroom again. I watch him walk down the long corridor lined with tables on one side to the single bathroom in the back of the restaurant. There is no line and he goes in.

"He's either got an inflamed prostate or he's feeding his cocaine habit."

Sybil looks at me and doesn't laugh but has a curious expression. There is, I imagine, a brief flicker of putting the pieces together as though she has all along seen the signs and just now understands what they mean and how obvious they have been. Is it possible that Oliver has been able to hide his cocaine use from his wife even when out to dinner together? I feel a happy sense of victory hoping I've just exposed this. That Sybil is collateral damage doesn't matter. She's better off knowing anyway. So is Julia.

Julia laughs. "Nick, you're awful."

I don't have a playful response, so I take another drink to have something to do, and I imagine Sybil's inquisition when she and Oliver get home later that night. In my mind, she pulls the white cellophane bag from his jacket breast pocket, slaps him across the face, knocking off the Harry Potter glasses, then goes for the kitchen knife.

"That osso buco was fantastic," Oliver says, sitting back down. Everyone smiles but no one says anything. I think we're all still adjusting to the new pieces of information that have come out to Sybil. "Julia, tell us more about your interior design business. It's very interesting. How does it all work?" Oliver seems to want to show that he is unafraid to go back to this topic. By brute force he will stamp out any suspicion of impropriety. The energy at the table shows reluctance to suffer the charade, but the only alternative is for one of us to expose Oliver's thinly veiled masquerade. I'm tempted. Julia knows me well enough that she answers before I can jump in.

"The business side is simple. There's an hourly fee for services plus a thirty-five percent charge on top of the items we purchase. Because I buy a lot across several clients, I usually buy at a discount from retail, so that extra percentage isn't as bad as it sounds." Julia now seems to be happy to go on about her work. Sybil feigns interest, but in a way that seems she wants to let us know she is only feigning.

"For the design part, I start with a few consultations with the client to see what kind of style to go with. Modern, classic, some Asian influence, what colors they like, et cetera. It's important to establish a theme. Sometimes we'll sit together and just leaf through a few magazines like *Veranda*, *House Beautiful*, *Elle Décor*, and the client will tell me what they like. Or just as importantly, what they don't like. The main thing is to understand the person and design something that will feel right to them. It costs a little more for people to do this, but where we live is too important not to make it a home we love. It's an investment in ourselves. As Oprah says, we all need a home that rises up to meet us. I had a client who's a single attorney, and she came into her home for the first time after I'd finished and she started to cry, she was so happy."

"You're kidding." Oliver says it and I'm thinking the same thing. I didn't know this story and I had no idea Julia was this good at what she does. I hadn't paid that much attention.

"She's a great woman. We're still friends. She's my age and divorced and single and never had a home of her own or any home done the way she wanted it. We spent a lot of time getting it just right. We also installed the sound system. I know what her favorite opera is and she loves candles, so when she arrived to see it for the first time, I had her opera playing and candles lit all around the home and she just burst out sobbing and hugged me. I started crying too. It was the best work moment I've had."

"You're such a romantic." This is not said mockingly. Oliver says this as though he's about to come across the table and start making love to her. He seems to realize this is too much to leave suspended, and he follows up to me, "Isn't she, Nick? What's it like? Being married to such a romantic?"

I feel vicious. I can't decide if it is Oliver or Julia I want to strike more. I decide on Julia.

"She's not romantic. She just likes romantic things. She likes candles, picnics, red wine, and dark chocolate, holding hands at subtitled films. But seemingly unromantic things can be romantic, because it's not the things, it's the people. Julia is always in control. Romance is giving yourself over to emotion and losing control. When your heart takes over your mind. When you do things not out of logic or reason, but out of passion."

The smile has drained from Julia's face. She is not enjoying my monologue. For the first time the entire evening, I'm beginning to enjoy myself, so I go on. "You know she lost her virginity her senior year in high school. How do you suppose it happened?"

"Nick." Julia tries to break up the story.

"It wasn't to some boy she had been dating and fallen in love with, or even didn't love but was lusting to have sex with. It wasn't even on a night when she'd had too much to drink and things went too far."

"Nicky," she pleads.

"It was because she knew she was going to college the next year and she wanted to have that experience before she went. The whole thing was a logically laid-out plan to prepare herself, and she knew a guy well enough to do the job."

The table is rapt with awkward attention, like watching a crystal vase teeter on a shelf but standing at too far a distance to do anything about it. I march on. "Does this sound like a woman driven by her passions? Like a woman who has been out of control for even a moment of her life? Julia is probably the least romantic person I've ever known."

I say this with a smile and in the most pleasant tone I can manage, as I watch the horror in Julia's eyes. There is a sociopathic disconnect between the smile on my face and the crime of my words.

For the first time I realize that if Julia starts anything with Oliver, it isn't about any passionate love affair with him. She has a need and wants to fill it. She evaluates options, sees that fixing me isn't working, and decides Oliver can do the job.

Everyone is eager to leave the table and the restaurant. My attempted pleasant tone didn't mask the malice and I'm also visibly drunk. We skip coffee and pay the check. After a mumbled goodbye to Sybil and Oliver, I take Julia's coat off the hook on the wall and help her put it on. Without turning to look, I notice Oliver doing the same for Sybil on the other side of the table. Julia and I walk straight for the door first. No one looks back at anyone.

I wonder what kind of asshole can turn as cruel to his wife as I do if threatened and angry. I tell myself I have a little mean streak, which plenty of good people do. Nothing more to self-analyze than that. I'm too drunk to have a conversation with Julia about it tonight, and that's my rationale to leave it alone for now, though I know damn well we'll never address it. It's too easy for us to avoid things and I hate that kind of conversation anyway.

We hail a taxi and ride home in silence.

December 16, 2005

WITH A CLEAR HEAD THE NEXT MORNING, MY GUILT IS more acute. Julia lets me out of the apartment without showing any signs that she's awake, and our avoidance is successful. I make it back in the office with a hangover no worse than normal. I take a coffee, a bottle of water, an egg sandwich, and two Advil back to my desk and begin to get my head straight. This is our version of an athlete warming up for a match.

I realize that I crossed a line with Julia. I compromised private information and used it in a sinister way. I don't even believe the awful judgments I made about her, but I had felt cornered and the instinct to be lethal. She and I are in new territory now. I don't know if there is a way to recover or if there is an urge to anyway.

I feel so unhappy that it's hard to keep a grounded view of what's happening around me. It's possible there's nothing even close to the beginnings of an affair. It's just an innocent flirtation that I've blown out of proportion because I view it all through the haze of my own morally bankrupt lifestyle and increasingly lonely marriage. It's hard to depend on my eyes when my imagination is out of focus.

William walks by. He still has his three-button suit jacket but he has at least taken it off and put it over the back of his chair. Progress. "Breakfast of champions?"

I nod, indicating I'm not in a mood for conversation.

"Farmer!" It's Jerry from his desk behind me. "Knicks game tonight?"

"Christ. No way. They suck and I'm exhausted."

"You'll be feeling fine by noon." Jerry will occasionally get the cocaine going in the office if the hangovers are really bad. It works, but I always feel lousy about it and don't want to do it today.

"Hey, Nick." I look across at Ron, who has a phone to his ear and is seated next to William. "It's for you on line four-four-two-oh." Anyone I know calls my direct line. If a person comes in through the general line for the desk, it is either someone I don't know or someone I know and don't want to talk to.

I pick up the receiver and press the flashing button for 4420. "Hello."

"Hey, Nick. Oliver." His voice sounds cheery, like an old friend I haven't seen for months who just got in town for a visit. Oliver. Jesus, what is this guy up to?

"Oliver who?"

"Funny. You dragging a little after last night?" I think he references last night just in case I was serious about Oliver who.

"No, I'm fine. Slept like a baby."

"Good. Good. We had a great time with you two. And Sybil really adores Julia." Really. This is the Sybil that managed about twenty words all evening.

"Sybil seems very nice." My Spidey senses are tingling. I feel like a field mouse being circled by a hawk.

There is a pause just longer than normal. "Say, Nick, I'm calling to see about that squash game. I have a court reserved at the Racquet Club. Six p.m. on Thursday. Can you make it?"

Incredible. He's like a Mafia don. Keep your enemies closer. "No, can't make it on Thursday. Got some stuff going on."

"Okay." He maintains his cheery tone. "I'm there all the time, so we can find a time that works soon." For a moment I worry that he's going to propose a bunch of possible dates to get together, making a casual brush-off more difficult, but he lets it go.

"Sure."

"And let's look into another dinner soon with the gals. That was a lot of fun." That is an impossible description. I had thought all four of us were having a bad time before I got drunk and especially bad after. His motivation can't be fun for the four of us. He seems like a tactician without conscience or remorse. I wonder if he spoke with Julia to contrive this plan to call me and befriend me and draw me in, but I dismiss it as paranoia. Julia doesn't have that in her.

"We'll take a look at calendars."

"And tell Julia we may want to contract her to do the interior design job for our Hamptons place." I can't imagine that will fly with Sybil.

"You can tell her yourself." If he is already talking with Julia, I hope he interprets this as a statement that I know what he's up to.

"Okay. We'll talk with you soon."

"Bye, Oliver." I hang up and dial Julia's cell phone. "Hi."

"Hey. What's up?" Her words are clipped and angry. The only reason she would pick up would be to hear an apology, and the edge in her voice says an apology over the phone won't cut it.

"I just got a call from Oliver."

"Really?" It feels like genuine surprise, and without alarm. I'm relieved.

"He wants to set a squash game with me."

"What'd you say?"

"I'm not interested in finding new ways to spend time with the guy. I told him I'm busy."

"All right."

"He wants the four of us to go out to dinner again. I would have thought last night was enough to put a stop to those."

She doesn't respond.

"Julia."

"Yes."

"I'm sorry about last night. I'm sorry for what I said about you. I don't feel that way, I was just drunk."

"Nick, I don't want to talk about this now. Certainly not while you're sitting at your desk."

This was only getting her angrier. What I said last night was bad enough and the implication that it could be handled by this form of apology was taken as an insult and making it worse. "I know. I'll see you tonight."

"Bye." I hear the phone click off.

I replay the tone of her voice again to try to determine any hint of guilt or nervousness about Oliver. Julia's an uncomfortable liar and something would show. I know I should be fixing the root of the problem, but now I'm too focused on how acute the symptoms have become.

I can hear her voice again in my head and I think she is too calm to be a person who has crossed the line. Julia could be just trying to get me to show signs of life in our relationship. And she could be trying to feel alive herself. To feel desired and sought after. A flirtation just enough to feel the emotional charge of what is possible but short of committing any act. Had she not forewarned me of her unhappiness, even this flirtation could be a betrayal. But it is within the bounds of her honesty and is innocent. She may have taken phone calls from Oliver and she may have allowed his adorations to go beyond what is appropriate, but I don't think she has started an affair. Although I do think she is starting to entertain the promise of something else.

I have an awful tightness in my stomach and groin. I know the feeling has nothing to do with Oliver. He's irrelevant. He's a single utensil at a great banquet. He can fawn on Julia all he wants, but he's not of her caliber.

My tightness is around the scale of the problem with Julia. What on the surface seems so simple to fix feels so out of control beneath the surface. I can't think of what to say when I get home. Like trying to stop a fire with only my own spit, I feel like I haven't even got the right tools for the job. But I know I need to get home tonight, even if I say nothing. Going to a Knicks game and avoiding home until the early morning hours would be a finger in her eye. I might as well send Oliver to my home in my stead for a candlelight dinner. Oliver who shows no conscience and moves like a cancer.

The phone rings again. "Nick, it's Fred."

"Hey, what's up?"

"You still planning to come to the meeting with Dale? It's going to be in January after year-end."

Jesus, this is a month out and he's calling me. I feel sorry for him. There's no reason to go except to offer moral support, which he obviously needs. I have no other role to play except to stick my neck out, and I'm starting to think it could be more dangerous than I previously had thought. But I said I'd do it. "Sure, Freddie. I'll be there." Damn.

"Okay, buddy." It's Jerry standing behind me and slapping my shoulder. "Drinks at Pastis, then we have courtside tickets for the Knicks. You can rest your toes on the hardwood."

I've already decided that I need to get home. If I show Jerry that I'm wavering at all or show any appreciation that it could be a fun night, he'll be relentless. I need to be defiant. More than defiant, I need to be angry. "I can't do it."

"Nick, c'mon. These guys love you. They've been asking if you're coming. We need you."

I turn my chair so my shoulders are square with him. "Jerry, I'm not going. Not tonight." I do sound a little angry and it feels good to release it. I'm ready to raise my voice if there's another iteration, and I want to. Jerry's smart enough to recognize this isn't just about me being tired and needing to rally. Something else is going on.

"Fine, fine. You pansy." I see he's disappointed by the way he shifts his bulk. I don't blame him. It feels strange to be the only thirty-something in a group of twenty-somethings.

"I'll make the next one. I've just got some stuff I need to do." I start to turn my chair back to my desk.

"Everything okay?" This has the tone of being a reflexive response rather than a reflective one. A human obligation to check in when another human appears to be struggling. Something most of us learn in our formative years or maybe is genetically coded, but is a noncognitive trigger response. I imagine the horror on Jerry's face if I turned to him and said, "Actually, I'm having a really difficult time. Do you have a few minutes that we could go somewhere and talk?"

"Everything's good. Thanks." I wonder if trying to solve problems at home will create more problems at the office. I don't know that I can make both work, or if I want to.

January 11, 2006

WITHOUT KIDS, THE HOLIDAYS CAN PASS RIGHT BY IF you want them to, and if you aren't happy, you want them to. We told our parents that we decided to celebrate alone in the city. I bought a tree, which we decorated without any ceremony and with the TV on. We kept it for a week, then I dragged it down to the sidewalk for trash pickup. I don't think we watered it once. I was relieved when activity picked back up at work.

Come January I'm on the trading floor hung up on a trade of casino bonds. The market for them is going the other way. The UBS salesman had asked me to wait on him, thinking he had a bid. By the time he confirmed he didn't have a bid with his trader, the whole buy side had dropped away and I'm screwed holding the bonds. If I sell at the current bid, I take a six-million-dollar loss to our books and Jerry won't shut his fat mouth.

But I'm not thinking about the bonds and I'm not thinking about Jerry. I can't get the squirrelly little bastard Oliver out of my head.

He's always walking around smiling and shaking hands, but

his eyes are never smiling behind those phony, prescriptionless glasses. The eyes are always thinking and working and making the smile work for them. The smile is never for the person he sees, because he isn't motivated by friendship. He's motivated by money, advancement, and power, so the smile is only for what that person can do for him. He acts nice because he knows it's better for him to have people say he's a nice guy. He's pleasant only for a purpose.

I recognize this sort of people around Bear. The ones who appear to dislike no one and to like everyone. But it isn't so much that they like or dislike anyone as it is that they are indifferent to everyone.

It's healthy to dislike some people. It's natural and honest. I've come to hate Oliver.

"Nick, goddamn it. Tell UBS they better make us whole on this. They hung us out!"

I don't turn around. My personal line rings and I'm relieved, thinking I can hide behind the phone against my ear.

"Hello."

"Hey, big bro." It's Sue's playful voice, and I feel calmer as though I've been transported to a comfortable wicker chair on a porch with lemonade on a sunny day.

"Sue, how are you?" I need to decide quickly how much I want to get into this.

"I'm fine. I want to hear how you are."

"The usual. Crappy."

She laughs. "What's going on? Are there some changes happening at work?"

"None. That's part of the problem. It's arrested development hitting a crisis stage."

"Sounds like it's time for a change."

"It's not all that easy. At my age I can't change careers like a T-shirt."

"Is anything going on?"

"Sue, I'm in the goddamn office."

"So whisper."

I look up at the television screen on one of the columns that hold up the ceiling and Rebecca is delivering a report on corporate earnings from the stock exchange floor. The volume is off but she looks gorgeous and I avert my eyes like I've been caught peeping in the women's dressing room. William and Ron are off the desk screwing around somewhere, so I have a little privacy.

"Julia and I are having some problems."

"What kind of problems?"

"We're barely speaking."

Sue has always adored Julia and I can feel that her level of concern has gone higher.

"Sue, there is so much hitting at once that it's hard to isolate, but the source of it is my job. I know it sounds like I'm pointing to something easy for a problem that is really inside the two of us, but I think work is playing that big a role. It's like the Marines— not a job, an adventure. It's a lifestyle adventure and it's a ride I can't get off."

"Well try, Nick."

"It's not a ride anymore, it's part of me. This is who I am; I just need to figure out how to correct course a little. I'm working on it."

"Nick. You're focused on the wrong thing." Her voice sounds fed up, which I don't expect at all. "People's lives are the way they are because of the choices they make. So before you focus on the job as the issue, you need to focus on you as the issue. What is it about you that got you here?"

I'd have hung up on anyone else, but I know she believes in me and is rooting for me. "Sue, I didn't have a crystal ball when I was twenty-two. If I had known, I'd have made different decisions."

"I don't buy that. I can see taking the job to start, but not sticking with it. You've had every opportunity to make a change at any point and you never have."

I don't want to say anything until I feel less defensive. All I can think is that I don't remember when I was last happy, even since long before Bear. Maybe sprinkles of happiness from Julia, but nothing independent. Nothing that would make a person think I was anything other than a miserable, cynical bastard. Maybe I choose to stay in this career because it is exactly what I deserve.

I've been silent long enough that I want to make sure Sue knows I'm not angry with her. "I'm not ignoring you, Sue. Just thinking."

"How bad is it with Julia?"

I haven't directly considered this before. I have never even tried to envision life without her. I always assumed the same laws of physics that make the rivers flow would also hold us together. This is to be our place in the universe even if comets collide around us. "I'm not sure. It's bad, and what's worse is I don't know if I can make it better. Every interaction we've had lately widens the gap."

"Take a few days off and go somewhere. Maybe it's better to go just by yourself to pull it together. You love Julia. That will take care of itself if you let it. You need to get your head screwed on straight first."

I have a mental image of myself in a remote hotel room, face down in a bowl of cornflakes next to an empty bottle of scotch tipped on its side. "I could take a few days and drive out to Sag Harbor. Quiet out there this time of year."

"Just focus on you for a little while. That has to be the first step. You don't sound good."

"I know."

"Are you and Julia coming to the birthday party for Andy?"

"Wouldn't miss it. Nine years old? How is he?"

"He's gone from threatening to leave home if we make him play soccer to now loving it. He's dying to see his uncle Nick."

"What does he want for his birthday? I could renew his subscription to *Penthouse*."

"I'm sure you'll think of something."

"See you in a couple weeks."

The phone hits the cradle. "So what did those rat bastards at UBS say?" I turn around to see Jerry with both arms up over his head like goalposts, one hand wrapped around a bottle of Pepto-Bismol.

I give him the finger and sit back in my chair. I'm still thinking about Sue's words and the emotion she had behind them. Sue still has the same fondness for Julia that she had when Julia and I first met, and it brings me back to a happier time.

I remember our second date. The first had gone so well that I had flowers delivered to her office before I picked her up to take her out again. The note said, "Looking forward to seeing you tonight."

At dinner she thanked me for the flowers. I thought I detected something odd in her thank-you. It was tiny but there was something about her that seemed cautious. After denying three times that there was anything to it, she confessed.

"I dated a guy who would send me flowers a lot. I love and appreciate flowers and I know they're expensive. But every time, they would come with a computer-printed card that said, 'Thinking of you.' It felt like it came from his secretary and could be going to girls all over town. And it's all he would ever do. No letters or notes or surprise drop-bys or even a long email. It got so I came to resent the flowers a little. They'd get dropped to my office, and every time I'd hope for something different from the computer-printed card."

"So no flowers."

"No, I'm sorry. I'm sorry. I don't want to sound ungrateful. I love the flowers from you. You're not that guy. Not at all."

"So no flowers with one-line notes?"

"Just don't substitute flowers for everything else. Flowers are great but not intimate."

"It's a deal," I said. Her smile was beautiful. These are the kinds of things people love to learn on early dates, and she's already saying how much more promising I am than an ex-boyfriend.

"Here's a deal. Never send me another flower. Just send me a letter once in a while."

"A no-flower policy. Not another flower ever?"

"Exactly. No temptation."

"Okay. I accept the deal." We shake hands and I think, damn, this will be harder. Getting the flowers to her took thirty seconds to dial the phone and read out my credit card number. I also think I really like this girl. She's different and honest.

Before our next date I sent to her office two dozen roses, a bottle of wine, a box of chocolates, and a singing midget who reads:

Roses are red
Violets are blue
Please forgive me
Breaking my deal with you

I'm using my words
To make sure that you know
I feel very strong
About how far we can go

They're no substitute
The flowers are real
I hope you accept
I'm changing the deal

It will be a big night
So rest up and get ready
I'm planning to ask you
Can we go steady?

I made sure nobody at Bear ever caught wind of any of this. It would have been humiliating, but sometimes it feels good to humiliate yourself if you can do it only to the person you care most about.

Four months later we're lying in bed in a suite at the Rock House in Harbour Island. We wanted a quiet vacation that would be just us in a place where we could sit on the beach, read books, eat seafood, and ride around the island in golf carts. The kind of place that requires two planes and a water taxi to get there.

She rolled over in bed so that she was sitting on my stomach and looking me in the eyes. "Nick, I love you."

I was so happy to hear this. I had felt this and thought about saying it and where, when, and how to say it, but she said it first. It didn't feel like losing a race because I really did love her. But it has always been a reminder of who is the more courageous of the two of us.

"I love you so much, Julia."

PART III

Nothing is more damaging to the adventurous spirit within a man than a secure future.

—Alexander Supertramp

January 20, 2006

CHAPPY CAN BROKER A SINGLE TRADE THAT GENER-
ates enough commission to warrant a celebration. These types of
trades can come together over a period of days or in an instant.
Celebrating only in response to a big commission would make
Chappy seem cheap, so there are also arbitrary parties. Celebrating without cause is the key to swagger.

Tonight is in response to a trade we put through Chappy. The
brokerage fee on the transaction is about six hundred thousand
and Jack Wilson will spend a good piece of that tonight. At any
rate, I'm in an elevator at the Soho Grand on the way to a suite
Chappy has for the night. I used to crave this kind of night. Like
rounding the bases after hitting a home run, I thought I would
always have the energy for it. Now I have the premonition of a
heroin addict who looks down at the needle in his arm with the
vague recognition that this crap will kill me one day.

Jack knows enough not to put the room in his name anymore.
He'll have some broker on his desk do it and let him know the
expense will be covered. I get off at the penthouse level and go to

Chappy's suite knowing exactly what I'll find. The Soho Grand has two penthouse suites, one with a view north and one with a view south. We're in the southern-facing one looking over Canal Street to the Statue of Liberty and Staten Island. I hope the northern one isn't rented.

There's a full bar set up but no bartender. Any other party would have bartenders and a few cute waitresses to pass hors d'oeuvres, but this party needs more discretion. I count five hookers in the room, each with a martini glass and a grip on the stem as though it were a ski pole. One bends down over the coffee table to rip a snort of cocaine. She straightens up like the yellow plastic bird in chemistry class that perpetually dips its beak in water, and her momentum pours her martini down her chest. A pimply kid who could pass for nineteen tries to drink it off her.

"Nick, good to see you. What's going on? What can I get you?" Jack Wilson seems to appear in a flicker next to me.

"Gin and tonic. I see I'm not too early." It's only 9 p.m. I usually try to avoid work functions on Friday nights. Even though I can sleep off the hangover, I'm hoping to make an early night of it.

"We got a jump on things." Woody comes through a bedroom door on the other side of the suite, arm in arm with two more very attractive hookers.

"Not bad." Jack follows my gaze to Woody and his two friends.

"Two grand each. They just got here. There were two others here earlier that were totally unacceptable and I sent them back. I gave the agency an earful, so they sent along these two in mint condition. Obviously it didn't take Woody long."

A person eavesdropping might have the sense that we're talking about pieces of fruit. Very expensive pieces of fruit. For a moment I imagine the cab ride home of the two hookers, scolded and rejected by a coked-up Jack Wilson. He passes my gin and tonic. My hand isn't visibly shaking but I can feel it and I force myself not to slurp down the drink.

The suite is huge, especially by New York City standards. The main room is the size of a tennis court with various sofas and chairs organized to create different pods for conversation. The room is elegant and conservative, lots of dark woods, dark carpets, and mostly dark blues in the fabrics. It would take a guest twenty minutes to try out every available place to sit. The suite is not designed to provide for every possible need; rather it is designed to provide the sensation of having so much excess that the notion of having to meet a need vanishes.

The rooms have been renovated to have the feel of a modern club room with high-end entertainment systems. There are two bedrooms, a bathroom, a study, and a balcony connected to the main room. Everything looks to be in use.

"Hey, Nick!"

"How ya doing, Woody?" He's still arm in arm with both hookers, who are surprisingly beautiful and no more than twenty years old. Poor things are probably fresh from some small town, just pretty enough to have a chance at a modeling contract with Ford or Wilhelmina, and like the rest of the new girls to the city, to pay the rent they end up waiting tables or promoting Bacardi rum in the bars. Or hooking.

"I'm excellent. Just survived a round with these two lovelies."

"Mazel tov." I'm looking down at my drink. The girls don't seem to mind being talked about in the third person. They're looking around but at nothing in particular.

"You should have seen the two that were here earlier. Jack traded up." He smiles at Jack and gives the girls a squeeze around the shoulders.

"Nice." I think I'm the only one feeling uncomfortable. "How's the balcony?" I take a step out of the conversation toward the balcony doors.

"Nothing out there," Woody calls after me. "It's freezing outside." I keep moving toward the balcony. "William and Ron are at Scores. They'll be over later." This is said as though it's information I've been waiting for.

I step outside and the cold snaps me alert. The wind blows much harder at this height. The balcony is the size of a suburban living room. I walk past some metal furniture to the rail and can see the activity up and down Canal.

"Hey, Nick. I see a little gray coming in on the sides. Hadn't noticed that before." Jack had followed me outside.

"It's premature."

"Yeah. Me too. Very distinguished-looking. You're not getting too old for all this?"

I wonder if Jack can see through to me. He's in sales, he must have some knack for picking up on things in people. On the other hand, it may not require any special gift to notice I'm miserable. "Maybe I am."

"You have any kids? That's when it really gets tough. I've got a kid with my ex-wife."

"No kids. I'm almost too old to start having kids."

"There are real advantages to starting at this age."

"Such as?"

"When you divorce, you can date a gal twenty years younger and she's still plenty older than your kids."

"I'll remember that." I sip the last of my drink. My lips are numb from the cold air and I can't feel the liquid but only the sting of the liquor. "Are you getting too old for this?"

Jack heaves a sigh as though he's already thought about this, and I can see a long trail of his breath blow in the cold night over the street. This is body language I've never seen from him before. Maybe he followed me out because he wanted this conversation. "I probably am. But I'll keep doing it until I'm such a pathetic hack that they force me out the door." His eyes briefly betray a fear that he's already a hack. It's just a flash, as though he may have wanted to talk about it but decided it is best not to be found out. In this moment of hesitation, Jack seems human, like a person who can get sad or confused, not an emotionless runaway train. For the first time I get the sense that he could have been a boy once. Maybe he has always just held up a front. No one wants to go drinking with sad. They want fun and fearless and invincible. Maybe it's not so easy being Jack Wilson either. Not at this age.

Jack finishes his drink, taking my cue, though now I'm a little interested. "Why don't you just walk out the door? Under your own power. Go buy a strip joint and run it."

He rattles the ice in the empty glass and answers me still looking at the ice cubes. "I used to think I would. I might still. Not the strip joint part." He looks up to me and smiles. "I had a magic number of fifteen million. Once I saved up that much, I'd walk away. The problem is once you get to that point, you're making so much money every year that it's hard to walk away. You're also spending so much that there needs to be some lifestyle changes for fifteen million to be enough to last."

I'm impressed he's cleared the fifteen-million mark. When you take out federal, state, and city tax, it takes a while to clear that much. Some people think brokers are second-class, but the good ones make more than most traders. I'm working the calculations. If Julia and I shed our expenses, could we make fifteen million last for the next forty years? With no kids and selling the Sag Harbor place it seems possible, with some belt tightening.

Jack pulls a cube from the glass and throws it like a dart across the balcony and it skids against the door. "So I don't think five years down the road. There's no point, it's too far from today." He seems to be slipping back into his carefree swagger and even his voice takes on a come-what-may tone.

"You don't love what we do?" I know the answer but there is a perversion that makes me need to hear it from him.

"Does anyone over thirty?"

"Right."

"I just make a deal with myself to get to the next New Year's Eve. When I get there, I can either quit or make a resolution to make it to the next New Year's Eve. Those are bites I can handle. The same way you eat an elephant. One bite at a time."

We're now both holding glasses with nothing but ice cubes in weather that is too cold to melt them without alcohol. "It's freezing out here. Let's get another drink."

I step back inside and the dry heat of the room makes my face flush as it comes back from numbness. Jack and I wordlessly split up like two little kids who have been doing something wrong and shuffle away with averted eyes so as not to get caught.

There have been a few more arrivals of young Chappy brokers full of excitement and pride to be here. They will retell their stories about tonight to their young friends back in their hometowns and dangle them all on a string of awe.

Eminem is playing but at a civilized volume. Probably a request of the hookers. I step through the crowd and more than half the guys here are only a handful of years out of college. The girls are under twenty-five and all professionals. There are the youthful expulsions of energy of a fraternity party, but while college has a jubilant venting of steam, this has already acquired a more sophisticated corruption. I get the feeling I need to throw myself a lifeline to pull myself out of this if I'm ever to have a chance. How can I find this to be an acceptable part of my life? I decide I need to force myself to imagine a different career. Even if it seems impossible, I need to go through the exercise. This weekend I'll get a pen and paper and draw it up. Maybe just by taking that step, I will make things start to feel more possible.

In the meantime I walk to the self-service bar. More gin. There's not a single person I'm interested in talking to.

"Hey, Nick!" Woody again from across the room. "I just spoke to Ron. He and William and a few other guys are leaving Scores now and bringing the bachelor party here. They're bringing a few of the Scores strippers with them." A few cheers and claps sprinkle the room at the news. I raise my glass in a silent toast. Woody does the same but with a yell and knocks back the rest of his drink. I feel like I need to get out of here and hope to make it through the hotel before Ron and William arrive. I don't want to seem like the old guy leaving early, but more than that I don't want to seem like the old guy sticking around not having any fun, and I can't be around all these kids and hookers.

I finish my drink and tap Jack on the shoulder for a quick thanks and make an excuse for the early night, and I'm out the door into the hallway. The heavy door closes behind me with a seal, and in an instant all the voices are gone like snapping off the radio. I wish things were good with Julia so I could have something I couldn't wait to get home to, but leaving here is good enough for now.

The elevator takes me all the way down without a single stop and I step past the two bronze Great Danes that line the elevator alcove. I'm almost to the door outside when I hear a collection of laughter and too many stories told at once in loud voices coming in from the other side. They're already here. Ron must have called Woody from a car close by.

They push through the door in a single mass, like an amoeba with forward body motion fueled by alcohol. Eight guys in designer jeans and untucked button-down shirts under navy trench coats. Like a uniform. I'm unavoidably in the path and I hear my name called in a chorus.

"William, congratulations on the big night out."

"This is an unofficial one, but it has all the ingredients. Are you coming or going?"

"Going. I need to get home." Less is more when trying to leave. Any information about why gives a foothold for counterargument.

"Nick, you can't. We have Scores dancers coming over."

"I heard. Where are they?"

"Coming at the end of their shift. We gave a down payment, and what stripper in her right mind would turn down a night at the Soho Grand penthouse with limitless blow?" In my mind this is said loud enough for the entire lobby to hear.

"I've never heard of such a stripper." William laughs at this. I need to go. "Damn, I can't believe I'm going to miss this one, guys." I try hard to sound genuine. "Take pictures and don't leave out any details on Monday."

"Okay. You sure?" I'm his boss. There's only so much complaining he can do.

"Yeah. Have fun. Stay out of trouble."

I get outside and the bellman gets a cab for me. I notice there's a voicemail on my cell phone and I check it.

Nick, it's Rebecca James. I hope it's okay that I'm calling you. I know you can't talk about Freddie's work, but I thought we might get together and talk about other things. Some nonconfidential things. Anyway, call me when you can.

I don't know how she got my number. I guess reporters have their ways. It's been more than a month since I saw her and I'm craving to call her back, but I know if I call her, I'll have created something that will take on a life of its own. I decide that if I call her, I need to wait until I'm in a place where I can concentrate rather than in the back of a taxi. This way I can just decide about it all later.

January 21, 2006

THE RING OF MY CELL PHONE BEGINS TO CRACK through my sleep and enter my consciousness.

"Hello." I answer because it's the fastest way to make it stop.

"Nick, it's Ron." I almost say Ron who, but another part of my brain narrowly wins the race and figures it out first. Why the hell would Ron be calling? I didn't know he even had my cell phone number. It feels like the beginning of a practical joke, but I'm only barely processing information.

"Ron. What time is it?"

"I guess it's about six a.m. We're in some trouble." I have an image of him mugged and beaten, lying next to his car, which is stripped and up on cinder blocks.

"Who's we and what kind of trouble?"

"Me and William. A few other guys. We're still at the Soho Grand. Things got a little out of control last night and the manager is here and he's freaking out and he's going to call the cops. I think we need your help, Nick."

When a person makes a habit of asking for help and abusing it, it becomes easier to say no, that I've already done my part. You've come to this well before and the well is dry. If a person has never abused it and sends out a distress call, the minimum human response is that I'll see what I can do. William and Ron have never asked for my help before.

"All right. I'll be there in thirty minutes."

"Thanks, Nick."

I turn back to Julia. Her face is angled slightly up from the pillow and her eyes are still closed. She never lets the pillow against her face. Her breathing is soft and slow. "Are you awake?"

"I was just wondering that very thing. What was that about?"

"Ron. A kid from the office. He and some other guys got into trouble last night."

"Are they in jail?"

"No, but they're about to be. They called to see if I can help."

"What can you do about it?"

"I have no idea, but I'll go see what I can do. They're at the Soho Grand now."

"Sounds like high-class trouble."

Her eyes have stayed closed for the conversation. I lean over and kiss her forehead. "I'll call you later. Maybe we can meet somewhere for breakfast."

I pull on jeans, loafers, and a long winter coat and put on a wool hat, which will flatten my bed hair. At 6 a.m. on a winter Saturday, the streets are strangely deserted like the setting of a Stephen King novel. The only movements are the few taxis roaming like fishermen on an unstocked stream. I hail one. I close the car door and lean forward to direct him to the Soho Grand as the smell of burnt lamb climbs up my nose. Some sort of god-awful gyro at 6 a.m. I crack the window for relief and start counting streets downtown.

Except for a skeleton overnight crew, the Soho Grand lobby is empty. I wave off a good morning from the bellhop and make directly for the elevator bay, retracing my steps from last night. I round the hallway corner outside the suite and see a cop straddling the doorframe where a closed door should be. One foot in the hall, one foot in the room, with his thumbs in his belt and leaning back against the frame and the hinges of the door to hold it open. He has the winter version of the NYPD coat, which is dark blue and leathery and thick enough to pass for ice hockey padding. He's big and burly and his mustache doesn't hide the fact that he's enjoying himself.

"You their boss?"

I don't stop but take smaller steps to slow my pace and give a single nod. His smile gets a little broader and he tilts his head to say go right in.

I squeeze past him through the doorframe and into the aroma of champagne spilled into carpet, like sweet mold. What must be the hotel manager is sitting at a writing table rifling through papers, making a show of looking furious but not looking up. No other bodies are moving and I see William, Ron, and Woody and three others that I recognize as Chappy brokers all sitting in a group. Eyes are shifting around the room but none meets mine.

I start out in a wide circular path to survey the room. Three sofas are upside down with legs in the air like upended, helpless turtles and bunched together as though a child had tried to build a fort. Shards of glass are crunching underfoot. I see the necks of what used to be whole bottles scattered across the room, and a shattered plasma TV that has been ripped from its mount on the wall. That must have been big fun, because the other two TVs are in the same condition. A coffee table is broken in two pieces with splinters the size of flatware hanging from the uneven break and all four legs ripped off. Glass still crunches with every step as though a uniform design of the carpet. I come to the open doorway of the master bedroom. The king-sized mattress is pulled from the box spring to the floor and a girl is asleep under the flat sheet. The dresser is turned upside down with all the drawers pulled out and stacked next to it. On the bedside table are four pairs of fake eyelashes neatly laid out. Classy. Probably the girls from Scores. An odd detail to notice, and I realize it is the only upright piece of furniture in the entire suite and so it stands apart like steel construction in a jungle. Soaked towels are balled up in a few places. Maybe early in the night there had been an effort to repair, like the finger in a dam.

I turn back to the main room and my foot lands in six inches of soil. A small tree in a huge ceramic pot had been brought in from the balcony and dropped like a bomb from a plane. The tree on its side looks like a bush against the wall. I stop to take in the whole room. There must have been a campaign to break each thing. Everything from the walls had been pulled off and thrown. Every piece of furniture, book, vase, phone, and pencil broken.

It looks like an Impressionist painting of a hotel room. This is the Black Hawk Down of bachelor parties.

Kicking the dirt off my shoe, I walk back past the six kids. "Nice work." They don't look up but this time the hotel manager does. I wave toward the hallway. "Can we have a word outside?"

He's a balding, bookwormy-looking man and his annoyed expression looks natural to him. "Fine," he says.

We both turn our shoulders sideways to get past the cop, who closes the door and follows behind us. The manager is still holding his papers and looks to be preparing to launch into his tirade. The only way to diffuse him is to launch into a tirade of my own before he does.

"Those goddamn idiots! Little pricks. They bring their drunken mess into your hotel and make my firm look bad. Those little bastards are going to pay."

The hotel manager had been about to start screaming his accusations and now his head is moving up and down in quick little movements. There's room for only one crazy man in a conversation. He realizes he doesn't need to argue or convince me of anything. He has an ally, a partner in generating the appropriate levels of outrage. "You're damn right! It was a freaking circus in there. Zoo animals! There have been parties in our suites, but in my twenty-five years in the hotel business I have never seen anything like this. Total abandon of anything resembling human behavior."

"You know I'm their boss. This was in no way a Bear event, but on behalf of Bear Stearns, I want to apologize."

"That's fine, but we're beyond apologies."

I look over at the cop, who has his arms folded and a calm smile. He's patient because he knows he'll have his turn. I'd guess there's a fifty-fifty chance he'll let this play out without making an arrest. He may be satisfied with making them squirm, a few jokes at their expense, then bleeding cash from their nose. The more cash that bleeds, the better chance they have of not getting arrested. Maybe he wants to avoid the paperwork of arresting a bunch of overprivileged kids.

"I understand that. And these kids are going to pay. For everything. And then some. I don't care if they have to beg from every friend and relative, but they're going to pay."

The cop nods and seems to like the sound of this. The manager takes this as a cue to return to shuffling his papers and crunching numbers. "I'm not finished with the inventory, but I'm at a hundred twenty-seven thousand in damages. And counting."

The cop's eyes nearly double in size and are almost perfect circles. This is good. There's hope to avoid jail.

"Keep counting then. I'll make sure they pay it. And feel free to estimate on the high side. If they don't want to be fired, they'll pay every penny and right away."

I turn to the cop. "Officer, about criminal charges. If they're arrested, I have to fire them. I'd rather bankrupt them with this bill, then put them through a living hell of my own."

"Well, I'm still looking into exactly what happened here."

"There were prostitutes in that room." The manager points a finger to the door of the suite to remind us of where we've just been.

I'm still looking at the cop. "I was told they were strippers who joined the party after a shift at Scores." This is true for at least some of the girls.

The cop is maintaining a calm tone, like a loving parent resolving a spat between children. "We sent a few girls home. I don't know who they were but there aren't any charges there. One more we couldn't wake up, but she's free to go when she does. I don't think they were the ones causing the trouble."

"Okay." I'm not sure where this leaves the others. "What about the six in there now?"

He nods to the manager. "Let's finish up the damages report and take it from there."

"I'll get back to work then." The manager walks back into the room, leaving the cop and me in the hallway.

"So these kids work for you?"

"Some of them. Some are with another company that works with us."

"Wall Street stuff?"

"Yeah."

"I never understood all that. What do you guys do?"

I'm trying to decide between a thirty-second and thirty-minute version of this. I also recognize it will be to my benefit not to sound proud about what I do, which is convenient to my state of mind. "Think about it this way. There are people out there who run companies that create goods and services. This hotel, McDonald's, Johnson and Johnson. They're the primary force. They need a way to interact with financial markets, to buy and sell companies, to issue bonds, give or get loans. That's what we help them do. We're the secondary force. They build and we help move around some of the pieces and then we take a slice for our work."

"Must be a big slice."

"Yeah. Over time it can get smaller, but then we find a new way to cut a slice. Wall Street always finds a way."

"You like what you do?"

My body language has been saying no. "No." I confirm it and I know I sound genuine. "You like what you do?" I wonder how much patience he actually has for this conversation.

The cop looks at me and he speaks slowly and evenly as though reading the words from the inside of his skull. "In seventeen years on the force I've pulled my gun thirty-two times. I've had a gun pulled on me eleven times and I've been shot twice. I have a cracked vertebra from when I was jumped by two drug dealers, and I have one dead partner. No, I do not like what I do but I'll keep doing it until I reach my full pension, and I don't have much time for the kind of crap pulled by your little friends in there."

The friendly rapport I had hoped we were building is up in smoke. The awkward moment is broken when the manager steps from the suite and I move to him like an expectant father to the OB emerging from the delivery room. "What have you got?"

"The total damages are one hundred seventy-four thousand,

five hundred twenty-seven dollars." The exactness of the number gives more credibility.

"Jesus." The cop whistles.

"Okay." I hang this out there like a question.

"If we receive prompt payment in full, I won't press charges."

I look over at the cop, who nods at the manager. "If he's happy, I'm happy."

"I'll make sure they pay it. Do you mind if I go have a word with them?" These two know that people in finance make good money, but they don't grasp the scale. They think these kids will be paying off debt for years. A young kid like Ron just pulled in a bonus of four hundred grand. He could pay this down himself.

"Be my guest." The manager smiles, starting to feel more re-laxed.

I want these six to feel relieved at the deal that has been struck. I walk back in the room and this time all eyes are on me, like kids hoping the teacher will announce recess.

"Jesus Christ, boys." I find myself enjoying this more than I should. "That cop wants to lock you up. You have cocaine, hook-ers, and unbelievable destruction of property. If that happens, I doubt any of you hang on to your jobs." I pause until every eye has dropped from mine to the floor. "I have good news and bad news." Eyes are back on me. A ray of hope. "You may not be headed to jail. There may be no charges at all, but you have to pay for the damages, including lost revenue while they fix this mess. Every penny, and today."

There are now some smirks and a few slide their hands back and forth on the top of their thighs as though ready to reach for their checkbooks now and get to work. "Sure, Nick," says Ron. "How much?"

"One hundred seventy-five grand."

"Ouch. I didn't know we had that much fun." Now that jail is off the table, one of the Chappy brokers is already feeling ready to dine out on this story.

"I'm going to go back in the hall and send these guys in. I suggest you act like this is a lot of money for you."

Ron squeaks, "This is a lot of money."

"Shut your mouth. Six ways, this is less than thirty grand each. One of you stay here and the rest of you get your checkbooks, get to the bank when it opens, and scrape it together. And go wake up that girl."

I step back in the hallway and see the cop and the manager standing in a way that shows there had not been any conversation since I left. "They understand. I suggested one stay here while the others find a way to go get the funds together. It could take some time."

The cop nods. The manager follows with a nod. "Fine. One of them can wait downstairs in the office." I don't know if I saved them from jail or just cost them some extra money. Either way, it's done and at a cost they won't even remember a year from now.

"I'm going home."

It's too early to call Julia and too late to get back to sleep. I pick up a couple newspapers on my way out of the lobby and go to French Roast on Sixth Avenue, which is open twenty-four hours and where I know I can get both coffee and alcohol.

The late-night club crowd has already come and gone, and the weekend brunch crowd won't show up for hours, so I have the place mostly to myself. I order a Bloody Mary, coffee, and a scrambled eggs breakfast and settle in with the papers. The first news article shifts my mind to Rebecca's voicemail from the night before and now my eyes are scanning words on the paper but my focus is on trying to repeat her message verbatim.

I'd like to call her back but I know it's a bad idea. On the other hand, it's rude not to return her message. I spend a moment considering which outweighs the other, then realize it's too early to call anyone anyway. I think if I still want to call her in a couple hours, I will. I conclude this deal with myself and order another Bloody Mary.

The waitress has taken me in like a boarder and seems happy for the company of someone to check in on. She matches my drinking rhythm, and each time the first few ice cubes in my glass are exposed to open air, she's back with a fresh drink.

After an hour and a half, I'm satisfied I've gotten all I can out of the *Times* and the *Post* for today. I'm also sure that no harm can come from calling Rebecca, and I want to do it. Actually, I'd like to see her. Not to get her into bed, but because I think this can draw out why I've been fascinated with her and why things have been such crap with Julia lately. I haven't before had an interest in another woman during my years of marriage. I've never even slept with a hooker. This new interest isn't boredom. Something is compellingly good about Rebecca, or inversely, something has gone compellingly bad with Julia. I think I'm equipped to confront it.

I work out my game plan, which is not to mess around with small talk on the phone. I'm better in person and if I want to see her, I should go for that directly and put her on the spot. The more we get comfortable talking, the more she can manipulate a plan. I'll just make this a tight yes-or-no offer.

The waitress stops by and I ask her to check back in a minute. If I get voicemail, I'll order another drink then. I feel jitters and I push my dishes to the far side of the table to symbolically clear space around me. I pull up the number that called me the night before and press dial.

She answers on the second ring and instead of saying hello she says, "Hi, Nick." I know she's using caller ID, but I don't expect it and it sounds seductive.

I ask if she can meet and she suggests she can be at Hudson Bar and Books in about an hour and it should be open then. It's a library-themed cigar bar in the Village and one of the last places in the city a person can still smoke. I haven't smoked in years but I don't mind. It seems like the kind of place where nobody would see us.

I have some time to kill, so I get another Bloody Mary to get my thoughts together. I have the sense that I'm cleaning house, but when it comes to Julia and Rebecca, I don't know what that translates to. Whatever the answer, I'm not sure I'm the type of person who can have a happy marriage anyway. I'm not that happy a guy and marriage isn't a magic ingredient. A happy career seems even more unlikely. Who the hell likes his job? Trying for more, thinking there could be more, is salt in the wound. Blissful marriages are for movies and storybooks. Blissful jobs are a goddamn farce. Not even the movies go that far.

I decide to stop getting my thoughts together. There's no way to prepare for something like this and it's only having the effect of depressing me.

I switch to beer and pass about forty minutes before the walk over to Hudson to meet Rebecca. The walk takes twenty minutes and the cold air combines with the alcohol to get me into a good state. I get there early, so I order a bourbon and sit at a table way in back.

The place is a single room shaped like a rectangle with an alcove in back and a bar to the side of the entrance. It's mostly a late-night place and now there is only a bartender, waitress, and one person at the bar smoking a cigar. I've forgotten what a stink that makes in a closed room. The walls of my alcove are lined with bookshelves and I browse titles to distract myself. There's a direct line of sight from the door to my table in back, so I adjust the angle of my chair a few times and try which elbow in what position will give me the most relaxed appearance. I keep watching the door but I want to time it so that I'm looking away at a book spine when she walks in and sees me first, then I can pass my eyes around the room and act the right amount of surprised to see her at that moment.

I can't keep my eyes from the door, and I screw it all up when she walks in and I wave hello before she even sees me.

I'm astonished all over again at how beautiful she is. There's nothing unusual in her face. There's nothing distinct or remarkable other than it is classic, perfect beauty, almost devoid of character as though it doesn't belong to her.

I marvel at her face as she walks toward me, smiling. The perfect angles, the perfect composition of her eyes, mouth, nose, and cheeks. I can't keep myself from staring and I can't imagine anyone has ever been able to. She must be used to people studying her. Her whole life, every guy turned on and intimidated. Every girl with a burst of negativity filled with resentment and competitiveness mixed with hopelessness.

Every relationship she's entered into has begun through this portal of her beauty. I feel sad for a moment that she has been dominated by this. She has been subordinated to her beauty and everything else has to fight to get noticed, if it ever gets a chance at all. I think better to be good-looking than great-looking.

"What's the emergency? You want to see me right away?" She bangs into conversation with poise and no fear.

"What can I get you to drink?"

"You're lucky I'm self-confident, otherwise I'd have made you wait and ask me to dinner on a Saturday night."

"Sorry. There's something I want to talk to you about and it just seemed like the sooner the better." I'm starting to wonder if I'm better in person after all. Maybe forcing this is a mistake.

The waitress stops by and Rebecca orders a pinot grigio.

"Okay. What do you want to talk about?"

"Let's wait for the drinks first."

We sit back in the chairs again staring at each other, and I can almost see the shift of gears in her head. "And since I've come all the way here, let me ask you a question."

"Shoot."

"In a few months they're going to fine Freddie Mac for illegal campaign contributions. They're also going to wrap up a two-year investigation as to whether Freddie Mac has been misstating earnings."

"Your question?"

Her voice takes on a tone of duty. "Since this is basically what you trade every day, maybe it's bundled into something or it's some related insurance product, but these home loans are the actual instrument underlying your trades of asset-backed securities. I'm wondering if you have any thoughts on the matter."

"Here's something you can put on the record. If you compensate a person based on volume, he's going to give you volume."

"Volume. You'll just trade volume, you don't care if it's toxic and dangerous."

"I didn't say that. I'm saying I'm not paid to care, I'm paid to deliver volume. If you want to fix the problem, you need to fix more than bad loans."

"I need to fix your motivation."

"Mine and everyone else's." This verbal volleying is not the flirtation I was aiming for.

"It doesn't motivate you that this can ruin the financial system? Globally?"

"It will change things a little, not ruin them. It's another cycle. In the nineties it was Long-Term Capital, and there were plenty of things in the decades before that. This might be worse. It might not be."

"So no laws broken, just a cycle." She can't hide her indignation or doesn't want to.

The waitress brings our drinks.

"I didn't say that either. I'm sure laws are being broken the same as they always are. Imagine the financial system is a heart, pumping liquidity all around. It's not a hundred percent efficient. Brokers and traders take a big percentage away from everything that moves. People move stuff that is unhealthy. Maybe they don't know it's unhealthy; maybe they do know and deceive. Whether it's deception or systemic inefficiency, let's call it corruption to be simple. Corruption is cholesterol in the heart. This is a high-cholesterol town. It's always building up and once in a while the heart needs surgery. Someone, maybe the attorney general or Congress, goes in and cleans out the cholesterol and plaque. As soon as surgery is over, the cholesterol starts flowing and accumulates in new places. The cycle starts again. We'll need another surgery again later. The thing is, this heart never stops beating."

She leans back with her wine and I'm trying to read if it's a smirk or a smile. "That's an awfully convenient point of view. What's your bonus this year?"

"No comment."

"Of course not. I can safely assume it's some number of millions."

"Are you still trying to work over Freddie Cook?"

"I was never trying to work over Freddie. He called me."

"Please don't push him. He's already got problems."

"You all do."

"That's true. Some of us more than others."

She sips her drink but keeps eye contact. "So, you wanted to talk about something?"

"I saw you do a reporter hit from the exchange floor the other day. You looked great."

"Thanks."

"There's something different about you. Some of the women come across flat on TV. With you there's something magnetic and exciting and it's not just looks."

"Thank you." It's a sincere compliment and she can feel it. I can tell by her eyes that she likes how the conversation is making her feel. And the eyes are on me. I haven't had playful eyes daring me to look back in too long. At home it has been dead eyes. I think to myself that married people still ought to find a way to flirt.

"Just an observation."

She looks like she's decided something and leans forward. "Nick, you know I'm not shy."

"I suspected that."

"Maybe I shouldn't return a compliment with a compliment, but I don't care about that and I will. You're very handsome. And you're exactly my type. Physically." I guess she adds this to be clear that married is not her type.

"What's your type?"

"Tall and dark hair." God, I'm loving the flirting. There's reckless energy passing between us.

I don't say anything for a while because I think it will make the suspense build. I'm getting goofy happy to the point that I'm not planning anything I'm saying but ad-libbing. "Sometimes we meet people that make us question the way we've set up our lives. Make us wonder about things." It feels risky to say this and I like it.

Her brows come together, trying to pull another sentence from me to discover my meaning. When there isn't another, she says, "Nick, you're officially flirting with me." I can see she's pleased.

"Maybe I am. A little. I think it's better to get it out in the open." I think I went too far. I brought our little fantasy back to earth where I have a wife.

"I see." She's having fun but doesn't seem to be taking me seriously, treating this as something futile. "Just what are you putting out in the open?"

"I like how I feel when I think about you." I hadn't put it into words before and I like how well I put my finger on it.

"Are you separated from your wife?"

"No."

"Have you talked to her about separating?"

"Well, no." This is starting to go sideways.

"So what are you telling me?"

Now I'm feeling indecisive and stupid. "I just wanted to tell you how I feel."

"Are you hoping I'll say something so we can do what you want and you can still be off the hook for it?"

"It's not that. Truly, I've just wanted to see you, and for the first time acted on it. I haven't thought about it much more than that and I haven't talked about it with Julia or anyone else." I hadn't meant to say her name.

I can't tell if she's irritated or hurt or both. "Nick, I don't know your wife. Even if I did, I can't give you advice about any of this. Relationship advice is always bad because nobody knows what they're talking about."

"I'd like to talk about it anyway." It occurs to me Julia must be talking to someone.

"I shouldn't be the one you talk to, Nick. Better not to choose someone you might end up in bed with. The only two people qualified to talk about this type of thing are relatives or friends of the same sex."

"Relatives of the opposite sex are okay?" I'm trying to be cute and should have known it would sound idiotic, but she lets it go.

"Unless there's a threat of incest."

"So the problem is always sex." The collapse into silliness might be saving the conversation.

"Of course. Even if it's minuscule, there's some percentage greater than zero that wants to have sex with the other person. Immediate disqualification from giving advice. You've seen *When Harry Met Sally*. The first half of the movie is true. The second half is a fake way to resolve the first half."

"There's not a third category? What about a shrink?"

"Nope. There too. Shrink needs to be same sex or at least fifty years apart in age."

"Have you slept with your shrink?"

"None of your business."

"Jesus." I clink her wineglass and sip my bourbon. "Despite the opposite sex part, I think I came to the right place."

We settle back in our chairs and are silent for a moment, a silence she finally breaks. "You shouldn't cheat, you know."

"Oh?" I feel like I was just starting to come around to the idea.

"The fact that you asked the question answers your question."

"Not in a very declarative way."

"Anyway, I don't want to sleep with someone who's married or on the fence about leaving his marriage. I don't think you're even on the fence. I think you're on the other side of the fence. With your wife."

I wonder if there's truth to this. I don't know if I brought up Julia because I'm in love with her or because I'm going a little insane with frustration.

She takes my silence as agreement and continues. "I'm thirty-two. Ten years ago this might have been fine, but not now. If you change your mind, and your circumstances, and get your act together, then we can talk."

I clink her glass again. I know it's a cowardly thing to do, but I couldn't have said it any better. "Since I got you all the way here, let me buy you another drink."

"Deal."

The waitress brings another round. This time Rebecca clinks my glass and says, "To getting to know ourselves."

"Cheers."

"And to discovering what may be right around the corner." She winks. God, she's gorgeous. "It was good to see you again, Nick." She says this in a sincere tone, and I feel that she doesn't usually say this in parting but reserves it for those it really was good to see.

January 24, 2006

PART OF MY POST-REBECCA PLAN IS TO TRY TO IM-
prove things with Julia and also with work. With my left hand
I'll conduct one side of the orchestra and with my right the
other side, and together I can bring calm from chaos. I feel the
momentum can be with me, that things can happen effortlessly.
I think this is the start of what it must be like to feel lucky. It's
only an idea now, just a secret project, but it seems to be expand-
ing. I want to be home more, and I make plans with Julia to cook
dinner at home like a normal night for a normal couple. Julia
has done the shopping and started the cooking by the time I get
home.

"I got swordfish and I'm trying a recipe for risotto with truffles."

"Sounds great." It doesn't smell great. So far it just smells fishy
but there is garlic in the risotto or the swordfish marinade that is
starting to make it better.

"There's a shrimp cocktail ready." She points toward the butler's
station just off the kitchen, at a dish of cocktail sauce with shrimp
the size of hot dogs hanging in a ring around the sides. "Would

you open a bottle of white? I picked some up. They're in the re-frigerator."

I step through the kitchen, past the empty store bags from Citarella cast on the floor, scooping and crumpling them up on my way. The grocery receipt is dangling from one. If we feel too loose with our money, cooking at home instead of eating at a restaurant is a remedy. It isn't enough to make a real difference in savings, but it makes us feel more responsible. Even though we have empty cupboards and have to shop for every item we cook, there is some-thing reassuring about preparing our own food, a sort of reminder that we might survive in the wild if necessary. I notice that the shrimp, swordfish, and truffles alone are almost two hundred dol-lars. With wine and a few other items, the total is over three fifty, more than we would spend in a great restaurant. In the annals of overspending, this will be in the top few. But she's cooking and I'm not going to discourage that. I toss the bags and receipt away and eat a shrimp.

"I talked to Abbey Roberts today," she says. Julia used to work with Abbey until about ten years ago when Abbey got married, quit work, moved to Philadelphia, and had two kids.

"How is she?"

"She seems very happy. Kids are six and eight now and both in school. I think she's struggling with the idea of being past the age of having a baby and now has kids that are growing up fast. And she wants to know when we're having kids."

"What did you tell her?" My fear that I wouldn't be a good father is stronger than ever. I can imagine Julia struggling with Abbey's question. We've told ourselves that we're putting off kids until we move out of Manhattan or something signals a change that we're ready for kids, but we don't know anymore if that is the truth. No action is a form of action if you wait long enough.

"I told her we're getting long in the tooth to start trying to have kids."

I don't say anything. We're not that old but I'm not sure if she is looking for me to agree or disagree with this statement. I know I don't want to start trying for kids, but I don't want to give away my position. I just nod.

"You know what she said? She wondered if I might have a medical problem carrying a baby. She offered to be our surrogate. To carry our baby for us." It's been years since I've seen Abbey. I think for Julia too. "What a kind person. I told her the problem isn't with that, but what an incredible gesture."

"Yeah. We better hope she never needs a kidney." Julia looks at me as though I've tortured a nun. I try to laugh up the joke but it feels awkward and as though I was partly serious. That's the thing about joking.

"It was one of the most touching things anyone has ever done for me. She said she had easy pregnancies and actually enjoyed being pregnant. She said if we need help, she'll do it. It's a serious offer."

"It's an incredible offer, but we don't know that this is something we need. Have you been to the doctor or something?"

"No. I don't know if we need her help, but now is the time, Nick. If we're going to try, I want to try soon."

"Julia, of all the years of our marriage, now feels like the worst time to try for kids." Her look says that she demands an explanation from me. My work is still an issue, but that's been a constant and one that she can dismiss. The other issue is that I don't trust what is happening with us and with Oliver and I can't decide if I can discuss this with her and not hear something that will gut me.

"What the hell is that supposed to mean?"

My mind is working furiously but making no progress, like a car stuck in snow. I'm not able to see two steps ahead in the conversation. "I just don't think we're in a great place right now. Our relationship." My phone vibrates in my pocket, announcing a text message. I hardly ever text, and I think about using this as a time-out from the conversation but I know that would make things worse.

"Nick, I know that. You know that I know that. I think I'd like to have a baby. There's a risk that our relationship isn't strong enough for this, but I'm running out of time."

"You're not out of time but we both have to want this. If we have a baby, it isn't just our relationship that we're risking anymore. Going in half expecting to fail isn't good enough."

"I don't expect to fail."

"Then what's going on with you?" I nearly shout this and my aggression confuses her.

"What are you talking about?"

I look away, trying not to say it, but I feel it coming on like a heave of vomit that I can't swallow. "Oliver." There, I've said it and part of me wants it back. I don't feel the relief that usually comes after throwing up. Julia stares evenly and seems not surprised but not guilty. "Not so much Oliver specifically. Just the prospect of someone. Julia, as long as I've known you, I've never felt even a hint of you glancing in another direction or trying to get a glance back. It's not an energy you put off. Until now. Now it seems like something you're open to."

"Nick, nothing is going on between me and Oliver."

"What does nothing mean? You never had sex?" I feel safe I know the answer to this.

"Of course not."

"Never flirted? Never felt anything?" I want to feel convinced now, to drive out the demons.

"No."

I think she's admitting to me as much as she's admitted to herself, which may be less than everything. "Julia, something is different. Worse. It used to be second nature that we're an unconditional team. Now I feel you're looking in another direction."

"I'm not happy. You know that. But you're my husband and I love you."

I realize it's not that I don't want to have a baby but that I'm afraid to. Julia deserves to be a mother. "I'm not saying no to a baby. Let's figure out the right thing."

Julia looks away, frustrated and silent. This sounds like the same commitment to dialogue that has ushered by the years, but I mean for it to be more now.

"This isn't just talk. Go to the doctor and see where we are medically. Let's get all the information first."

"Okay. I'll get in to a fertility doctor next week. Sooner if I can." She seems suspicious this is just a delay tactic but is still claiming whatever ground has been made. Possibly she's already been to the doctor and has a loaded deck. At any rate, it seems clear she feels the current form of our relationship is worth putting at risk. The outcomes of a baby with us together and a baby with us apart are both better than more of the same. She's not going to settle for no action anymore.

I walk into the living room to check the text message. I open the flip phone and it's Rebecca's number.

where are you?

This is amazingly appealing but not the best timing. All of this will be hard enough without temptation. The phone buzzes again while I'm holding it open and it startles me.

where's the fence?

I close the phone. Crap.

January 25, 2006

FREDDIE'S IN A PANIC AND TRYING TO FOCUS HIMSELF by memorizing his first few lines. We're waiting outside the conference room for Dale Brown to admit us so Freddie can deliver his report.

I hear Freddie muttering to himself, "Gentlemen, thank you for coming. This report is a summary review of, a comprehensive analysis of, crap. Gentlemen, thank you . . ." He's dressed slightly better than normal. Everything's been pressed but the clothes have the wear and the style of being at least fifteen years old and show the ill-fitting pushes and pulls from the changes in his body over that time so that it looks like he does his shopping at the Salvation Army. His ugly tie is pulled tight and straight around his neck in a knot that looks impossible to undo. He tried hard this morning and I feel sorry for him. He did the best with what he knows.

"Freddie, take it easy. You're going to work yourself into a lather."

"I just need to get the introduction down. I'm not a very good public speaker."

"It's going to be only a few guys. You know the information cold, just take people through it. You'll do fine."

"I know, I know." He sits down and closes his eyes and seems to be focusing on his breathing.

In a moment the conference room door opens and Preston Palmer steps out into our waiting room. He's the assistant to the president and I don't know him but have heard plenty. When he's not around Dale Brown, he assumes the full authority of the office of the president to throw his weight around and act like a jackass. When he is around Dale Brown, he acts like a manservant. "Okay. Let's go, guys." He gives me a curious glance, then gives Freddie a condescending stare.

We follow Preston back into the conference room. Dale Brown is at the head of an empty table. His appearance is the other end of the spectrum from Freddie. His suit looks expensive and fits perfectly, and I see the stitching around the border of the lapel that is a sign of handmade work. His silk tie is in a fat Windsor knot and his hair looks like it was cut just this morning. He's handsome and young for his position, maybe only ten years older than I am. I imagine he's had some sharp elbows during his career.

Freddie looks around the room a few times, checking and rechecking for invitees to the meeting. I develop my own conspiracy theory that Dale Brown wants as few people as possible to witness his exposure to this information. Nobody wants a piece of this meeting, and I wonder why the hell I'm here. Dale also gives me just a passing glance, then stares at Freddie. I don't know Dale very well. We were in a golfing foursome once about five years ago, and we were at a twenty-person dinner once. With a prompt he might remember me. "Take a seat." Preston points to seats on the opposite side of the table from Dale, then he also sits across from us.

Freddie pulls a stack of copies of his report from his bag and passes one to each of us, and the remaining copies lie in a pile on the table as a reminder of his unmet expectations of attendance. He clears his throat and begins. "Gentlemen, thank you for—"

"Listen, Freddie," Dale interrupts. "I don't want a big preamble. Let's just get started and get through this." He already knocks Freddie off balance. Dale would have said this no matter how Freddie started.

"Yes. Well, thank you for coming." Freddie picks up the report and turns back the cover page. I pick it up and fan the pages. It's seventy pages of charts and graphs and block paragraphs of analysis.

Dale's arms don't leave the armrest of the chair. His eyes don't drop to the report on the table in front of him but stay locked on Freddie.

"As you can see in the executive summary—"

"Freddie, I don't have time to turn pages on your report with you. Let's bottom-line this."

Freddie's hanging on by a thread. To his credit, as with many analytical minds, his anxiety forces him to slow down rather than speed up. "Okay." He closes the report and slides it forward a few inches and releases it. "I have developed a framework for analysis." His words are slow and plodding. "The result is a risk scale from one to ten, one being the least risky and ten being the most risky. The optimal level of risk to return for our firm is five point three." His words are starting to come faster as he talks about his risk engine, which has become a living and breathing best friend to him.

"Fine." Dale plays along. Preston is leafing through the pages, stopping at parts and reading closely, not listening to Freddie.

"The only thing I have yet to correct is that the one to ten isn't exactly to proportion. Meaning that if you move from a six to a seven, that is more than just ten percent additional risk. It's exponential. Like an earthquake on the Richter scale."

"Why didn't you fix it?"

"I just, well, I haven't gotten that part right yet."

"Continue." Dale looks bored but happy he's been able to make a criticism already.

"So moving higher than five point three can be significant. To use the analogy of a car, a score of six five would be redlining the engine."

Freddie stops and looks over at Preston, who is focused on a page of the report. There are crinkles of concern on his forehead. He seems to notice the room has gone silent, and he looks up at Freddie, then over at Dale. Dale looks like he is about to ask Preston a question, then changes his mind. "Continue, Freddie."

"Last year we were at a nine point one."

Dale scowls. I think he was ready for a high number but I see real surprise that it is this high. "What the hell does that mean, Freddie?" He likes to say the name Freddie in a mocking tone like it's a disparaging word. "You tell me nine one and I'm supposed to use that information to manage the firm? You want me to act because we're a nine one on the Freddie scale?"

"It's all in the report, Dale."

"I don't care about the goddamn report!"

Freddie is silent. We all are and we take turns looking at each other.

"Holy crap. Just keep going, Freddie."

"Well, this year the scale can't account for the risk." He quickly realizes his phrasing will lead only to more criticism of the model itself. "What I mean is, we're off the scale. We're higher than ten."

"What in God's name does that mean?"

"It means that given external market conditions, the positions of the other firms, and our own positions, we're leveraged through derivative instruments to such an extent that the scale can't fully capture the risk. It's like trying to divide a number by zero."

"I still don't know how you expect me to interpret this information." Dale is staring at Freddie, ready for a duel and positioning for his denial that he learned anything here today. Preston is back to poring over the report and has a concerned look like he is trying to wish away the facts.

"Dale, the conclusion here is that this strategy could wipe out more than just Bear. Other firms are doing this too. Once we have a dip in the market, this will magnify the problem because there isn't anyone healthy to absorb the mess. There'll be no place to hide. The whole system is at risk."

Preston keeps his eyes down on the paper, but he doesn't seem to be reading anymore. Dale smiles, and this time it's a friendly smile, as if to a child that doesn't understand and that he wants to help. "Freddie, that seems a little fantastic. You can't expect me to react to statements that the sky is falling."

"It's not fantastic."

"We had our best year ever. We're going to keep it going."

"You mean your best bonus year ever." Freddie is like the angry geek who somehow finds the nerve for a moment to stand up to the captain of the football team.

Dale tries to keep his smile, but this time it's dismissive. "I said we're going to keep it going."

"That will risk the firm. Maybe more than that."

"Don't be dramatic. You're here to help us make more money. Not less."

"I'm here to help us manage risk in the optimal way. Not set us on a suicide course with the market."

"Listen to me. We're making money. We're going to continue making money. We'll alter course when this cools off."

"You have to alter course now. Now. We can't unwind these positions overnight. We have to gently unwind starting now and do it over a period of a year, maybe two, and hope the market doesn't turn before we're finished. We have to do it slowly, and even that comes with risk."

"Risk from where?"

"People are going to start to wake up to how exposed the major banks are. Then they're going to start to make bets on the correction. The bets on the downfall will accelerate the downfall. That will push assets in the same direction as our unwinding needs to go and make it more difficult to complete. It will become self-fulfilling. We may not be able to get all the way out, even if we start today."

"Then why try to get out at all? Let's keep our high earnings. We'll increase our bets and fight off the correction."

"Because you will lose the whole company. Everything. The underlying bet isn't there."

Dale knows Freddie is brilliant and he also knows that he himself is incapable of grasping the analysis in Freddie's report. The root of his disdain for Freddie is fear. Dale's belief system about success is that men get ahead on guts, vision, and persuasion. Freddie doesn't lead; he's someone you pay a salary to play a supporting role. If Freddie challenges this belief, Dale will defend himself the way insecure people in authority do.

Dale bangs his pen down and looks at Preston. He gives another friendly smile to Preston, then to me, inviting people to agree with him and condemn Freddie. If his smile could speak, it would say, Can you believe this guy?

"I've got to make money with a bunch of little girls around me like this Cook. No balls and weak stomachs."

Freddie holds his ground. He sits up a little straighter. I can tell it's his last shred of courage before he runs home hyperventilating and locks himself in a room with pizza, soda, and computer games. "This is my official report and I'm submitting it for internal publication today."

"Get out."

"Then there's still the issue of the three-strike loans."

"Shut your mouth right now, Cook, and get the hell out."

Freddie is up and gone like a swimmer off his block at the sound of a gun. I wait a full three count before getting up, just to make clear that I don't work for Freddie and any anger or command to get out isn't meant directly for me.

When I reach the exit, I look back over my shoulder as I close the door behind me, and I see Dale staring down at his pen lying halfway across the table from him. He looks scared.

Freddie is standing on the far end of the waiting room, wanting to leave altogether but waiting for me. He looks like he isn't yet sure whether or not he should cry.

"Let's go," I say. We walk down the hall in silence until we get into the elevator on the way out of the building. I wonder if there's another Freddie at another firm blowing whistles about the high leverage of bad assets. Nobody wants to talk about this.

"Oh my God, Nick. He's pissed."

"Yes."

"What am I going to do? I think I need to find a new job."

"You did your job, Freddie. And you stood up to him. You should be proud of that." I feel I should be fully honest with him.

"It wouldn't be a bad idea to polish up your resume." I think I may do the same.

"You think they'd fire me for telling the truth?"

"Like you said, he's pissed off."

"I was trapped, Nick," he says, looking dejected. "What else could I report? Damned if I do, damned if I don't."

"That's not true, Freddie. You did the right thing. That took a lot of courage." I mean that. It's always easier to see it clearly when it's someone else.

"I need to go outside and take a walk."

"Okay. I'm heading back to my desk."

The elevator stops on seven and I step out and turn back around to Freddie. I hold the elevator door open.

"Freddie, you did fine. Screw him." He nods and I pull my hand away and let the doors close over him like water over something sinking beneath the surface.

I get a coffee, wishing it could be gin and tonic, and start to my desk. Ron is walking around the area looking excited and sees me coming.

"Jack's coming by."

"Wilson?"

"Yeah, he should be here in a few minutes."

"Why's he coming here?"

"I think there's a Knicks game or a Duke game and he's taking some people."

"And why's he coming here?"

He shrugs. "I don't know. I guess he gets to see more people this way. You know Jack. He's a politician on the campaign trail."

"Yeah. Try not to kiss him."

I get in my chair and check to see where the market has moved on the bonds I'm following.

"Hey, Nick. Can I ask you something?" William walks up to me with a tone of voice that tells me this is something he should have apologized for long ago. This is going to be bad.

"What's up?"

"You remember the night at the Soho Grand?"

"I do." His timidity is putting me on edge. It would be much better if he'd blurt it out.

"Something happened that night that I've been dealing with. My version is what happened, not her version. But I think I need your help with it."

"Come to the point, William. Jesus Christ."

"I've been accused of assault. By a stripper. Who was there that night."

"Rape?"

"Technically, yeah. She agrees we started consensually, but she says I got rough and she wanted to stop and I wouldn't."

"And what do you say?"

"It was consensual the whole way. We got into some bondage, it was a little rough but totally consensual."

"You're sure?"

"I'm sure." William doesn't sound indignant. He sounds nervous. I don't bother to ask how much coke he did that night.

"Is this the girl who was passed out in the bedroom?"

"No, she's not one of the girls who spent the night. She left early on during the party, just after we were together."

"Why do you need my help?"

"She wants to file charges. Criminal charges." He's starting to gather some indignation. "I've had to get a lawyer and I've managed to keep it from my parents and my fiancée so far. It hasn't gone anywhere yet and my lawyer is talking to the cops and the

DA's office. He's trying to see if the whole thing can be dropped or at least handled without charges."

"You mean pay her money to make her go away."

"Basically. Yes."

"William, I don't want any part of this. Why the hell are you talking to me?"

"I have a meeting with the assistant district attorney. He needs to decide whether or not to proceed with a case. It's me, my lawyer, and the ADA. He's also going to meet with the girl, but separately."

"I'm sure he'd love to get a case off his desk. I still don't know why you're talking to me."

He clears his throat. "The ADA would like to speak with you since you were at the party, at least the beginning of it. My lawyer also thinks it will help me to have a character reference."

"If you want a character reference, try your fiancée."

"Nick, I can't. She can't know about this." He pauses. "Oh, were you kidding?"

"No."

"Oh. Well, I can't. She would kill me. That would end things between us. My lawyer thinks it would be good to have someone who's known me for years. Ideally my boss."

I lean back in my chair and break eye contact for a long time. I'm not trying to send him a message. I really don't know yet how to handle this. "Jesus, William."

"I'm sorry, Nick."

We sit in silence together for a while. "Tell you what, William. I'll talk with your lawyer first. Privately. I'm not going to lie to the DA. I'm not going to tell him you're a goddamn saint. After I talk with your lawyer, if he still thinks it's a good idea for me to meet with the DA, I'll do it."

"Okay. Thanks, Nick." He seems just happy the conversation is over rather than truly appreciative.

A few minutes later there's commotion over by the elevators. I know Jack has arrived on the floor. I can't see it but I can hear distant rumbling and I know something's happened, like standing in the stadium parking lot at kickoff. The commotion is moving closer.

"Hey, Jacko!" I hear a few other morons making catcalls.

Jack comes through a ring of people, and when he sees me, he points at me. I'm on the phone and I give him the finger and he does a belly laugh. He walks over and takes the phone out of my hand. "I'll call you back in five minutes," he shouts down the phone before slamming it into the cradle.

There's no point in complaining about this, even in a joking way. "What are you doing here?"

"We're on our way to a game. Thought I'd stop by. Press the flesh. How are you? What's going on? Everything good?"

"Great." I stand up and give him a hearty handshake where we're wrapped more around the thumbs than the palms. "You look the same. Bloated and happy."

"Hey. I'm sensitive about that. Don't make fun." He laughs and gives me a half hug with his right shoulder lined up with my right shoulder. It's more of a bump than a hug.

His left hand comes around to pat my back but instead gets a fistful of my shirt and clenches it. His body tips forward and his right shoulder leans into mine and presses. "Hey, Jack. Jesus." His face lowers so his cheek is resting on top of my shoulder. His full weight is on me so I have to drop step a foot back to hold him up. He's mumbling words I can't understand and it sounds like he's saying "apple."

"Jack, what are you doing?" It's a stupid question. I know he's not choosing to do anything right now. Something's very wrong.

He lets out a muffled yell of pain and his knees buckle. His grip on my shirt pulls me down too, and I lower him on his back and I'm on top of him.

I look up and see a few dozen people standing around us, open-mouthed. "Call an ambulance!" I look back down and Jack is red-faced, eyes clenched closed and barely breathing. I'm not sure he's breathing at all and it actually crosses my mind how much I don't want to give him mouth-to-mouth. It might have to be me. We're practically spooning and nobody else is within ten feet.

Jesus Christ, I don't want to be here. "Does anyone know CPR?" I think it's twenty chest compressions, then a breath. Or fifteen compressions. Maybe I'm supposed to tilt his neck to clear the airway. "Any of you idiots know CPR!"

"Nick, I called an ambulance." It's William.

"Good." I look down at Jack. There's shallow breathing. His eyes are watery and open in little slits. "Hang in there, buddy."

He starts to speak. I can't hear a voice. It's more like he's shaping his breath into words. He brings his right hand up to clench my shirt too and brings me closer. We're nose to nose with about four inches to spare. His breath seems to be coming a little easier. I can tell he's already had a few drinks.

"Nick. Tell my wife I love her very much. She knows."

"What?" I have an image of standing over Jack in a casket holding hands with a woman I've never laid eyes on before, telling her how much Jack really loved her and how he spoke of her often.

"You're right. Screw that. She's a pain in my ass and she's my ex-wife anyway."

"What!" He's clowning around with his last breath.

"Seriously, Nick." He tightens his grip and brings me closer. We're down to three inches from touching noses. He's grimacing away the pain. "If I don't make it, talk to my kids. Tell them something nice about me. You can do that."

I think I can. I may have to get creative. "Sure, Jack. You're going to be fine, though. Stop talking and try to breathe slowly."

I'm pretty sure you give CPR only if the person isn't breathing, so I think I'm in the clear for the moment. "Where's the goddamn ambulance!"

"Two more minutes, Nick." It's William again.

"Hold on, Jack," someone shouts from rows away, and this starts a ripple of encouraging words from dazed-sounding voices.

"Does he need some water?" William is trying to help again. He feels like he's part of the rescue team.

"William, I don't know what the hell he needs. Just clear a path for a stretcher."

William goes about this, parting the ring of people and walking the shortest route to the elevators just as one opens and three paramedics come running out.

"Follow me," William yells, feeling very involved now. They all run up, and I roll away from Jack and watch seated on the floor while they check Jack's vitals and get ready to move him. They're fast and decisive and relaxed. They've obviously seen a lot worse than this.

In a moment, Jack is up on the stretcher, wheeled to the elevator, and gone. I'm still sitting on the floor by my desk. Everyone is still standing around in a looser formation of the ring they had been in while Jack was on the floor. They're shocked and everyone is talking in whispers.

Most of the people are like kids having watched their sports hero fall with a career-ending injury. I feel more like the player one locker down who's been taking the same steroids for the last ten years.

I'm still sitting on the floor with my legs straight out. Ron walks over and offers a hand up. I take it without thinking or looking and he pulls me over and into my chair.

If I can't find the fearlessness to make a change, maybe I can find the fear of not making a change.

January 27, 2006

I'M RATTLED BY JACK'S HEART ATTACK AND HAVE been leaving work early. Today I cut out for home instead of a bar and I notice Julia's bag for the gym isn't in the usual place by the door. I'm excited to be at home on a weekday afternoon, like a child skipping class and being in a place he shouldn't be but no one knows. I go to the kitchen to fix a drink.

When problems at home get truly bad, a perspective takes over to remind a person that these are the most important problems to solve. I can't get this off my mind, and if I can't get it off my mind anyway, I may as well be at home. I told William I had a client lunch and left. Just by being at home, I feel I'm working on making things better.

I go in the living room and sit with my drink resting on the edge of the chair armrest and my fingers only loosely around the glass. I look at the remote control for the TV on the coffee table in front of me and decide to leave it there. Now I just want to sit.

I swirl my glass, trying to get the ice cubes to move in an orbit.

I'm making an effort to think through issues but I can't find the starting point for any one of them.

I finish the drink and wipe the sweat from the bottom of the glass onto my suit pants. I drank fast enough that there wasn't much. Once I've had two or three, I can slow down my drinking, so I go back to the kitchen to fix another before changing out of my suit. I make it with more gin and less tonic this time, since the gin is already getting harder to taste.

I walk past Julia's office. Sketches of rooms in someone's suburban home are lying out with catalog photographs of furniture and bed linens. A crib and rocker for a baby room. I keep walking to our bedroom. My suit is starting to feel like it's made of shrinking burlap and my feet are hot in my shoes.

I hang the suit, lining up the pant creases, and fill the shoes with the shoe trees. As a kid I used to watch my father do this. I walk to the dresser to get a T-shirt, and on top of the dresser is a book with the kind of leather cover that can bend like a paperback. I recognize it as Julia's diary and see there is a pen in the pages poking out for my attention. I flip the diary open to where the pen is and look up and down the pages without reading the words. I understand the hand is Julia's. It feels like a stranger's. I realize I rarely see her handwriting at all.

Before I can look away, my eyes have begun to decode words and take in sentences. I do it without thinking. Without allowing myself to think, so I can avoid the guilt that might otherwise stop me. The page is opened to an entry on December 19, 2005, and it looks like there are several more since then. She must have been rereading old entries.

I am fat. FAT! Emergency fat. So fat am I that I am mortified at the thought of Oliver seeing my giant . . .

Oliver. My eyes passing over the name knock me right off the page. I'm scrambling and unscrambling the letters to make sure that I've read it right. O-L-I-V-E-R. It's actually written there, in her diary. I feel like I've been punched in the stomach. Everything about me has been threatened and is under attack. My hands are shaking and my body is weak as though I've had a lethal dose of caffeine. I peer back down at the diary and I find the word as though it was written in a different color ink.

> . . . Oliver seeing my giant and ever-expanding ass making its way to the dinner table.

I stop again. Everything about this moment feels perverted. Maybe discovering infidelity by sneaking a look in another's diary with drink in hand and in your own bedroom is the best way to find out.

This entry is more than a month old. My mind flashes to a confrontation with Julia coming home from the gym and me waving the diary like the prosecutor with exhibit A. That would spell the end and I know I'm no good at confrontation. Not just with Julia. I hate any kind. Some people thrive on combat, but I'm averse. I've been able to manage confrontation at work but never in my personal life. The stakes are too high and the damage is permanent.

I feel guilty having read any of the diary now. I've never read it before. Never thought about it, even when seeing the familiar binding on her nightstand or sticking out of her travel luggage. Sometimes she'd read parts to me. Unpack an old diary to read to me about her self-confessions and excitement when she got home from our first dates years ago. These are my experiences with the diary and I don't want to contaminate them.

I lower the book. There is a strong argument that it is no

violation to read the diary of a woman who has betrayed me. Or may have betrayed me. A woman who at a minimum cares enough about how fat her ass looks in front of another man to come home and write about it.

I need to read more, no matter how masochistic the impulse. My heart races with nerves and I look in the direction of the front door, which I could see only if I could look through walls. I'd make a terrible spy.

I skim pages braced for a sex scene with Oliver that she writes about wistfully, saying that but for her domestic prison and abusive husband, she could be with her true love. I skim over an encounter with a challenging client of hers and a conversation with her father that was so meaningless she got upset. Then I see

Nick hurt me last night. So deeply I may not recover. It revealed something about his view of me. Maybe it is something I need to consider, but his disgust with me was so thorough that I don't know if we have anything left.

I check the date and it's about the time of the Da Silvano dinner. Damn, I'm an asshole. I keep skimming but with less steam. There are only a few pages left anyway and then I see it.

Oliver called again. We had a long conversation and I have to admit I appreciate the attention. Where can I be honest if not here. Not sure how to handle this one.

I'm at the end of her pages and I put the diary down. There isn't a sex scene but there's confirmation of contact. Oliver is trying to have sex with her and she hasn't been telling me about that. My instincts are telling me something is very bad.

I look around the bedroom and make an uncomfortable pivot of my feet, turning in a complete circle like I'm lost in the woods. I need to get out. I need to get out before she gets home. I'm in no shape to talk, no shape to be seen.

I'm in a sudden desperate rush. I need to clear the apartment, hallway, elevator, lobby, and city block before she gets near. I have pants, a sweatshirt, loafers, and a coat pulled on just enough to stay with me, and I get my keys from the dish in the foyer on the third frustrated swipe and I'm out the door. Time enough to straighten myself in the elevator.

I round out of the elevator and into the lobby with arms pumping as fast as can still be considered a walk and not a jog. Charlie sees me coming, and I can see he looks worried for me. My face is telegraphing trauma and in my mind Charlie perceives the cause and knows all. I'd appreciate talking to Charlie now but it's more important to put distance between me and this building, as though I can hear the bursting, burping alarm sound that signals a nuclear reactor breach. I tighten my body language and stare to make sure there is no mistaking that I will leave the building without stopping to talk.

"Take care of yourself, Nick."

"Thanks, Charlie."

The gym is right, so I turn left and I'm away. I have no destination but keep a course going north and pull out my phone.

"Matt, it's Nick. You have time to get together?"

"Sure, for a couple hours. I need to be at the theater by five thirty to get ready for the show."

"That won't work. I need someone who can get drunk."

"Everything okay?"

"No. Nothing is." It's taking too much energy to collect my thoughts and talk on the phone. "I have to go. I'll call you later." I realize I'm walking fast and moving between people on the sidewalk.

I'm about to lose this woman. She's on her way out of my life. We're no longer two people in love but two people held together by a contract without the magic that makes you see the other person in a generous light. That spell is broken.

I love Julia and I want to save my marriage. I hear Sue's words again and I know the common thread of the problems isn't with my job and it isn't with Julia. It's me. I need to make a change. I ask myself what I'm prepared to do, and this time I demand an answer.

I suddenly stop in the middle of the sidewalk like Forrest Gump stopping his cross-country run. People behind me have to alter course to the side or they'd run up my back. My swirl of emotions is coming to rest at pissed off. I'm wired and I need a release. My anger is directed mainly at Oliver and I want to see him. He's not the heart of the problem but he's the heart of the symptom and that seems like a great start. I don't know if it's sadistic or masochistic, but I want to be in the same room with him, come what may.

It's still office hours, so I take out my cell phone to call him at Bear. If he answers, I'm going to tell him I'm on my way to see him, then hang up before he can say anything. I want to get to him face-to-face and tell him to stay away from us. I won't reveal anything about what I know and don't know, I'll just scare him. If I scare him enough, I might learn something.

The main reception puts me through. "Mr. Bennett's office."

"Hi, it's Nick Farmer from fixed income. I need to speak with Oliver."

"He's not in the office at the moment, Mr. Farmer."

"Back later or is he traveling?"

"I don't know, sir. He won't be in today."

"Vacation."

"Yes, sir. Yesterday he mentioned that he won't be available today, but I don't think he's traveling. May I try to get a message to him?"

"No, thanks." I hang up. What the hell is he doing?

I dial 411 for Oliver's home number. And address. Even better if I just drop in.

I'm already about ten blocks north of my place and near Bar Six, so I stop in for a few drinks to get myself ready and to pass an hour. I want to get closer to early evening so there's a better chance he's home. Bar Six is narrow and deep and looks like an old-world Italian trattoria only a little fancier. On the left by the entrance is a small bar with a copper top and it's wide open. I order a shot of tequila and a Stella. The bartender seems to recognize that I'm on serious business and am taking my drinking seriously.

I want to get my plan together but I realize I don't have a plan, I have only a motivation. I don't have enough information for a plan. I don't know if anything has happened, but I know he wants something to happen and I want to get rid of him.

I have two more beers and get ready to leave. Oliver lives all the way on the Upper East Side, so for good measure I have one more tequila shot while I put on my coat and leave. My stomach feels full of tequila and nervous acid. As I'm waving for a taxi on Sixth Avenue, I think about what I'm about to do and that I hardly know myself right now. This is the lowest and sickest place I've ever been. Surely this must be rock bottom, and I tell myself that it is.

Oliver lives across from the park on Fifth Avenue in a nice building, where the taxi drops me off. I hadn't contemplated getting past the doorman, and I decide quick and obnoxious is the best way.

I walk in fast and right by him like a resident. He was expecting me to stop and inquire after someone, so I'm a few steps past him before I hear, "Sir?"

I don't say anything because I'm searching around for the stairs as I get deeper in the lobby. It would be too awkward to wait for an elevator.

"Sir, who are you here to see? I'll need to call ahead."

"Oliver Bennett." I offer this over my shoulder and I see the stairs.

"Sir, if you'll wait here, I need to call ahead."

I'm at the base of the stairs. I turn around and point right at the doorman. I'm not angry with him at all, but I'm angry as hell. "Five A. You call him!" This has the effect of completely stunning him, and I'm up the first flight of stairs and maybe more before he recovers.

I take the stairs two at a time and it feels good to release some energy and recalibrate myself. By the fourth floor I'm getting spent, so I slow down to catch my breath and get ready for Oliver.

I'm standing in front of 5A and about to ring the doorbell but stop myself. I think better to knock and knock loudly than to ring the doorbell. It's a small detail but will make a nice difference. I want to do this just right.

I knock as loud as I can without hurting the door or myself. I finish a second assault and hear the door latch turn. The door opens only a quarter of the way and Sybil fills up the available space.

"Nick?"

Damn. I hadn't thought about this. Kids could be here too. I'll just tell her I need to speak with Oliver privately and we'll find some room. "Hi, Sybil."

She firms up her position and her arm tenses behind the door, giving the sense that she would like to close it. She's backlit by a huge chandelier and it makes her skin look cold and out of focus. There's an opalescent sheen to her like a Renoir bather. "What can I do for you?"

"I'd like to speak with Oliver for a minute."

"He's not here."

Son of a bitch. She reflexively leans back a bit to get out of the way of the door she'd like to slam. She seems to be operating on instinct and her instinct is screaming that I'm not a friend to her.

The phone starts to ring and she looks behind her, torn. I guess it's the doorman sounding the alarm. Her manners prevail over instincts. "One moment, Nick. Come in."

I step into a small foyer that opens to a huge living room lit by the chandelier. There's a hallway to the left that looks like it leads to bedrooms and one to the right leading to the kitchen. I don't see any kids.

She picks up a phone from a writing table in the living room. It's one of those new phones meant to look old, made of brass and porcelain with a fancy cradle so the phone hangs vertically. "Hello . . . Yes, he's here . . . Yes, fine . . . Thank you, Sam." She cradles the phone.

"Is Oliver out of town?"

"He is." I'm certain she knows exactly as much as I know, which is an incomplete and unhealthy amount, but she's chosen defiance over sharing sympathies. She's lumped me into the enemy camp and I have the urge to break her veneer and see her whimper through a confession.

"Business or pleasure?" I try to make it sound as customary as exchanging a greeting and that I don't care about an answer.

"He's golfing. He flew to Palm Beach early this morning to play. He might be back tonight. Probably first thing tomorrow."

"Avid golfer."

"At least once a week, year round. In the winter that means more travel." She catches that this could sound like a complaint, so she brightens her face and rambles on. "He's at the Everglades Club today, which is a great old course. One of Oliver's dear friends is a private client money manager in Palm Beach who's struggled with alcoholism. He moved to Palm Beach after rehabilitation for a quieter life, and Oliver visits him often to support him and help him along."

This all sounds hollow. She's trying to make his golfing seem altruistic, but it sounds false and makes me think of potpourri spray over crap. The mix is worse than just the crap. "I just can't get into golf. It seems like a holdover from nineteen fifties misogyny. Who wants to spend a whole day on a golf course except a person who would rather not be at home?"

Now it's her turn to brush away a comment. "With Oliver it's really about helping a friend. They bond over golf and Oliver's helped him to be two years sober, which he credits almost entirely to Oliver." I get the sense she badly wants to believe this. She seems like a person acting not in the pursuit of life but in the avoidance of death, a child under a bed hiding from an intruder.

"Rehab is for quitters. I think Keith Richards said that. Genius." Even I don't know what I'm talking about now. I'm still pissed but I've lost sight of what I can accomplish here. It might be good if Sybil passes on to Oliver that I was here and that I know, but I don't think she's able to confront him and she'll say only that I stopped by to say hi.

She smiles at my comment, willing to pretend that she thinks I was trying to be funny. Is it possible that Oliver is in Florida helping a friend in need and being a good guy? No way. He's a fraud. He's a movie set of a western town.

"The Everglades Club is sort of stuck-up, isn't it?"

"Oh, well, we always have a nice time there. Oliver has made some very nice new friends."

I know she knows. We each know everything the other knows and I'm sick of this game. "Sometimes people can have more fun with new friends than with old friends. Don't you think?"

At this point it would be reasonable for her to tell me I'm rude and ask me to leave, but she acts dumb. I'm sure she'd like to kick me out, but she's not comfortable doing it. I feel a little like a bully, but I'm just trying to shake some sense into her.

"I don't know. I love new friends and old friends."

"What about Oliver?"

"What about him?" This isn't a challenge. It's asked timidly, hoping I won't answer in a cruel way.

"Has he found new friends to love?"

"Nick, I don't know what you're insinuating, but you sound awful."

"You don't know what I'm insinuating. Not at all?"

"I do not."

I pause and shake my head, piling on as much judgment as I can. "You two have the perfect codependent dysfunction. You pretend to like the same things and dislike the same things and you accept each other's lies and wear it around thinking nobody's going to notice. Even worse, you recycle his crap and expect to be congratulated for it. But you know it's lies, don't you? He hands it to you and you know it and you don't care. It's not real."

She's at a loss for words. Then she finds one. "Asshole."

"Asshole? Oliver tries on new personalities like a change of clothes. I'm the one helping you and I'm the asshole?"

"You like being ironic?"

"I can't stand it."

"I'd like you to leave."

"Of course." The door is still cracked and I'm through it. I wonder if she'll tell Oliver about our little chat. Probably not. Probably I just made her more alone and unhappy.

PART IV

In theory, there's no difference between theory and practice. In practice there is.

—Yogi Berra

January 28, 2006

MY MARRIAGE IS ABOUT TO SHATTER AND I MAKE A connection to my parents that I have never made before. It isn't that any of the four people in the two marriages are at all similar, but there is a dynamic that is relevant. My father's easygoing way, which I have always counted among his best qualities, I now call into question. My mother is a bitch, and in plain view. Not once did my father ever challenge her on this, even when on the receiving end of her coldness. Not a single word of reproach. Now I see that he taught himself to deny that my mother was a bitch at all. Rather than have the conversation, he was more comfortable living in a self-fashioned fantasy. I now understand that he could have done better by all of us.

Julia's parents to me are just something to be suffered. If anything, the roles are reversed and her dad is the active pain in the ass while her mom goes along.

Our dinner plans with them have been set for this Saturday. This is the type of thing I usually might find an excuse to miss, but tonight I sense it is an opportunity. Blindly doing the opposite of what my impulses have been in the past seems like a sound plan, so I try to be cheery about the dinner. The problem is I hate spending time with her father even under normal circumstances. The mother isn't actively horrible but she's complicit in her husband's jackass behavior and so I can't stand her either. My cheeriness sounds a little hyper and false.

I had made sure to come home late Friday and she was up early Saturday, so this afternoon is our first time together since my reading the diary. I've been avoiding her, steeling myself for how to act around her. She doesn't know I've seen the diary, so her interpretation of my avoidance could be anything. Probably she thinks I'm just sour about having to spend the evening with her parents. There's some truth in that.

It's an hour drive to the restaurant in Oyster Bay. "It feels nice to drive out of the city. It's a mini getaway." It feels like I'm working for every minute.

"It's nice to get a change of scenery," she responds, and I pat her left knee with my right hand, keeping my eyes still on the road.

"It'll be good to see your dad. It's important." My new rule is to say only positive things. If I have a negative thought, I'll filter it before it gets to my mouth.

We're through the Midtown Tunnel and on the Long Island Expressway going east. I'm in the passing lane doing about seventy. In the rearview I see a black Nissan bombing up the right-hand lane. It has a spoiler on the back and performance tires with fancy hubcaps. It has racing stripes down the side. It has a weird suspension like it's meant for drag racing. Probably a twelve-thousand-dollar car with twenty thousand worth of extras. Absurd. I think all of this but don't say it, keeping with the new rule.

The car is screaming up toward us and there is a gap where he can pass me on the right and slip into my lane before he reaches the car in front of him. There's a car about fifty yards in front of me, so he'll have to switch lanes back again. I hate this kind of idiot driver.

I press down on the accelerator to get even with the car in the right lane and close the gap to pin in the Nissan. I want to see him smack his steering wheel and scream into the dashboard.

I had meant to subtly accelerate, but the rpm needle jumps and the pitch of the engine makes everything feel urgent. Julia moves her hands from her lap to the sides of her seat and hangs on.

"Crap," I mutter under my breath. I get off the accelerator and touch up the brake. The damn Nissan is on us in a second and its engine sounds like a blender. I see the teenaged bastard behind the wheel, and he slips into our lane in front of us with about three feet between his bumpers and the cars on either end. He's in our lane for about a three count before he passes the car to his right and is back over in that lane again. I feel a little proud of myself for granting passage. Julia's hands come off the seat. I think she's relieved but hardly proud.

The restaurant is cedar-shingled and looks like a converted old inn. The parking lot is a driveway that has been expanded for more cars and winds around the side of the building. I pass a few open spaces and park around the corner from the entrance. There's no benefit to doing this. I realize when I've stopped that it just isn't the way a person who wants to get inside would do it. I shut off the car but don't make a move for my door.

She turns to me. "You ready?" She's trying to sound cheerful too.

"I'm hungry."

"Nick, at least try to fake it. Just for a couple hours. Please."

"It'll be just fine as long as he doesn't talk much."

"Just take the high road."

"I'm kidding, I'm kidding." I flip the door handle and get out.

Alistair Pembroke, the great retired attorney and royal pain in my ass, is already there seated on a wooden bench along the wall in the waiting area. His legs are crossed knee over knee with his hands resting uncertainly on top as though the legs are something extra, a piece of luggage next to him on the bench and not connected to the rest of his body. He's tall and tan, with thinning black hair combed straight back and small amounts of gray at the temples left skillfully undyed. He has a long, thin nose that isn't so bad on a man and fortunately didn't get passed down to Julia. He's wearing a blazer with a black turtleneck shirt underneath. The outfit looks ridiculous on a man nearly seventy. It belongs in Miami Beach on a man half his age running a nightclub.

While he sits, Patricia Pembroke is up across the room like his receptionist checking on the table with the host. She's at least dressed sensibly in the sort of pants and blouse you'd expect from a woman her age. Julia gets her looks mainly from Patricia. Tall, thin, athletic, pretty eyes, pretty lips. She looks much like Julia might in thirty years. She has a nice way about her too, but I can't forgive her the sin of what she chose for a husband. Show me who you love and I'll show you who you are.

The one positive thing I can say for Alistair is he didn't drop Patricia for the fresh-faced secretary. Knowing him, he probably had affairs, he just never had the guts to be honest with everyone, especially himself, to go the whole distance and set everyone free. But Patricia sticks around for it. They don't seem very loving, more as though they have a good professional relationship but one that obviously fills needs, because they're both here.

Alistair uncrosses his legs and stands. All his movements seem to happen sequentially like a kid moving the parts of a toy robot. I go to shake his hand and muscle up a smile. I can't stand the way he talks, always in run-on monotone sentences that force the listener to do the punctuation for himself. It has a schizophrenic quality and is probably why he couldn't be a litigator and why he worked in corporate law.

"Good to see you Nick glad you both could make it out this way and I suppose traffic wasn't too bad and you were able to keep my daughter safe must be nice to have a little break from that city if only for a night, eh?"

"Good to see you, Alistair. Patricia, you look nice." She had appeared at our sides for the handshake like the dutiful aide. I give her a kiss on the cheek.

"How are you, Nick?" Patricia always seemed to like me. She seems to get along with all men, especially those she thinks are handsome. But she's also cautious of the tension between me and Alistair.

"I'm getting by."

Julia hugs each of her parents and we start for the table, a round one in the middle of the room. Fortunately Alistair is quick to order a drink and I get bourbon on ice. Neither of us wants to be here, but it's the only way he can see his daughter. I have no reason for being here.

"So Nick how are things on Wall Street seems like a good year never does seem to matter though you traders can move it around whether it's going up or down."

"Should be an okay year. I'll fax over my W2 if you're interested." He irritates me. I can't help it.

"Ha nothing like that very funny though it seems like only you and the baseball players get paid no matter what got a guy getting ten million and bats two hundred ought to give it all back for turning in a rotten season like that what a joke, eh?"

"Well, I couldn't get into law school."

"I say I was there in the heyday of it all billion-dollar oil and gas mergers and saving thousands of jobs at airlines through structured bankruptcy and fighting Carl Icahn in a proxy war to take him for a billion it was fun and one hell of a time we did things."

Alistair's stories seem to grow by twenty percent each time I hear them. With compound growth, a person needs to know him only a few years before they've doubled and tripled in grandeur. I can hardly tolerate his indulgences to preserve some legacy for himself. Corporate lawyers really have a chip on their shoulders about having done anything exciting. I look at Julia and widen my eyes, which I hope communicates to her that I'm nearing a breaking point already and she better jump in and shut him up.

"Mom, you look great. Where'd you get those earrings?"

The drinks arrive and I order another one before taking the first sip. Patricia glances at me but I've already decided that if I'm going to make it through dinner, I need to focus on me and my survival and there might be collateral damage in doing so.

"Honey, I've had these earrings for years. Your father gave them to me on our tenth anniversary."

Alistair reaches over in a fumbling way to touch one earring, and I half expect him to yank Patricia out of her chair the way one of the Three Stooges might pull another by gripping a nose or an earlobe.

"Yes yes beautiful they are the way a man needs to be for a woman there's a sparkle and I remember the jeweler was a good man and he and I designed a few pieces together you remember dear." Of course any comment at the table he needs to relate back to himself. I think the only way to contain him is not to make any comments at all.

The waiter arrives, so I barge in to announce that I won't have a salad or appetizer and I order my entrée. This seems like a good way to shorten dinner by thirty minutes. Alistair is put off by my behavior, but the girls go next and go along with just an entrée and so does he. It feels like a small win.

I have the pork, which turns out to be very good, and I switch to wine. I don't know what the others are having or what they're saying. I'm playing a game with myself to think back through a whole story start to finish, whichever story comes to mind first, then come back to the table and conversation to see how much time has passed. It's usually only two or three minutes, so I keep playing. No one seems to mind.

The entrées are finished and taken and Alistair orders dessert. He eats it slowly, and I notice Patricia is looking concerned for Julia, several times placing her hand on Julia's forearm in a comforting way and without prompting. Julia looks happy for it, which isn't normal, and I can see it makes Patricia feel happy and needed. It makes me want to leave faster.

The waiter delivers the check directly to Alistair though I had wanted to pay. I don't want him to feel like he's doing anything nice for us. "I'll get that, Alistair." I reach over with my credit card.

"Nonsense the least we can do you coming all the way out here to sit with us."

Short of ripping the bill from his hands, I'll have to let this go. Alistair completes the tip and transaction with the waiter, then quietly surveys the table with his hands folded in front of him like a rancher looking over his pasture from up in the saddle of his horse.

"So when are you two going to deliver us a grandchild not getting any younger here and neither are you would be nice to know the child you see in our day we raised children when we were young and they were the focus and family the priority." He starts talking while looking at Julia and ends looking at me.

"That's none of your business, Dad." Julia is uncomfortable but firm and looks him right in the eye, meaning to shut this down before it goes a comment further.

"Alistair, please." Patricia puts her hand on Julia's forearm again and slowly strokes.

I let it all pass but Alistair doesn't want to end dinner having been rebuked. He moves on like a pitcher who has thrown a called ball and goes right back into his windup for the next pitch. He decides to press what he clearly views to be a related point.

"Nick, how long do you keep it up on Wall Street younger man's game you know could buy a little business to run and live in a house with a yard find a little business that does some good and gives some back could be fun."

He knows very well this hits a nerve with me, that some part of me agrees with what he says. Coming from him, I can't see it as support but only as antagonism. Maybe he's pissed that even average bond traders make more than partners in law firms. I lean back first to think about the best way to respond, and I decide direct is best. "Alistair, every time we see each other, you find a way to criticize me and my job and try to convince me to make changes as though you're not happy with who I am. As though you think I'm soulless, my job is soulless. Why would you say that to me? Is that what you think?" I lean forward at him to show I intend to get an answer to the question.

There's no sound but the clinking of teacups in saucers. Alistair clears his throat. Like any passive-aggressive, he's not used to direct confrontation or an honest interpretation of his question that forces him to defend why he asked it. He prefers to have his subtlety returned with subtlety.

"It's a fine job provides for the family and all to be sure not at all soulless just there comes a time and people try things make career changes see what's out there and this is what you've done for a dozen years and just a thought."

Confronting Alistair like this is one step. I could smile and shrug it off now and everyone's temperature would drop and it would all be forgotten. I could stop it at this level of damage. Or I could take the next step and say what I've thought but held back for the sake of keeping the peace, keeping Julia out of the cross fire of open war. To take the next step with Alistair would be irreversible. If I fight with Julia, we have a foundation of years together and a contract that means we work to fix it and we want to forgive. To fight with Alistair would poison the soil we've been trying to build on and we'd abandon the effort and the toxic ground. On the other hand, to confront him is the honest thing to do. I want to make the changes in my life to cut away the negative and focus on the positive. If I believe in this, then Alistair must go. These are the kinds of decisions I need to make.

This is a turn down a one-way street with no U-turns. I feel myself press down the accelerator. "Just a thought," I repeat back to him. "Here's a thought for you, Alistair." I look for a moment at Patricia, then at Julia, then settle back on Alistair. Patricia looks horrified at what she knows is coming. Julia looks calm as though this is something she's been predicting for years would come and is happy to see it and feels vindicated. There's even a small smile curling up one side of her mouth, and in the middle of this it strikes me how beautiful she looks. Alistair shifts in his chair with hands clenching the edge of the table like an airline passenger hitting turbulence.

"You're incapable of being honest with yourself, which is lucky for you because you don't have to come face-to-face with what a pompous clown you are. You reinvent history and yourself to be whatever makes you feel happy and secure. What's unlucky for everyone around you is that we're stuck with you. You're just as incapable of changing from the piece of crap that you are because you can't or won't face how twisted up you are, and so we all have to sit around and indulge this illusion you've created of yourself, for yourself. Just a thought." I remember my commitment to filter the negative and say only the positive. My new rule lasted about two hours before I overwhelmed it.

Alistair looks stunned and angry. I don't think he heard anything specific that I said after the first few words. He internalized only that it was insulting and insolent and he dismissed it. Patricia has her hand to her mouth.

I play back in my head what I've said, and I know it is immature bordering on irrational. I'm tempted to apologize, throw up my hands and say hey, let's forget the whole thing, but that feels impossible and might make me look even crazier.

Julia takes a final sip of coffee and, putting the cup down, says, "Okay," with more emphasis on the *kay* than the *o*, which seems to signal the end of dinner. All four chairs push back from the table at once. The simultaneous precision is comical. And tragic.

January 29, 2006

JULIA GAVE NO EXPLANATION AND NONE WAS ASKED for. She simply said she wasn't going to come. I simply nodded and said okay. It's hard for me to gauge the damage from last night's dinner, given she's not a fan of her own father, as well as the context of the already catastrophic level of damage in our marriage.

I park behind a line of cars along the street of my sister's home. It's the kind of town that averages about a half acre per house. Hundred-year-old renovated homes with manicured lawns are close together, creating a real neighborhood with enough kids always nearby to meet in groups and play in the streets.

Ted Golb is walking in front of the house carrying bags and wearing a tall hat that looks out of a Dr. Seuss story and that says "Happy Birthday" around it.

"Nicholas, my man." Never Nick. He never calls anyone by the name they go by. If I went by Nicholas, he'd call me Nicky. He always changes everyone's name to some form of nickname he can use. He feels it's the chummy thing to do, that it breaks down barriers and means we're old friends. It's part of his social awkwardness.

"How are you, Ted."

"Hey, pal." He raises his hands a few inches to show they are full of bags. "Would you mind getting some beer and soda and ice from the refrigerator out back and bringing it in? See if anyone needs a refill?"

"Sure. If you have a mop, I can do the kitchen floor. Maybe sweep out the garage?"

"No need, buddy. All set." I assume he's choosing to ignore my sarcasm rather than having missed it entirely. I want to be sure, though.

"I must have skipped over the part in the invitation that said this is a barn raising." As I say this, I realize I must be in a worse mood than I had thought. I'm not lashing out at Ted as much as I am at Julia. But the fact is I do hate people that host a party, then hand out chores to arriving guests.

"Barn raising?"

"Hasn't anyone ever told you that you can hire people who come over and do this sort of thing so your guests can actually be guests?"

"Listen, if you don't want to do it, that's okay." He looks a little off balance and is trying to be friendly but isn't quite smiling. He's a sort of Fred Rogers type, plus I'm his wife's brother, so he probably feels he can't get angry with me.

"It's no problem. I'm on it. See you in there." I start for the back door to the house before he can apologize or tell me how rude I am. I don't know which it would have been.

On the back porch they have a refrigerator that lies down like an oversized coffin. I get twelve Budweiser and twelve Mountain Dew and fit a bag of ice under each arm and enter the house from the porch into the kitchen. They have a huge Victorian house built in the late 1800s. The house has a main central staircase, and each of the rooms connects in a ring around the main stairs, so a person can move from room to room in a circle around the first floor and come back to where he started. I go from the kitchen to the dining room, where I see Ted and drop my load next to him like I'm delivering a summons. "Here you go." I smile and again move on before he can react.

I cross through the foyer of the front door and into the living room on the other side, where I get Susan's eye. She's surrounded by the parents of Andy's friends, I imagine talking about soccer leagues and flute lessons. Between me and Susan is my mother, talking with a couple, and she beckons me over with one hand while still finishing her sentence. I step toward them just as the front door of the house opens. Into the foyer behind me run Andy and several young birthday revelers who were playing outside.

"Uncle Nick!" Andy runs directly for me. He still has his jacket on and I can feel he carries some cold air with him as he gives me a leaping hug. He smells like soap and leaves.

"Happy birthday, big man."

"Thanks! See ya." He runs off past his mother and my mother, with a herd of others like him trailing behind and all shouting words communicating nothing more than a train whistle blowing.

"Children, mind yourselves," my mother says with no playfulness, like the kids are dogs and she's not a dog person. They run by her and she takes a dramatic step backward even though they weren't close to her. "Oh, the humanity."

"Jesus Christ, Mother." Although she's not fat, my mother is a big woman with a physical presence. She always looks elegant without being overdressed for the occasion. Usually it's a dress from St.

John or Chanel. The kind older women with money wear. Today it's a pale-blue dress with a pearl necklace and earrings. She's never worn a pair of jeans in her life and the image seems impossible.

"Nicholas, I beg your pardon." Sue's friends take an exit.

"Where's Dad?"

"He had some work to finish. He'll be along in an hour or so."

"Okay." I turn and walk away. I don't want to spend more time with her. That was plenty. I'm reminded of how oddly adolescent my relationship with her remains, which makes me dislike her even more. Ironically, she seems to like me more now than when I was a child, probably because I'm not so inconvenient anymore. I'm an adult with my own life, so now she needs to engage me only as much as she would a friend from a book club.

Susan uses the commotion to break with the other parents and come over to me. "Hey, big brother."

"Sometimes I still can't believe my little sister's a mom at all."

"I used to have those moments. The kids pounded them out of me very quickly. Where's Julia?"

"She's not coming." There is no excuse like a sprained ankle or car trouble that I can deliver in an easy manner. It's just a brief statement of fact that lands with a thud.

"Let's go talk upstairs. The first floor's overrun."

"Okay." I smile my appreciation and am surprised to find how much I'm looking forward to talking with her. "I'm going to stop by the bar on the way. Can I get you something?"

"Gin and tonic. I'll escape now. See you in the den upstairs."

I walk back through the foyer into the dining room, where the bar is set up on one end of the table. I move workmanlike with a lowered gaze to avoid making any accidental invitation to conversation. In a moment I have two glasses loaded to the rim with gin

and tonic and I'm back to the foyer and up the stairs without having uttered even a grunt to anyone.

They've styled their den in a classic way with wood paneling on
the walls, a dark walnut desk, and built-in bookshelves full of old
books that give the room the smell of a library's old book room.
Susan's sitting on a two-seat leather sofa against the wall, and I
hand her a drink and lean against the desk in a sideways sit.

"Mom's her usual charming self. How's Caroline?"

"She's good. She was cute this morning with Andy for his
birthday. It's funny having two. One day they're best friends and
loving and supportive. The next day the opposite. But either way,
they know each other better than anyone else."

"Like you and me."

"Yup. How are you, Nick? Any special reason why Julia isn't
with you?"

"Hm. Special reason. Probably. I can start with the most recent
reason, which is that last night at a casual dinner for four with her
parents, I managed to punctuate the end of dinner by calling her
dad a pompous clown and piece of crap."

Some people reflexively say "You're kidding" or "Seriously?"
when hearing a story like that. Susan never does that, which I appreciate. "I would love to have seen Alistair's face." She smiles and
takes a sip of her drink. "Jesus, Nick, are we out of tonic?"

"I only barely saw his face myself. A little red, a little contorted,
then turned to the door. There wasn't a discussion."

"He is a pompous ass. Once he calms down, he ought to realize
you did him a favor."

"Not likely."

"How did Julia react?"

"About like you. Except our problems run pretty deep. I've

always kept things in check with Alistair, just going along to get along with him because it's better for us, but now I feel like I'm losing my grip. I wasn't mad at Alistair. I don't care enough about him to get mad at him, but I carried some old wounds into dinner and he hit a nerve."

"And you went after him."

"Whatever I used to value enough to keep the peace with him wasn't there. It wasn't that I was thumbing my nose at Julia. I didn't want to hurt her or make things hard for her. It was just a reshuffling of priorities so that I did something more for myself without worrying about consequences."

"What nerve of yours did he hit?"

"The usual raw and exposed nerve. That my career is meaningless and juvenile. Which is also part of the problem with Julia. Some form of what he said, she thinks."

"You're not your career, Nick. She may not love what you do, but she loves you. She respects you and your character. She and I have had enough conversations into the early morning hours that I know this."

"Well, my career is still in the picture. Distinguishing it in the way you do may not be enough. She would prefer to exorcise it and kill it."

"You already know how I feel about that. I agree."

I do know and I don't want to retread this ground. It also isn't what has all my senses in a panic. "It's possible Julia may be having an affair."

Susan's expression doesn't change but she leans back into the sofa, staring at me. I notice how long it's been since she last blinked, and I find myself counting the seconds and the number of times I blink before she next does. "You buried the lead. What makes you suspect her?"

I don't want to describe how I read through Julia's diary, that it was just lying out and I happened to see it and read a few pages. "We've spent some time with another couple. Julia's behavior's been a little weird, his has been weirder. And there've been some clues around the apartment."

We both sip our drinks and sit quietly for a moment. "Nick, Julia is not the type for affairs. Of course, people who are not the type still have affairs all the time for one reason or another."

"Meaning it takes two? Meaning I drove her to it?"

"Meaning there's no point in talking about whether she crossed the line. We don't know and I can't comment on it. It's not the most important thing anyway. What matters is why she would even consider it in the first place."

"Look, I know I have a role in this, I'm not an idiot. But starting an affair with another man is a different matter."

"Nick, let's leave the affair question to the side for a moment."

Susan is treading lightly around this. My relationship with Julia is potentially till death do us part, so she may be speaking carefully about a person who is supposed to be a permanent member of the family, but it's frustrating me. "How are we supposed to put an affair to the side?"

"Because the affair itself isn't what matters. It's your relationship with Julia."

"It's been on a slow and steady descent to unhappiness for a long time."

"Do you want to work on it?"

"Yes, we're trying to figure out how."

"You need to believe you're worth it. Not just Julia or your marriage, but you. Sometimes you seem a little self-loathing, whether it's you or your job."

I'm following along with what Susan's saying and actively

weighing whether it has any relevance to what's happening. "I wouldn't be so sure."

"I know the type of stuff you get up to at work. It's easier to be a sister to than a wife to. I also know it's not really you."

"I don't know anymore, Susie. I've changed since you really knew me well. I'm not the person you grew up with."

"Nick, the last thirteen years don't define you and never have in the slightest. You're the same person you always have been from the beginning." She stands from the couch, steps to me, and pokes the center of my chest. "Before you were ten years old, the man you would become was already in there. The point is that I do know you well. You're a good person. Nothing else can be saved if you can't believe that."

I finish my drink. "Maybe you're right."

She smiles and her tone gets more offhanded. "If anything, you're a little closed off. You never take chances with yourself."

She's right about that and I don't want to talk about it. It's easier to be closed off. Sometimes it's just easier to say nothing, or even to let yourself slip into a pattern of self-castigation because it's easier to accept the punishment than to try for better. Sue knows she's close to the heart of it and I'm uncomfortable, so she lets me off the hook.

"You are a good man, Nick."

"In that case, please apologize to Ted for me. I was in a bad mood and might have been a little rude."

Susan makes a sigh mixed with a laugh. "Oh, God. How bad?"

"Not horrible."

She stands and hugs me.

"Thanks, Susie." She pulls my face down and kisses my forehead. "I'm going to give Andy and Caroline a hug, then slip out."

"I love you, Nick."

"I love you too."

I avoid my mother on the way out and am in Susan's driveway when I run into my dad arriving to the party.

"Hiya, Nick."

He slips between bumpers of tightly parked cars to give me a hug. Not the kind that is slow and sentimental but the kind that means in our relationship we always hug. The thing is, this has started only since I've been in my thirties. I think the old man has always had it in him, but it wasn't until this stage of his life that he decided it's important. Maybe he got some therapy.

He looks a lot like I might in twenty years, only more professorial. He's always wearing tweed jackets and old leather shoes. He still practices as an orthopedic surgeon.

Two types of people go into medicine. Some because they manage to get tuition together and it gives them a safe and lifelong career. Even if they aren't very good, they won't go unemployed, and it's respectable enough for cocktail parties. Susan's husband, Ted, is one of these.

The others choose it because it's a noble and intellectual profession. Dr. Tom Farmer is one of these.

"How are you, Dad?"

"How's city life?" He lives only forty-five minutes away but is still fascinated by the city and can't understand how a person can live in it.

"The same. It's where the action is."

"How's your lovely wife?"

"She's fine. She had some errands to run, so she couldn't make the party."

"How are things at work?" Dad likes to stay in regular touch. I can tell when he's short on time because he asks the punch line questions, then signs off.

"It's a living." It doesn't feel obnoxious to respond with punch line answers.

"Nick, what do you say we get together for duck hunting? Your mother and I fixed up the old blind this fall. We could get a hunt in before the end of the season."

I expected some form of this. He ends every conversation trying to make a plan to see each other the next time, as though he's convincing us both this is important to him. I think he hasn't come to terms with the moment on the train platform when he saw me off to boarding school and sent the message that spending more time with me wasn't a priority. "That would be great, Dad. Maybe in a few weeks."

"Sure. Sure. You can use my old Browning. I just had it cleaned and restored." This is a prize possession of his that he bought while in his twenties in Belgium when he didn't have much money. He feels that a gentleman always buys the best that he can afford, then takes great care to maintain it. His gun is a classic in mint condition and a reminder to him that he has acted like a gentleman.

"It's a deal."

"Great, then. I'll see you in a couple weeks."

We wrap the conversation in a bow. He's a kind man, but Mom is the dominant person. I think every kid needs to like at least one of his parents, so I suppose I'm lucky to have him.

I'm back in the car and away to the city.

January 30, 2006

I CALL WILLIAM AND TELL HIM I'M NOT COMING IN AND to cover my accounts. I don't tell him I'm sick or try to sound sick or even tired. He can probably hear that I'm calling from the car.

I had told Julia that I wanted to take the car to check on our house in Sag Harbor and stay there a couple days. She seemed to find as much relief as I did in the plan. We slept in the same room last night, though I had thought about moving to a couch to ease the effect of the silence in such close proximity, but there's something so official about dragging a pillow and blanket to the next room, like ringing the bell at a prizefight. Anyway, I was up and out the door by 7 a.m. before she was awake.

I love driving in winter with my jacket still on and the windows down, and I do it the whole distance I'm on the Long Island Expressway. It feels like camping out. There's no traffic at this hour heading in this direction, so I'm out to Sag Harbor in about two hours. I love it here in the winter. The whole town seems to be resting. Even the trees seem to be lounging with coffee and a book.

When we bought our place a few years ago, we decided on the

philosophy of buying the worst house on the best street. Even still, our house is not at all bad with its large bay windows and working fireplace. I pull into the market for ground coffee, the paper, and firewood before going there.

I stop the car at the head of the driveway and admire my house for a moment. I think how it looks old and nice and that I own it. I can claim this as my own and others can attribute it to me. It is something I use and that feels substantial.

I think how I should buy only real things and not stock in some company. When I buy stock in IBM, I never visit the offices to walk the halls of the company or sit down with management. The stock will move up or down based on the comments of an analyst, and I have no real connection to the company. The whole thing could be a fiction or a board game. It's like buying a vacation property that I know I intend never to visit or even see, then adjusting the value each day based on the weather forecast.

But this is a real home where I can step inside and get warm or shower after a day at the beach and others can drive by and admire it and decide they would pay an amount for it. It feels good to possess. Something in our nature promotes that, and I know too much about the manipulations on Wall Street to find any comfort in a paper investment.

Julia and I used to take off as many summer Fridays and Mondays as we could, pack the car and fight the traffic to get here. We'd pull in and notice the city sounds had been replaced by quiet and salt air and feel that these are the moments that make life good on balance.

I walk in the front door and slide my hand up the wood frame, admiring the sturdiness more than I have in the past. I start the coffee and a fire and sit in a reclining chair so I can feel the pulse of heat from the flames. The chair is old and leather and so worn in places that the brown has turned yellowish. All the furniture is so rustic and otherwise uncoordinated that it creates a theme of its own that nearly works for a comfortable beach home. Or maybe Julia has put more thought into it than I know.

I pick up the paper and start reading and wait for the calmness to come.

I have the *Journal* and the *Times*, and between periods of closing my eyes for a rest and getting up to freshen the fire, I make my way through most of the articles. I turn to the crossword puzzle. Nothing signals being on vacation like spending time on a crossword. It's the Monday version, so there are some easy gimmes that help establish a whole corner of the puzzle. I find myself starting to care about completing the puzzle and it feels good to see progress and to have a corner I can count on as a foundation. It's a shame that life doesn't come with the same little victories and affirmations of correctness of a crossword puzzle.

Within an hour I've gotten all I can get without cheating, which is disappointing because it's only Monday and I used to be able to complete these. But it's been a while since I've done one, maybe since a vacation with Julia a few years ago.

I put the paper down and recline back in the chair to rest my eyes again. My mind reverts back to Oliver, as though he was there all the time under my eyelids just waiting for them to close. I have an image of accepting his invitation to play squash and crushing his slight body into a side wall as I pretend to go for a ball but angle directly into him instead. Then I stand over his body writhing in pain from cracked ribs and his broken glasses lying at an angle on top of his wincing face, and I offer him a hand up with a look that says, This is your fault because you shouldn't have been standing there. You should have stayed out of my way and not come anywhere near me. My hand comes off the armrest of the leather chair and extends to pick up Oliver's crumpled body as though I'm on the squash court, and my body acts out the scene the way a little kid will mime a rock star in the bathroom mirror. This scene is something I can make happen in real life if I go just a little bit crazier, and it makes me happy to think that.

Then my mind races on to Julia tending to his broken body still lying on the court. She kneels beside him and looks up at me with appalled eyes that know that I wasn't trying to get to a ball at all. Then she turns back to him to straighten his silly glasses and smooth over his hair with the other hand. I drop my racquet and walk off the court, and in real life I straighten up from the reclined chair, open my eyes, and put another log on the fire.

My plan for calmness isn't working. Being so focused on acting calm never made anyone calm. I think maybe I should start a diary of my own. Maybe I can take all of this and dump it onto the pages of a journal. This wouldn't be a document to memorialize things so that years from now I could leaf through the pages and recapture the feeling. This would be the opposite. Like removing a wart, I want to cut it out of me and cast it into the pages and never see it again.

I wonder which of these roles Julia's diary plays for her. I also decide that I'm starting not to like my own company very much. Being alone strips away all the little distractions and corners I can use to hide away from my own thoughts. It unveils me to myself. I know it should be good, like shaving down a callus to bring out the virgin skin. Two days of this will be enough and three too many. Right now I'm not sure I like myself enough to be alone.

I'm a cynical bastard stuck in relationships that I should let go. Churchill said a fanatic is a person who can't change his mind and won't change the subject, and I think I'm a fanatically cynical bastard. What I need is a good crisis to help me clean house.

I know I could go stir-crazy here, and I don't like the image of getting drunk home alone in an emptied beach community, living out a clichéd version of rock bottom. I decide I'll leave early in the morning to get a workout at the Racquet Club, then get to the office. I'll be better off if I'm not alone.

My phone rings and it's William calling. A few days ago I had spoken with the lawyer representing William in the assault charge. It turns out the assistant DA wants to speak with William's boss, so the idea to include me had never been William's or his lawyer's.

"Hello."

"Hey, Nick. It's William."

"What's up?"

"The ADA is hoping to meet tomorrow at ten a.m. Will you be in the city? Can you make it?"

I'll have to do it sooner or later. "I'll be there."

"Thanks, Nick. I haven't even been charged yet, so my lawyer thinks this is a good show of confidence that I'm taking this meeting. The DA is One Hogan Place. I'll be in the office early until about nine a.m., then go to the meeting."

"Got it."

January 31, 2006

I FINISH MY MORNING SHOWER AND SHAVE AT THE club, where I keep a suit in my locker. I want to keep my distance from William's problem as much as possible, so I tell him I need to run some errands and won't be in the office first but will meet him at the appointment. I get a taxi to the DA's office all the way downtown. I haven't been there before, and the taxi drops me in front of an office building that looks as though the architect's instructions were to make it look as drab and depressing as possible. Across the way is Columbus Park, which has a few sickly trees, patches of grass, and benches sunk into concrete. Only Manhattan would call this a park.

Getting through security is easier than the airports. I put my wallet and watch in a plastic dish and pass through the metal detector while lawyers and staff with badges just breeze around the whole setup. There are three elevators and I take one to the sixth floor for our meeting. I step off the elevator into a main corridor that must be fifty yards long with small tributary halls shooting off the sides. The floor is the plastic-looking Kentile from the first half of the last century, made worse by the inconsistent fluorescent lighting hanging from a ceiling that hasn't seen new paint since they stopped making Kentile floors. The corridor is lined with cheap metal filing cabinets and natural wood benches outside the office doors. There's a big difference between a government office and a Bear Stearns office. For the price of one piece of our lobby art, they could redo this whole place.

I walk to the conference room the ADA has reserved for our meeting. A man in a suit is standing by the door and sees me approaching.

"Mr. Farmer?"

"Yes." We shake hands. He must be the defense attorney because his suit is too nice and his hair too perfect for a government employee. His hair is completely gray but so full and groomed it's hard to believe it's gray. It has the thickness that usually only a kid can have. He has a ruddy face and is otherwise unremarkable. Average height, weight, and looks. Probably relates well to a jury.

"Thank you for coming. I'm Alan Gallagher. The ADA is inside. Peter Jeffries. You can go right in. William is waiting down the hall. I'm going to visit with him briefly, then I'll be back and we'll get started." He smiles but it's awkward and he looks around. I follow his eyes and see a woman seated on a bench near the door. She's in a plain, matronly dress that can't hide her stripper body, stripper fake tan, bleached hair, and ankle tattoos. The clothes are overwhelmed by the woman. She's very attractive, though she looks like she's been crying. This must be the girl.

"That's fine."

William's lawyer opens the door for me and I walk into a small conference room as drab as the building exterior. Nothing on the walls but white paint, a single window with bars across it, and a rectangular table that fits six chairs that don't roll but need to be scraped across an ancient plastic tile.

Peter Jeffries stands from the head of the rectangle and comes to shake my hand. "Thank you for coming, Mr. Farmer."

"Of course." There's also a uniformed detective in the room, which is jarring but shouldn't surprise me. It's not the same cop who was at the Soho Grand.

"This is Detective Kelly, who has been handling the complaint. This shouldn't take much of your time, Mr. Farmer. The DA's office is determining whether or not to proceed with criminal prosecution in this matter. Your input will be taken into consideration as a part of our evaluation."

Lawyers always use too many words. "All right."

"I'll ask you a few questions about Mr. William Lansing. We'll begin once his lawyer is present. Answer honestly and fully."

I nod. We wait less than a minute in silence, then the door opens without a knock and William's lawyer walks in. The ADA stands, then sits without shaking any hands, more like someone bumped the back of his chair. I never leave my seat. I assume William's lawyer is here because the ADA wants to make some kind of deal.

"Let's get started." The ADA is already out of patience. "Mr. Farmer, your presence here will be required for only a short time, after which I will conclude my meeting with Mr. Lansing, then with the accuser." He clears his throat. "Mr. Farmer, I'm going to ask you a few questions about Mr. Lansing."

I nod again.

"Mr. Lansing is currently in your employ?"

"He's employed by Bear Stearns. He reports to me."

"Fine. As part of your supervision of Mr. Lansing, do you conduct performance reviews?"

"I do."

"Would you be willing to share these reviews with me in cooperation with my investigation?"

"I can fax the paperwork this afternoon. A lot of the review happens orally."

"In addition to faxing the reviews you have filed, and please fax from as many years back as you have, would you please also describe the nature of the most recent review you gave Mr. Lansing?"

"William got an above-average review. He's a reliable employee, he shows up on time, rarely calls in sick, works hard, gets along with other employees, and his sales numbers are above the average for his position."

"To your knowledge, have there been any disciplinary incidents with Mr. Lansing?"

"No."

"Okay. Fine." He seems like he's about to take a different tack with the questioning and he physically adjusts also. "Some of the following questions will be more subjective. Please do your best to answer."

I nod.

"Please describe, in your own words, Mr. Lansing. His character."

Jesus Christ. "I don't socialize with William much out of the office. We're very different ages and I'm his boss."

"Did you attend the party at the Soho Grand on the night in question?"

Goddamn it. "Yes, for less than an hour early in the night. It started as a work function for clients."

"Was Mr. Lansing there when you were there?"

"He arrived as I was leaving."

"So you occasionally see Mr. Lansing outside the office?" He pauses for effect. "For drinks from time to time."

232 | DOUGLAS BRUNT

"Yes." I'm starting to dislike the ADA.

"And in the totality of your experience with Mr. Lansing on these occasions, please describe his character."

He sounds smug and my dislike for him is probably going to play to William's benefit because I'd really like to shove something down the ADA's throat. "He seems like an okay guy." I sound a little smug now and immediately regret it.

"Does he drink liquor?"

"Yes."

"Frequently?"

"He drinks with customers. I don't know about other times."

"Does he use illicit drugs?"

I pause. Damn. Whether or not I do shouldn't be relevant, but managing an employee that I know uses illicit drugs could be a problem. "I've not seen him take an illicit drug." This is actually true. Thank God for private bathrooms.

"Do you suspect that he does?"

"It's possible."

"Okay. Fine." He's enjoying this but doesn't go after me further on this point. I'm sure for the purpose of this evaluation he knows William does cocaine. The police report from the Soho Grand would probably take care of that. "Does Mr. Lansing attend strip clubs?"

"Yes."

"Does he hire the services of prostitutes?"

"Same as the illicit drugs. It's possible but I've never watched him having sex." Jesus, I need to be careful.

The detective laughs a little, which is the first evidence he is listening. He otherwise seems bored and not motivated to pursue a case. The ADA is not amused and continues. "Okay, Mr. Farmer.

Mr. Lansing is accused of aggravated assault and rape. What is your reaction to this charge?"

This is the one I really don't want to answer. I've been thinking about it so that I'd be prepared but haven't been able to come up with the answer, so now I'm still stuck and hesitating. I want to be noncommittal, but noncommittal hangs him out to dry and I can't do that.

The ADA slides three photographs across the table to me. One is of the girl's face with a black eye and swollen upper lip. She looks like she hasn't slept in days. Her hair is oily and hangs in strings that are pushed out of the way of her bruises. The other photographs show raw and broken skin around her wrists and ankles.

I can't take my eyes from the purple and black colors that stain the young girl. The things I hate about work, or about anything, I keep at arm's length, but the ADA won't let me get away with that here. He shoves the images into me like a knife with practiced technique, then watches the physical changes in me. I can't just intellectualize about a rape anymore because it's in my face now. I'm staring at what the girl says William did, and I'm trying to keep my face still but I'm disgusted.

The truth is that I don't know William well enough to vouch for him, but I've known a lot of guys like him. Wall Street guys like coke and hookers, but violence isn't in the gene. They tend to get off on power in a different way.

"William's not a rapist." I say it though I'm not sure of it.

"Okay. Thank you, Mr. Farmer. We're done here."

"Okay." I stand and nod to each of the three of them.

I step outside the room and close the door behind me. I turn and find the stripper now standing by the bench. I don't know why I can't identify her as the woman and not the stripper, but I can't. She's looking right at me.

"You work with him?"

"I do." I break eye contact and make for the elevator.

She lets me get a few steps. "He's a sick bastard. He'll do it to someone else." She hurls the words into my back. In that moment she seems more like a girl and less like a stripper and I feel sick.

I don't turn but get in the elevator and leave the building. I feel too claustrophobic with my own thoughts to get in a taxi and I want to walk, so I head for that crappy Columbus Park and just walk in a circle around it, then sit on a bench in the cold.

Thirty minutes later my phone rings and it's William.

"Heya, Nick."

"Hey."

"The ADA indicated to her lawyer that there probably isn't enough to proceed criminally. Apparently there are some real credibility problems with the girl. I think she's cried rape before. Anyway, my lawyer headed off a civil suit and just brokered a deal with her lawyer for twenty-five grand. I'm sure your interview with the ADA was a big help. Thanks. It's over."

"You happy?"

"Extremely."

"Right." I hang up.

A minute later from my bench I can see William come out of the building and hail a taxi. He has a big smile. There's nothing about Bear or the DA's office or this city that will stop William or even slow him down. The only thing that might punish William is inside William, and that won't happen because the system is rigged to reinforce to him that he's doing things exactly the right way.

◆ ◆ ◆

An hour later I force my freezing body from the bench and get a taxi back to the office. I walk across the massive trading floor with coffee and an egg sandwich, navigating through the long desks like aisles in a grocery store. I have an empty and friendless feeling.

I see my vacant desk chair and Bloomberg terminal and wish I could pass it by as though it were a hallucination that I could medicate away. But it's still there when I get to it, so I put down my coffee and sit.

Before I've reversed my momentum to roll the chair forward to the desk, Jerry has a hand on my shoulder. "Good to have you back, buddy."

"Hey. You really had your eyes peeled for me."

"I need to get you up to speed. We have some telecom bonds we need to buy. The i-bankers are structuring a new debt issuance. You know the one."

"Yeah, sure."

"We need to buy up the secondary market bonds from the last issuance. Keep buying up to ninety-three."

"They're not worth ninety-three."

"They will be. Keep buying and push up the price. They want to see some upward movement in support of the new issuance."

"Crap."

"Ninety-three."

I eat my sandwich and make a few calls. The bonds are well offered at ninety-two, and I lift from a few different shops.

William walks to his desk across from me with a smile on his face suggesting that something must be going his way. Maybe the same smile he has always had, but today it strikes me that he will succeed in this place and without hesitation or compromise.

William's success will be different from the roly-poly and gruff Jerry Cavanaugh's. Jerry is indifferent to all the crap of our industry, but William enjoys it. He revels in it and will be able to manipulate it to work for him. I find myself staring at his face as though I'm alone in a room studying a photograph, and I no longer see a person but the face of a virus. A virus that can fill a suit and wear a tie and is massive in ambition, limitless and insatiable, consuming the physical world and destroying souls because it has no soul of its own to care for, sacrificing everything spiritual for meeting the primal with excess. Everything you can eat, drink, and screw and snort up your nose. But I know the happiness can be only on the primal level too, like a smile on a dog.

Still staring at William, I wonder what will be his happiest day. He's made it clear it won't be his wedding. For the birth of a son, I imagine he will spend the hours of his wife's labor with friends in a bar around the corner from the hospital and be very drunk when the baby arrives. His happiest day will not be connected to anything external to himself. It will be the day he consumed the most. The day he gets a ten-million-dollar bonus or a twenty-four-hour stretch in Las Vegas when he wins at the craps table, covers the spread on the Super Bowl, takes a few hits of ecstasy, snorts a gram of blow, and has sex with five strippers who are all sisters.

I know I can feel more than this. I can feel good and bad on an order higher than what is only primal, away from a virus eating through flesh.

I look away from William as though I'm coming out of a trance, trying to decipher the images that have just come to me and not conscious of how long I've been under.

On William's desk is the Jenny McCarthy *Playboy* centerfold spread over his computer keyboard. "William. We actually have a few women working here."

He seems to acknowledge but draw no conclusions.

"Why don't you put that in a drawer before someone has to fire you."

"Sure, Nick. Sorry."

I want to sit up from my desk as though I sense it causing an allergic reaction, constricting the air passageways in my throat and making my breathing weak and shallow. I feel like I'm cracking up. I need a vacation from this place. The days away have shown only that I need many more.

"Hey, Nick."

"Yeah, Ron?" He's gotten out of his chair and walked over next to me and is speaking in a quiet tone.

"Can I ask you something?" I can never get over the irony of this question.

"Sure."

"Do you think that it can be the same person for both love and sex or that the two things are different enough that it would have to be two different people and that to make it one person necessitates a compromise?"

I give Ron a look that I hope says I want no part of this conversation, but I make the mistake of not actually cutting him off. He somehow interprets it as curiosity.

"See, what I mean is, with love there's this trust and intimacy. That's all great but it's kind of safe and it's not the person you lose control over and want to tear her clothes off. With the best sex there's total abandon and maybe some risk and doubt and then physical heights. It can be aggressive and conquering and not so safe and trusting, with everything already explored and understood. It's wilder and dirtier and probably not with the person who would then be your first choice to talk about your favorite books with. And the person you talk about books with may not

be the first person you want to have crazy sex with. I'm not saying one person can't be good at both things. I'm saying one person
can't be number one in both things. There has to be a compromise
to choose one person. Right?"

"Jesus Christ, Ron. I don't want to know you like this. Go ask
William. He seems to have all this figured out."

He looks at me wide-eyed and blank. Of possible responses,
this is not one he had anticipated. "You're an ass."

"Exactly how you should feel about me. Get back to work. Go
sell some bonds."

I stand up and walk away before he can leave. I think Ron may
not be such a terrible kid and has about a year left to be saved
from all this. I could fire him but that wouldn't be enough to do it.
He needs to fire the industry.

I grab my coat and walk to the elevator and leave the building. I decide to walk to the subway station for the 6 train and the
walking feels good, like I'm occupied and getting somewhere. The
sidewalks are full of brisk walkers, but each is closed off from the
others like letters dropped through different mail chutes. Their
eyes are ahead and slightly down as they travel over a path they
have beaten many times before. Their focus is entirely on delivering themselves to the destination and not on what they may
encounter along the way. There is no interaction among people,
but possibly because there are too many people. To pass a single
person in an entire block would require a hello. To pass one hundred people in a single block requires efficiency and skills of self-
preservation.

When I stop at a street kiosk to buy a newspaper, I see the
most closed of all. His eyes averted, he looks ready to collect my
change and move me on like a package on a conveyor belt. But in
response to my smile and hello, his veneer cracks. In one moment

he mentions the plight of the Knicks, the NFL playoffs, and the weather. His pent-up niceness comes bursting through like a volcanic eruption through the crust of the earth. Each of the people on the sidewalk may have their own lava to come out with only the prick of a pin.

I tuck the paper under my arm and walk down the steps to the subway trains.

In my subway car alone I see East Asian, Indian, black, Hispanic, and white people, from young to ancient, from suits to tattoos. The mixing process is so complete that even in this car of thirty people, they're all here. This is the real New York, all the rest that is outside the walls of the investment banks. It reminds me how small and pathetic my life inside those walls can be. Rich but pathetic. I can't remember the last time I rode the subway.

I climb out of the subway near Union Square and start for the Cedar Tavern for an early lunch and a drink. I haven't spoken with Julia in a few days now, and I pull out my cell phone to call her. I dial her cell phone so she'll see my number on her caller ID and she can decide whether or not she wants to pick up.

"Hi, Nick."

"Hey. How are you?"

"Okay." She pauses. I guess we both do. "Where are you?" Her question is not accusing or demanding. Just soft and curious.

"I'm back in the city."

"How was your trip?"

"Fine." There's another long pause. I start to regret having called. It's too clear that we're talking without saying anything.

"Are you coming home tonight?"

"Yes, not till late, though. There's a dinner I have to go to." This is part truth, part lie. There's no work dinner but I intend to stay at Cedar Tavern drinking by myself until late before going home.

"Okay."

I clear my throat. I want to change the conversation but I can't begin to put the words together.

"Nick." She says my name but seems also to fail at the next words. She leaves it hanging in the air, and my instinct is to help it the way a person sees a pencil rolling off a table's edge and flashes a hand toward it by reflex.

"Yes?" I've helped. I wait again.

"I miss us."

I'm silent now, thinking about those three words, and in particular the last one. She didn't say that she missed me. She didn't say that she missed the Nick Farmer who is walking on Fourteenth Street on January 31, 2006. She said she misses "us," an entity neither of us has seen in a long time and which is possibly irrecoverable. She doesn't say she wants me to come home. She seems to say she wants me to go back in time and recover something I've lost, then for that person to come home. I don't know how to respond to this and so I tell her the truth. "I don't know what to say to that, Julia."

"No." She utters this, it seems, more to herself than to me. "Well, I guess I'll see you later."

For a moment I wonder if my interpretation of her words is too negative. She had reached out and I shut it down the way I shut down every other person's attempt to reach me. "Yes, I'll be late tonight, so maybe in the morning." She still seems able to open a door for us. I need to pull myself together and walk through it before it's too late.

"Look, I'm sorry. I just had to tell the assistant district attorney that a guy who is a piece of crap is actually all right."

"What?"

"Never mind. Can we talk later?"

"Okay. Bye."

I put the phone back in my pocket and I see the sign for Cedar Tavern a block away. I feel more tense than ever and fear that I've just made a colossal and avoidable blunder by not going to Julia right now, and the consequences are already falling on me like lead weight. I can feel the muscles in the back of my neck.

Cedar Tavern is so dark inside that it's a strange place to enter in the middle of the day. I walk to a booth in the back while my eyes adjust. I pass by the bar stools. I don't want the persistent and stalking presence of a bartender while I pass the hours. I slide across the leather seat of the booth and angle my back to the corner against the wall and settle in with my first drink. I get only a beer as I want a drink but also want to make it the whole day here and not pass out.

The booth feels safe and comfortable to me. I don't have another place to escape to. There's no home and no place of work I can run to. Like DiMaggio in his late years trying hopelessly to make a home of an upstairs room at the Olympic Club with not much to do but meet a dwindling number of old buddies and admirers for a drink in the club bar. I'll make it home eventually, but I think late enough and drunk enough to avoid a conversation.

My cell phone buzzes with a text message and I assume it will be Julia but I recognize it as Rebecca's number.

lost in the village—come help me ☺

I think about dropping everything and getting a taxi to wherever she is. Then I think about what I would do tomorrow. I think most single or married guys I know would jump at this, but I'm already so dejected with myself I can't handle the idea of it. It would be great for a few hours, then I'd feel miserable and trapped in a prison I made for myself. William's theory on this is right. If I feel that urge, it's safer and easier just to get a hooker, but I don't want to do that either.

out of town. ur on ur own

I stare at the phone in my hand like a woman waiting for the double lines of a pregnancy test and wishing I hadn't shortened *you're* and *your* to *ur* because it looks so ridiculous.

some hero you are

Right. I turn off my phone for the night and get a bourbon. I sip it and think of my phone turned off and feel that I've conquered some small thing. I start to drink a silent toast to myself and then decide screw it, I need to say it out loud like taking an oath. With bourbon at eye level I say, "You're a good person, Nick. You deserve better. Settle for more."

Anyone overhearing this would think I'm speaking to a departed friend, and I hope it does signal a death and rebirth. It's up to me.

I stare at the bourbon left in my glass and issue a silent challenge. In a violent sip I finish it. I don't only finish it, I vanquish it. I don't want any more, and I think in a few minutes' walk from this bar I can be to St. Vincent's Hospital to visit Jack. I haven't seen him in a while and I need to.

It had been a massive heart attack, and I know from William that Jack is still in the hospital getting tests. I hadn't thought of visiting Jack as something I would do, but now I'm certain it will make me feel better and might be good for him.

I walk into the cardiac ward and ask at the nursing station for Jack.

"Oh, Mr. Wilson," the nurse says, smiling. "He's made quite an impression on us already."

I take her meaning literally. I could make a joke here but hospitals always make me so damn uncomfortable. I feel like I'm supposed to be sad and respectful, so I don't say anything.

"He's in three forty-two. He's awake."

"Thanks."

I walk into Jack's room and he's lying in one of those mechanical beds that has his head slightly elevated. There are all sorts of wires connecting his body to machines that are beeping like crazy. He's watching TV and looks as white as the sheets.

"Hey, buddy."

"Nick!" He lights up seeing me but his voice is still weak. I'm watching the numbers on the machines like a hawk and I see one of them start to rise. I think it's the heart rate.

"You've looked better."

"Yeah. I feel fine."

"Good."

"Thanks for the help. I appreciate the soft landing."

"I didn't have a choice. You had a hell of a grip on me."

There's a chair under the wall-mounted TV and I sit. The room is all white with a little window looking over Seventh Avenue. We could probably squeeze two more people in here with all the machines and crap. "What did the doctors say?"

"They say I'll recover. I need to take it easy."

"Yeah? You're going to take it easy?"

"I am. No booze, no coke." He pauses. "No work."

"For how long?"

"For however long I have left. Hopefully a while."

"You're quitting?"

"Already did. Only took a phone call."

"When?"

"This morning."

I lean back in the chair trying to digest this. Jack is delivering this like happy news. It also feels like genuinely happy news. "Great."

"Chappy said to take as much time as I need but I'm done. I told them I'm resigning. I can't go back." He smiles. "The doctors said keeping on with a job like mine is a death sentence."

"Yeah."

"You and I knew that a long time ago."

I nod. "Yeah."

We're silent for a while, listening to the TV over my head. Jack is watching me, though. He continues, "I thought about getting out for years and never was able to bring myself to do it. In a way, I got off easy. My body put its foot down and it didn't kill me. It's amazing, but I feel happy. Even my ex-wife seems to like me now."

"She's been to visit?"

"Round the clock. She'll be back in about an hour." He puts his hands up to say, Can you believe it? "We've been pouring our hearts out, so to speak. It's been weird but interesting. Who knows?"

"Good for you, Jack." He looks calm and happy. He seems different. Better. Even the way he talks is a little different, like he stopped trying to win over the whole world all the time.

He can still read people, though. "How are you doing?"

The true answer is probably not as well as Jack. "I'm going to leave soon too. I'm going to do it."

"I recommend it. The water is fine."

A nurse comes through the door and goes straight to Jack.

There's no pause for an invitation or even a hello. "I'm going to check your vitals, Mr. Wilson."

"Hi, Krista. You know, the best a woman can look with clothes on is in a nurse outfit. I tell you what."

Krista the nurse has a modicum of cuteness, nothing more. And that's beside the point. Or maybe it just adds a very little something to the main point. It's clear some things with Jack are going to take a while to change and I decide that's reassuring.

Neither Krista nor I acknowledges the remark and she goes on about her business. It's a private moment and a good excuse to go. "I'm glad you're okay. Take it easy on the nurses." I stand and give him a handshake, picking up where we had left off the last one.

"I'll see you around, Nick."

February 1, 2006

I'M STILL THINKING ABOUT MY BOURBON OATH AND MY visit to Jack and I feel great this morning. The early trading has slowed down and I'm finishing up the *Wall Street Journal* at my desk when Freddie's number rings through to my cell phone.

"Hey, Freddie."

"Hi, Nick. Are you at your desk?"

"Yup. How are you?"

"I've been better."

I wait a moment for more information. "What's going on?"

"Nick, have you talked to your boss?"

"No. Why?"

"I'm sorry, Nick. I shouldn't have involved you at all."

"Freddie, what the hell are you talking about?"

"I've just been escorted from the building. By armed security guards. I'm calling you from the sidewalk, sitting on a cardboard box that has all my personal effects."

"They fired you. They actually fired you." It isn't a question or even an incredulous declaration.

"My report. What else could it be?"

"Did they say anything?"

"They asked if anyone worked on the report with me. They asked about you."

I don't say anything. My silence is a more effective prompt for information than smacking him across the back of the head.

"Obviously I told them you didn't have anything to do with it."

I don't feel relief. I don't care enough to feel it. "I'm sorry, Freddie."

"It's okay. This whole thing has stressed me out so much, I'm just glad it's over. It feels good to be outside the building."

"Now you can go sell your story to the papers."

"I don't think so. They made it clear that would be a very bad idea. There were two lawyers as part of my escort who made it clear about nine different ways that if I violate my confidentiality agreement, they'll make life very difficult for me."

"Jesus, Freddie. I'm sorry. Have you talked to Rebecca?" I'm also curious for an update on her generally.

"Not in a while. Not about this. I think she backed away from the story." He exhales right into the phone receiver and it sounds like a train in a tunnel. "It's like they're selling vacation property they know is sitting right over a fault line, and not only do they not disclose that to the buyers, they won't even acknowledge it themselves." He pauses again. "Well, if something happens now, I'll have a clear conscience."

I see my boss enter the trading floor and his eyes are searching and they land on me and he nods and starts in my direction. "Freddie, I have to go. Let's get together soon. I'm buying the pizza and Pepsi."

Joe Sansone has a bald head and the rest of his body seems to match the bald roundness the way a dog will sometimes match its owner. He has bright blue eyes that are the only attractive feature in an otherwise mass of unattractiveness that reminds me of Howard Stern even though he looks nothing like Howard Stern except for the eyes.

"Hiya, Nick."

"Joe." He's got an oversized smile, that phony son of a bitch. He's going to try for a friendly execution.

"You have a minute to talk right now?"

"Sure."

"Let's go downstairs around the corner, get an iced tea. It's almost noon. Maybe something stronger." Impossibly, the smile gets bigger and more fake.

"What's wrong with right here?"

"I have a few private things I need to discuss with you. It'll be better there. Come on, I'm buying."

I look over his shoulder to check for the thick-necked security guards. There are none. "Fine."

We take the elevator downstairs and walk all the way to the Bull & Bear at the Waldorf. A little too fancy for an execution. We sit at the bar and get two beers. A few other people have come for an early lunch but the restaurant is quiet. Nothing is said between us. When we've each had some of our beer, I decide I won't be the first to say anything. I can sit in silence longer than he can.

"Nick, I'll just come right out and say it." He's still forcing his smile and I want to knock it off his face. I wonder if I look as angry as I feel. "You're doing a great job and I want to keep you. I want to make sure the firm keeps you."

I'm washed over with confusion. "What do you mean, Joe?"

"I got approval from upstairs. I'm prepared to offer you a two-year deal at three point five million per year. Guaranteed. Seven million bucks to commit to twenty-four months." He slaps me on the arm.

I try not to look so shocked. I put my face in my beer for as long a sip as I can do. It occurs to me that the timing of this and Freddie's firing is suspicious. "Thanks, Joe. You really went to bat for me, huh?"

"Hey, I'm always supporting you, Nick." He's so fluid with his false pleasantness. "So what do you say? I can show you where to sign this afternoon." Still a salesman trying to close a deal.

"It's a two-year commit. I can't sign without running it by the wife."

"Give her a call. I can step outside if you want a moment."

"She's traveling with her parents for a few days." Now I'm the one fluid with falseness. "Can it wait a few days?"

He shrugs.

"It's a great offer, Joe. Thank you. I just need a few days."

"No problem. A few days."

We finish our beers and get another round, and Joe seems to have something else on his mind that he's trying to get to. "You a golfer, Nick?"

"Time to time. I like it but I'm not a fanatic."

"Me too. I'll tell you, Dale Brown is a fanatic. He's out on the course whenever he can be. A few times a week probably."

"Yeah?"

"Absolutely a nut. You ever golf with him?"

Joe looks over with a casualness that doesn't ring true. This feels like the area he's tried to get to and the source of all his falseness. "Once, about five years ago."

"Five years? Not since then?" He seems disappointed with my answer and tries to think of something else to cover his reaction. "We need to get you back out there."

"Sure."

"Dale's a good guy." His awkward probing for some link between Dale and me tells me the offer of a guaranteed contract didn't originate with Joe. He's as confused by it as I was a minute ago, and he wants to know where it came from.

"Great guy."

"Yeah, great guy." Joe hates not knowing the political map of the organization. There's something driving decisions from the top about his team and he doesn't know what it is. I'm enjoying his frustration. I feel empowered to start calling the shots.

"Well, Joe. Thanks for the talk and the offer. I need to get back upstairs to follow up on a few things." He has a flash of annoyance that he missed the opportunity to end the meeting himself.

"Thanks, Nick. A few days."

I do have some follow-up to do and I wonder if a few days is enough. I could put up with a lot of crap for seven million bucks. Maybe that's enough then finally to leave things behind.

February 2, 2006

SOME KID WHO LOOKS LIKE HE WORKS IN THE BACK OF-fice walks up to my desk. "Are you Nick Farmer?" he asks in a tone of apology.

"I am."

"Some guy outside asked me to bring you this." He hands me a sealed envelope that has "Nick Farmer" handwritten on the outside in block letters.

"Okay, thanks." I take it and release the kid by now ignoring him. I open the envelope and there's a single page with a typed message:

Meet me at the deli on the corner of 56th and 2nd ASAP.
I'll be waiting inside.
F. C.

Freddie has lost his damn mind. I put the page back in the envelope and fold it up. I'll throw it away in a trash can outside the building, just in case there's a legitimate reason for this idiocy.

It takes me about ten minutes to get to the deli, which is a typical-looking New York convenience store. It isn't the kind of New York–style deli that people who are not from New York think they should visit for real New York food. It looks like a tiny 7-Eleven that hasn't been washed in years. I make a loop around the single island of shelving in the small store and see Freddie isn't there. As I go to leave, Freddie appears in my path, blocking the door on his way in.

"Hey, Nick. Sorry, I wanted to see you go in first."

"What the hell is going on?"

"Let's move in to the back of the store."

I let Freddie pull my sleeve. This is too weird to argue about yet.

"Bear Stearns has had me under surveillance."

"You're nuts. Don't be a moron."

He pulls out a tiny piece of black plastic.

"What's that?"

"A bug. A listening device that I found in my apartment after they fired me."

"That's crazy. They would never try to pull something like that."

"Sure they would. They just hire a private investigator to do it for less than five grand. The PI gets money from a third party and he wouldn't even know he's working for Bear."

"You better be careful what you say then."

"It's late for that. There's more." Freddie looks sick.

"What?"

"They sent me a photograph."

"Of what, Freddie? Don't make me draw this out piece by piece."

"It's a compromising photo of me."

"Sex?"

"Just before, but I'm meant to assume they have photos of that too."

"Okay, so what? You should be pounding the table. You're not married, so good for you."

He looks away from me and at a row of cereals on the shelf. "With a man."

I let this piece together through my history of knowing Freddie. Poor guy is in hell. "So what, anyway? Screw them."

"I can't have that find its way to my mom and dad. I just can't even imagine that."

We're quiet for a while. "I'm really sorry, Freddie."

He picks up with what seems to be the main point of coming to see me. "Did you read my full report to Dale?"

This should come as no surprise. "No."

"I want you to understand exactly what happened. What the report means. They think you understand it anyway, so you should."

"Are you putting me in danger?"

"I think you're okay. At this point, having the information would protect you. Several people are already saying what I've been saying. Some hedge fund guys, even a senior trader at Deutsche Bank is saying anyone holding these positions is screwed. The only thing Bear cares about now is that nobody can point to a person inside Bear who was saying early on that Bear had the facts and knowingly pushed around toxic securities. That way they can just claim stupid instead of evil. I think either one is criminal, but they'd still prefer stupid."

I'm pissed I'm getting deeper in this with Freddie, but there's nothing else to do. "Fine, go ahead."

"Here's the sequence. The government passes legislation that facilitates and encourages every American to own a home. This may be the only well-intentioned piece of it. Well-intentioned but stupid because that set the table. Everything else is greed. Lenders start lending because that's how lenders make fees and profits. They lend recklessly and irresponsibly. There's a whole category of loan called a no-doc loan, meaning the borrowers didn't show any documentation at all about how creditworthy they are. The lender just wrote the loan and charged a fee. So now you have a bunch of bad loans out there. Really bad."

"Okay."

"Then guys like the ones you work for get involved. They take all these loans and bundle them into a security and claim the diversity of a thousand loans or so makes the overall security of a higher quality. Nobody actually looks at the individual loans within the security, but if you do, you see the security is going to be a mess. Normal default rates are two to three percent. If ten percent of the loans were to default, the security would blow up. If anyone actually does the analysis, they'll see these are geared for forty percent default rates."

I nod. It's incredible an entire industry could be in on something this extreme. I can imagine individuals doing crazy stuff, but not institutions all at once.

"The worst is yet to come. So far you have lenders making bad loans because they're greedy and shortsighted. Then you have banks packaging bad loans together and reselling them because they're greedy and stupid. Finally you get credit default swaps. These are so complicated, it took a while for me to understand, but they're basically like insurance and allow two things. First, people who have positions in these mortgage securities that tie up their need for collateral will buy insurance for cheap on the securities so they free up collateral for more leverage. The second thing is more interesting. It allows people to make a bet against the mortgage market. Right now, for about a hundred grand, I can buy insurance on a one-hundred-million-dollar security. If it fails—when it fails—for a hundred-grand bet, I get paid a hundred million."

I kind of know this but hadn't thought it all the way through.

"There are a bunch of hedge funds catching on to this already. And the guy at Deutsche Bank too. Part of the reason this can happen is the guys at Moody's and S&P are asleep. They should be rating these securities as high-risk, but they're putting A ratings on them. These may be the worst idiots of all."

"What am I supposed to do with this?"

"Nothing for now. There are a few people who know all this, but mostly people who refuse to believe it."

"Like Dale."

He nods. "One thing more. You're sitting on a time bomb. Most of the bad loans started the first half of 2005. These loans typically had a two-year teaser rate on the interest. At the end of two years, the real and much higher interest payments kick in. I'd say around May 2007 the bomb goes off. Things won't be the same around here after that. You should be prepared."

"What are you going to do?"

"I'd like to invest in one of the hedge funds betting against Bear, but I don't care enough about making money to get involved and risk what might happen if I do. I could talk to a journalist, but I won't for the same reason. I'm going to swallow it and walk away just like they want me to."

Somewhere, someone at Bear has sized Freddie up and knows he's not a fighter. They know he studies risk for a living and never takes any. They didn't care if he discovered his phones were tapped. All the better. That and a compromising photograph from an anonymous source would send him under a rock. "I'm sorry,

Freddie." He looks battle-weary but not broken. "Is there anything I can do for you?"

"I just need someone to know. It doesn't matter if it's only one person. I just needed someone to know the things I've told you."

Thanks a lot. "Okay, Freddie."

I walk back to the office realizing that I shouldn't be surprised that an industry made up of sleazy people would act sleazy on an institutional level.

I get back to my desk feeling exhausted before the day has even begun. Jerry is in my personal space before I can sit.

"Nick, Jesus. I have the story of the week for you. Maybe the year."

Jerry never has good stories. I don't know if it's in his retelling or if he just isn't clever enough to recognize the truly good ones. He grabs the back of a chair with one hand and rolls it around in a wide arc toward me in the motion of a rodeo cowboy getting a lasso started, and he plops into the chair flush-faced. All his movements and expressions are happening in double time. "What have you got?"

"You know Oliver Bennett? Investment banker?" Something odd happens in my stomach. The muscles of my midsection grip down tight on whatever it is, trying to control it, like hands clenching a slippery snake.

"Yeah, sure. I know who he is." I feel confident that whatever is happening to my expression Jerry will interpret as my effort to recall the name Oliver Bennett and put a face with the name.

"My wife's best friend and her husband live next door to Bennett and his wife. Somewhere on Fifth Avenue. And this gal and Bennett's wife have become pretty good friends. They've shared a wall for a bunch of years."

"Yup." I try to sound impatient for the story to end but am hanging on each word.

"So late last night my wife's talking with her friend because the friend had just spent a few hours with Bennett's wife, who was beside herself."

The snake is squirming fiercely in my clenched fists. I know vomiting would help me feel better. "At some point this story starts to get interesting?"

"Believe me." He leans forward as though someone put a strip steak in front of him. "Bennett's wife gets home last night and there's a voicemail from Bennett calling from his cell phone. He says all the normal stuff—honey I miss you, I love you, be home late tonight, don't wait up. Then he says bye and hangs up the phone, only the moron doesn't hang up his cell phone. The line's still connected and he has no idea."

This is starting to get good. No wonder Jerry's so excited. He's come across his first good story. "And so he started reading out loud from Verizon's income statement."

"No. He was with another woman."

I feel the blood drain from my face as though an SOS had been sent and all the blood raced back to my heart to try to save it. I let out a low whistle and lean back into my chair. I'm light-headed and have lost my balance and need the support of the seat back.

"Not only was he with another woman, but he starts getting into it with the other woman. Immediately."

Like a punch-drunk prizefighter after a blow, I try to keep my hands up and recover before the next words put me down for good. "Everything into the wife's voicemail?"

"Yup." Jerry nods, satisfied that he's impressed me.

The image of Oliver with Julia that comes to me is so real and vivid that I know it had to have happened. There is a level of detail in the clothing and the placement of limbs that I couldn't have painted myself but had to come to me from across the universe. For a moment I wonder if Jerry knows the identity of the other woman and he's come here to torture me or to find out if I even know I've been made a cuckolded man. I look at him with a new interest, as though discovering the rumor of something extraordinary about an ordinary person. But all I see is genuine enthusiasm for chaos. Jerry isn't so sinister as to come torture me under a pretense of ignorance. He doesn't know the woman is Julia. For the moment only I hold that information. "What happened?"

"Right after the dope does his non-hang-up, there's some rustling around and some kissing, heavy panting." I think of a split screen on TV capturing the simultaneous moments, one side with me at the Cedar Tavern behind a ring of empty pint glasses and the other side of the screen with Oliver and Julia throwing their clothes into piles around the room. I manage to say, "Huh."

"Then they go on to say they wish they had all night and it's the best sex they've ever had."

For Oliver this I can believe. Whatever Julia said had to have been just bluster. "This whole thing sounds like an urban myth."

"Bennett's wife played the whole message for the neighbor."

"Really."

"Over and over." Now Jerry leans back, swallowing the last bite of his strip steak, contented.

"What did the wife do last night?" I'm careful not to say the name Sybil.

"She dead-bolted the door and put a note outside that said, 'I hope you had fun tonight and don't bother coming home again, you can speak with my divorce attorney.'" Jerry's laugh is the kind of full, loud laugh you hear at a comedy club, with his body rocking back and his hands moving up as though trying to grab something for balance. Nobody turns to look though. There's already plenty of yelling and other noises on the trading floor.

This story is less than twelve hours old and already is racing around Bear. Jerry is so focused on the telling and not on my reaction that I'm in no danger of being identified as a character in this drama. And even so, the story is so bizarre that there is no inappropriate reaction. I could have passed out cold or jumped up and down on the table or anything between and Jerry would have laughed along with it. "Doesn't sound like there's any coming back from that. It's already playing out in public."

"This guy Bennett is screwed. This is going to be like lead around his neck."

"An albatross," I mindlessly correct, for some reason wanting accuracy.

"Exactly. It'll be the first thing anyone thinks about him the rest of his life. It's that good a story."

It is sensational, I think. Except for the part about my wife, it's sensational in every way. Oliver blew himself up, but I'm collateral damage.

I don't want Jerry in front of me anymore. I try to think of something to end our conversation and make him go away. "Wow, mission accomplished, Jerry. Good story."

"Incredible. And the moral of the story is don't be a moron. Hang up your goddamn cell phone."

Really? Is that the moral? "Yup. It's a new age."

"Okay, buddy. See you later." He starts his waddle back to his desk and I swivel my chair to change my view. I make several attempts to process the information and to conclude how I feel so I can pack it away like a fact I would write down and put in a filing cabinet where it can't touch me, but I can't reach an answer. I try more scientific approaches to solving the puzzle—if-then statements, and a plus b equals c. If Julia slept with Oliver last night, then I am angry. Then I am depressed. Then I am suicidal. Then I am homicidal.

But every time I start down a train of thought, it is obliterated like a TV screen going to white fuzz. My mind isn't functioning right. It's compromised and I notice I'm sweating and my heart is beating fast but not hard. It's beating with quick and tiny pumps that don't seem to move the blood but just blow on it lightly.

I stand up without knowing where to go next, and so I just stand by my chair. My mind is working furiously and producing nothing. I think maybe I should sit back down, but I don't complete the thought and I stand rubbing my hands over the top of my thighs in a slight crouch like a toddler wetting himself.

"You okay?" William calls from across the desk, not with genuine concern but with genuine amusement and a half smile.

This is what I need. Like hearing the siren of an air raid, it means one preprogrammed thing. Evacuate—get to safety. "Fine, be right back." My hands come off my thighs and start to swing in a steady cadence. I get to the elevators and my dizziness starts to pass and anger plants my two feet and straightens my back. I can remember our couples dinner with Oliver and Sybil when I lashed out at Julia by telling my version of her first sex. It was a weakness of mine to be so defensive and cruel.

Now I feel just as vicious but not weak. This time I'm an avenger. And this time I want Oliver first. I press the up button for the elevator and wait. None of the noise around me registers as anything. I take the elevator to the twenty-seventh floor and walk out to the right, where I know Oliver's office is. My walk is unhurried and my breathing is normal, but I can hear it like a scuba diver. My peripheral vision is gone. I can focus only on a narrow band in front of me and the sides are a blur. My veins carrying an extra force of blood are squeezing my sight.

Oliver's door is closed and I open it and walk in. "We need to talk."

His calm charade is stripped away and he looks up frightened and ten years younger. He's sitting in a lounge chair around the front of his desk. "Nick." His voice cracks. He's panicking. I must look as crazy as I feel.

"Now."

"Nick, I'm with people." He gestures with palms up at two junior bankers sitting on his sofa with laps full of binders and loose papers. He offers them up, hoping for a human shield. I only barely notice them.

"They can stay. They'll enjoy this." I sit on the edge of Oliver's desk. The three of them are sitting around the coffee table. The two junior guys look at each other and I'm looking only at Oliver. He's frozen. He's used to working with information and manipulating situations, but now he has no information. He has no idea what I'm capable of and I know he's worried I'll hurt him. I want to feign a punch and watch him leap out of his chair.

"Nick, please. This is out of line."

"How was my wife?"

The kid on the sofa closer to the door shoves the papers from his lap to the coffee table. "We can just go." He starts out of the room with the other right behind and they close the door after them.

Now I stand and walk slowly to Oliver with my arms crossed until I'm standing over him. "How was my wife?"

He's rigid and staring at me, waiting for the first punch and dreading it. I reach down and pull the glasses off his face. His eyes clench but he's otherwise still. With a lens in each hand, I start to bend them back and forth.

"I asked you a question."

"Did you talk with Julia?"

"Shut up." The wire bridge snaps and I toss the pieces of his glasses.

"Nick, what are you talking about? I—"

I cuff the back of his head, hard, the way I would hit a forehand. His head rocks forward and his shoulders hunch up, bracing for the next blow. He has gel in his hair, which holds it in an upright position like there's a steady wind blowing on the back of his head.

When another blow doesn't come, he lowers his shoulders and looks up at me. It felt so good to hit him that I know I'm going to do it again.

"Nick, please."

"Do you love her?"

"What? Nick, wait a minute."

"Do you?"

He doesn't know the right answer not to get hit. "Nick, I like Julia very much but there's been nothing."

"You're pathetic. You're just a toy. A plaything to her." God, I hope I'm right.

He looks like he's coming out of shock and looking for more conversation with less violence. "Nick, I'm not sleeping with Julia."

His face is angled up to me just so, and I wind around with an open hand that catches his head flush and sounds like a gunshot. It's as hard as I can hit and he doesn't expect it at all. I can feel the weight of his head go from heavy to light as I swing through, the way hitting a baseball or golf ball just right has the sensation of transferring beautiful energy.

My swing rips him out of his chair. His body knocks over the coffee table and he lands crumpled over his knees in a ball with his forehead on the ground. He doesn't make a noise and I'm not sure he's conscious.

I jab his hip with the bottom of my shoe to topple him on one side and I can see his face. One hand is covering where I made impact. His eyes are a watery mess and staring at me, both accusing and pleading.

I lean over him with my hands on my knees. "Don't ever come near me or her again."

He chokes out a few words. "I swear I didn't sleep with her."

"No? Not last night? Sybil didn't just kick you out of the house?"

"That was a hooker, you asshole. Not Julia."

He's indignant and definitely not lying to me. I stand up straight and breathe a few times. I don't have a chance to feel relief that Julia didn't sleep with Oliver, because a new awful feeling has taken hold and this time I'm not on offense. Jesus, this is bad. I got this very wrong. It's not a slow realization—I see it and feel it right away. I crossed a line almost as bad as sleeping with someone else. This is humiliating to me and more so to Julia. I can't think of a single word to say.

"I've talked to Julia many times but never slept with her. It wasn't like that."

It wasn't like that because she wouldn't consent to it. He's sort of guilty, so I don't feel as bad about hitting him. What I've done to Julia is far worse.

I walk to the door and open it. I can hear him rustling to his feet. I step into the hall and Oliver steps to the doorframe behind me. He has found new courage now that he knows I'm leaving and won't strangle him.

"She was unhappy, Nick!"

I turn around. Oliver is outside his office door and takes a half step back in. One hand is still holding the side of his face, streaked with tears. He takes a quick glance around to be sure there are enough people immediately nearby that he's safe. There are about a dozen gawkers, but I'm leaving anyway. I turn back around for the elevator.

"Unhappy, Nick! You hear me?"

February 2, 2006

I TAKE THE ELEVATOR DOWN, AND OUTSIDE THE OFFICE there's an open taxi at the corner as though it knew I'd be coming. I burst into the back seat and out of the cold and give the cabbie my address. It's nine fifteen in the morning.

What I've done is a betrayal of faith, and I did it publicly. Instead of going to Julia, I condemned her and looked for retribution. I need to get to her quickly to tell her what happened, to let her know it was my insecurity that blinded me. If she hears about what happened with Oliver from anyone else, it will be much worse. I picture entering the apartment, interrupting her from something, and holding her hand while I confess.

When I open the apartment door, I find her sitting at the breakfast table with her coffee just a half room away, surprised to see me. I felt prepared and ready only moments ago. Now I'm like a sprinting dog yanked to a stop by the limits of his tether. I stare at her while still standing in the open doorway.

"Nick, what are you doing home?"

It feels absurd to say, *I just punched out the guy I thought you were sleeping with, so I came home early,* but it's the truth. "I had an incident today. With Oliver." I pause. "I heard some things. Some rumors. And I made some assumptions. Some very bad, very wrong assumptions."

"Oh, God, Nick. What did you do?"

"I confronted Oliver. I'm sorry. I thought you were sleeping with him."

"Nick." She puts the coffee down and brings her hand up to her face.

"I hit him. He was sleeping with someone other than Sybil, but obviously it wasn't you. I should have known that. I should have just known that, but I thought maybe you were."

I'm expecting anger but there is none. She's just slowly shaking her head and not looking at me.

"I'm sorry, Julia. I'm so sorry. And I'm sorry it was so public. I should have come here first."

"Oh, Nick." Her voice is resigned, which is much worse than angry. "I wish you knew I'd never do that. You used to know that."

We're silent and unmoving. I'm standing and looking at her; she's sitting and looking away. My arms hang at my sides feeling useless and needing instruction.

"When did everything change?" she asks, as though she is trying to work out the answer herself.

She's right to ask. But it's hard to pinpoint. Our connection has faded, so slowly we didn't notice it happening until we started feeling unhappy and asked why. My job is the easy scapegoat. I'm away a lot, distracted when I'm here. We don't know each other anymore. She asked an important question and I'm working it out, but because of my silence she treats it as rhetorical and goes on.

"At least you still care enough to be angry that I might have slept with someone else. We've still got a pulse. I guess that's something. Or was it just your bruised ego?"

There's not much I can say.

She brings her hands to her lap and shakes her head one firm time. "I can't do this anymore. I can't be your wife anymore, Nick."

"Julia, wait a minute."

"It's not about what you did today. That's just an example of what's so wrong. You don't know me, we don't talk. Our relationship is broken."

It's broken but I know we can fix it because I know what's changing in me. I want to tell her that I've found myself again and that I'm right here with her. I hope it's not too late.

I'm coming up with my plan and she says, "We should have made this decision a while ago. We could have saved ourselves some pain."

"There're a lot of things I should have done a while ago," I say. "I'm going to do them now." It's all clear. I know I can never work another day at Bear Stearns. Keeping Julia, getting her back, is the only thing that matters.

She's only half listening.

I stand. "Julia, we're broken, but not beyond repair." I squeeze her hand.

"Nick, I want you to get out. You need to leave this apartment, or I'll leave, I don't care which, but I can't be with you."

I want to ask if she means forever or just for right now. Even if she means just for now, once I'm gone, she'll probably feel such relief that she'll realize she means forever, so it's better not to ask and make her face the question yet. I want forgiveness and to make amends, but she doesn't want me in the same room. I know enough about Julia and any woman that being pushy now will blow things up.

I feel motivation and suddenly clarity—the *Wonderful Life* moment I had thought was possible only in a movie. I just don't know how to share it. I need a plan that will give me the opportunity to prove to Julia that I can change in a true and permanent way. I can start by proving it to myself.

"Okay. I'll go." I walk to the bedroom to pack a bag and whisper a wish that she doesn't leave me alone to do it. I pull a suitcase from the closet and start to put a half dozen of everything into it.

Julia walks as far as the doorway but doesn't come in the room.

I stop packing for a moment and look at her. "I'm going to go to the office tomorrow for the last time."

She leans against the doorframe and crosses her arms. She's evaluating my statement and seems to conclude that it's not too little but it is too late. She smiles through tears. "I'm happy for you."

My instinct is to hug her and lift her from the ground, to tell her everything can be okay now, but I know I need to give Julia room to come to believe in me rather than to try to persuade her with words. She needs to have enough time to want to see me again, at least a little.

"Julia, don't answer me now. I want you to know that I love you. Those aren't just words. You're everything that matters to me and I feel that with my whole heart. I have no right to ask for it, but I want a second chance. I want to give us a second chance. If you feel anything for me still, if you think there's a chance for us, meet me tomorrow. I'm going to buy two tickets to somewhere quiet, some island in the Caribbean. At nine a.m. tomorrow I'm going to quit and I'll be outside the office by nine fifteen and I'll wait for you. We can go to the airport together and we can try a new start, away from here."

Julia nods. Tears are running down her cheeks and falling from the line of her jaw. They're not tears of happiness. She's too exhausted to wipe them and she won't make eye contact with me.

"Julia, I'm still the person you fell in love with and married. I hope you'll give me the chance to show you that."

February 3, 2006

THE TAXI TAKES PARK AVENUE AND I WATCH THE FEW trees that are planted in the median as we pass by. I can look up through the naked branches like cracks in a windshield. We turn on Forty-sixth Street toward 383 Madison. My breath comes easy. I'll walk through these doors for the last time.

When I was twenty-two coming to work, I never did things with a plan. I didn't do things based on how I wanted my life to be. I never stopped to think about what that life would eventually look like. I was paying the bills and living life. It all felt like a dress rehearsal and there would be plenty of time to get things exactly right.

But then the years go by and only belatedly do I realize there never was a dress rehearsal. It's all been happening in a single take and it all counts.

I'm halfway across the lobby to the elevators and I hear, "Hi, Mr. Farmer."

She's a small, middle-aged woman and I know the face. It's round and happy. Her clothes are inexpensive but neat and her hair is permed in a way that went out in the 1950s. "Hi, how are you?" My smile is real. There's something comforting about her. I remember that she works in the back office, processing trade orders. She's been at Bear for about two decades and might make fifty grand a year. She probably thinks I have the world at my feet, though right now I'm the one envying her happiness.

"Great. I like a little chill in the air. I'm going to get a coffee. Can I get you anything?" She smiles.

"No." I wish I knew her name. I'd love to be able to say it to her now. I'd love to be able to go back thirteen years to tell myself that it's an important thing to know and those are important things to care about. "But thank you."

For thirteen years I haven't been in my life, I've been hovering above it like a phantom, all the while with the nagging feeling that something isn't right, that I'm not real. Jack Wilson is a phantom too. A ghost who still thinks he belongs among the living. He can't understand the source of his confusion, why the only people who can see him are other ghosts, but he doesn't know that they're ghosts too. He knows only that they resemble him in some way.

With my mind made up and certain, I feel more powerful. I have nothing to lose anymore and everything to gain. I'm as eager to get upstairs as a child reaching to open a present.

In the elevator I press 6 for the executive offices, stopping short of the trading floor on seven. I roll my shoulders in a way to release tension and I find that I'm not tense at all and it occurs to me that the most dangerous person is not the one with the most strength or weaponry. The most dangerous person is the one who feels he has nothing to lose. I've tapped into this strength. I feel it flow through my body. My fingertips tingle with it. Nobody has a claim on me and I care nothing for a claim of my own on anything else. There is no consequence left for me to fear. It's liberating, exhilarating.

I exit the elevator doors onto the sixth floor, as though concealing my weapons through a security checkpoint. The sixth floor is nothing like the trading floor. Here there are actual hallways and partitions and offices with doors to close them off. There is no line of sight from one end to another, but there is a main hallway that runs the perimeter of the floor, connecting all the executive windowed offices like an old post road. On the one side sits the executive in an office with sofas and an expensive desk, artwork, and lavish furnishings and with a view of the city. Steps across to the other side sits the secretary in the more humble setting of a cubicle, wishing she had enough privacy to pull up solitaire on her computer.

This is where Dale Brown comes to work. I don't want to see Joe Sansone because my immediate boss might treat me as a friend, try to persuade me to change my mind and give me time to do so. I want this to be official, cold, and friendless.

I haven't seen Dale since the meeting with Freddie. I don't know if he recognized me then or will now. I know his office is in the southwest corner, though I've never been there. I get on the post road and start my journey south, then west.

When I get near to the corner, I strain to see the office name-plates out of the corner of my eye without appearing as though I need them to find my way. I see "Dale Brown, President" across from an alert secretary who is watching me coming. She's cute but not stunning and she seems to sense the danger in my gait. Dale hardly knows me and she certainly doesn't know me at all. She starts to rise, then hovers inches above the seat of her chair as though she's decided it's best to get in a ready position.

"Is he in?"

"Do you have an appointment?"

I don't answer and don't stop. I've already got position on her and I'm to the door. I turn the knob and step into the office.

"Sir, excuse me." I close the door behind me to shut out her protests.

The opening and abrupt shutting of the door startles Dale. He looks up from his computer screen. An expression of panic travels across his face before dissolving to one of annoyance. A man in a suit who must be a Bear Stearns underling has interrupted his reading. There is a flicker of recognition, and probably an association with Freddie.

"Can I help you?" He says this in a way to let me know that helping me has nothing to do with his question.

The door opens behind me. "I'm sorry, Mr. Brown." She snaps out her words and comes around to stand next to me, glaring and with the corners of her mouth pulled flat back toward the hinge of her jawbone.

"I'm Nick Farmer. I quit."

His eyebrows rise in symmetrical arches of surprise. He seems to be trying to decide if this is something he should care about before he commits to a response.

I don't care to wait. I turn and let myself out and close the door behind me and shut them in. They're left to stare at each other, each to confirm for the other that what they think just happened actually happened.

I retrace my steps to the elevator and press Down for the lobby. I see the 7 button for the trading floor and I think of all the souls trapped in there. Not against their will, but against their knowledge. I wonder if corruption can reach levels to be self-defeating, or if Bear will always be here.

I think of Freddie and his prognostications putting a date on the end of the world. A nerd-like Nostradamus predicting that Bear's insane bets and manipulation of securities will create a black hole. Once critical mass is reached, the global economy will crumple in on itself in an instant. Bear will be compressed to the size of a grain of sand. I imagine people and banks throughout Europe and Asia ripped from their foundations and screaming across oceans, the way things are sucked with violent force toward a gash in an airplane at altitude. Everything colliding into Bear.

Is a person like William the first to be destroyed, or does he show up in a post-Armageddon world like a cockroach? I'll find a safe place far from here to rebuild, and if the rest of the world has to rebuild around me, so much the better. I answer my own question as I realize William will survive too, because there's always a place for a soulless soldier.

Traveling down in the empty elevator, I already sense a change, like a fever breaking, and I think I could like myself again. Enough to be alone, and I hope that's the first step to not being alone.

As the elevator drops, so does my strength and certainty, because I don't know what's coming next. I never get nervous when I know what I'm going to do, and I had known exactly how I was going to quit. It felt like an actor was playing the role of Nick Farmer and delivering the lines I had already written and I wasn't there at all. But now I don't know what's going to happen. I can feel the nerves bunch up in my throat and my stomach feels light, as though I need to weigh it down, but I'm too nauseous to eat.

The elevator doors open and I hope to see Julia waiting in the lobby with a reluctant smile, but I know right away she's not there. In my periphery I can tell all the bodies are moving with purpose to destinations. No one is waiting for anyone. I circle the lobby to reaffirm what I already know. It's 9:15 a.m. exactly.

I walk outside to the cold air and the sounds of city traffic. The sidewalks are still thick with people though not with the crush of an hour earlier. I take a few more steps away from the building to look up and down the sidewalk, knowing I can pick out her movements from the crowd.

She's not there and I don't blame her. I'll wait until 11 a.m. for her, then go to the airport by myself and hope she just needs a couple weeks to herself before she'll see me.

I turn back around to move against the building so I'm not standing still in the middle of a stream of brisk walkers. My eyes stop on a woman seated on the backrest of a bench, at an angle so that I see her in profile. I recognize the posture and the tilt of her head.

Seeing her is the kind of gift that changes everything. I am the luckiest. I don't realize I've been holding my breath until I hear myself exhale. We have a chance.

She hasn't moved and doesn't see me. She's resting against the empty bench, her body facing into the wind like a seagull on a pylon.

ACKNOWLEDGMENTS

It feels funny to thank Megyn Kelly. She and I are so far beyond that. Not only is a "thanks" beneath the proportion of what she has given, it is also the least profound of the ways that we express what we mean to each other. But there are limits to the Acknowledgments piece of a novel.

Megyn is my biggest supporter and fan, despite the fact that she gets the first read of the first draft (before even I read it) when the novel is in its crappiest state. Her ideas for plot and character development as well as editorial judgment are unsurpassed, and her influence shows up across this novel. Megyn, thank you. I'll express more outside the confines of these pages.

Thanks to my agents, Lane Zachary and Todd Shuster, for being early believers in the novel and helping to develop it. Also to Jane Rosenman and Jacklyn Brunt for their early feedback. Thanks to Peter and Linda Kirwan for their support. Thanks to Manly Yates Brunt Jr. for instilling in me a love of literature.

At Touchstone, thanks to my brilliant, fun, and dynamic editor, Stacy Creamer. Her ideas and encouragement brought the novel to its final form. Thanks also to Meredith Vilarello and Megan Reid for educating me in the ways of the publishing world.

Thanks to Yates and Yardley. Their presence has changed my life and inspired me to reach for things that make me happy—things like this book.

Ghosts of Manhattan

Douglas Brunt
Reading Group Guide

INTRODUCTION

It's 2005, and thirty five-year-old Wall Street trader Nick Farmer appears to have it all—a successful career at top firm Bear Stearns and a beautiful wife. But after more than a decade of soul-crushing work in a field dominated by greed, drugs, and hypocrisy, Nick is looking for a way out. Yet the prospect of a bigger and better bonus keeps him tied to the lifestyle he now loathes. As this high-powered world of excess and immorality faces an unimaginable crash, Nick struggles to save his career, his marriage, and himself.

Topics & Questions for Discussion

1. Discuss the ways in which Nick Farmer's story echoes the classic Faustian motif of selling one's soul to or making a pact with the devil. Who or what is the "devil" in this scenario?

2. Nick describes many of his colleagues as soulless and seduced by money. Is Nick a hypocrite? How similar or different is he from those around him? Would you consider him an "outsider" or an "insider"? Is he a sympathetic character? Why or why not?

3. Substance abuse is a normal part of daily life for many of the characters depicted in *Ghosts of Manhattan*. What role does alcohol and drugs play in Nick's decision-making process? How does drinking affect his actions?

4. Each part of the novel opens with a quote—ranging from Friedrich Nietzsche to Guns N' Roses. How do these quotes foreshadow the events that follow in the narrative? How do they frame your reading of *Ghosts of Manhattan*?

5. Many of the employees at Bear Stearns feel they are above the law. What actions contribute to this attitude? Do you consider Nick to be part of this group?

6. "It occurs to me that in the same way a person can have a kindred spirit or soul mate that they seek out, a person can also have a nemesis that they would like to remove from their life, a person to conquer or be conquered by." (Page 70) Do you agree with Nick? In what ways does Oliver provide a foil for Nick's character?

7. How has Nick's tense relationship with his parents affected his choices as an adult? How would you characterize Nick's upbringing?

8. Were there any points in the novel that you found to be both humorous and unnerving? How would you describe Nick's narrative voice? How did this writing style relate to or mirror the themes and plot of *Ghosts of Manhattan*?

9. "Whatever the answer, I'm not sure I'm the type of person who can have a happy marriage anyway. I'm not that happy a guy and marriage isn't a magic ingredient." (Page 160) How would you describe Nick and Julia's relationship in light of this passage? How does their relationship evolve over the course of the novel?

10. When Nick quits his job, he doesn't appear to worry that Bear Stearns may threaten him the way they did Freddie. In your opinion, should he have cause for concern? Why or why not?

11. Do you think Nick can ever fully escape Wall Street's grasp? Consider the following quote in your response: "A happy career seems even more unlikely. Who the hell likes his job? Trying for more, thinking there could be more, is salt in the wound." (Page 160) In an ideal world, what do you think he should do next with his life?

12. Freddie confides his suspicions to Nick, whom he enlists as an ally. Did you find Nick to be a particularly trustworthy character? Were you surprised by Nick's reaction to Freddie's discoveries?

13. Discuss the role money plays in *Ghosts of Manhattan*. How are the haves and have-nots defined? What does money equate and what power does it hold over those seeking it?

14. What did you think of the novel's conclusion? Did you have any lingering questions? Were you satisfied with the ending?

Enhance Your Book Club

1. For another perspective on the financial crisis watch the HBO film *Too Big to Fail* (2011) or read William Cohan's *House of Cards: A Tale of Hubris and Wretched Excess on Wall Street*. How did these nonfiction accounts influence or complement your reading of *Ghosts of Manhattan*?

2. Discuss an area of your life in which you have felt trapped, similarly to how Nick feels trapped in his job. What changes, whether small or large, could you make today to improve the situation?

3. Read through the headlines of a current publication like *The Wall Street Journal, Financial Times,* or *The Economist.* How has the economy changed since 2005? In what ways does today's economic climate echo the events in *Ghosts of Manhattan*? Discuss with fellow members of your book club.

A Conversation with Douglas Brunt

You are the former CEO of a private venture-backed Internet security company. What inspired you to start writing?

I've always loved literature. I was very shy as a kid, and for shy people, literature is a great thing. It's a safe place to go. I'm a bit less shy now, but still love to lose myself in both reading and writing. The writing has generally been something I did as a hobby. During a fairly stressful career as a CEO sometimes in order to relax—usually on an airplane or on the weekend—I would choose to write rather than read. That's how this novel began.

This is your debut novel. Can you describe this experience? What was the most challenging part of the process? The most rewarding?

I had a clear idea for the big picture of the novel from the beginning. Writing the first draft was a pleasure, and as I mentioned, became a way to relax. The hard stages were the many iterations of edits and refinements when I hadn't yet made writing a career and didn't have a clear path to anyone other than family ever reading it. The most rewarding part was seeing how much better the novel became after those many iterations.

***Ghosts of Manhattan* centers around the now-defunct Bear Stearns. What kind of research did you do before writing *Ghosts of Manhattan?* Why did you choose to base Nick's story in the year 2005?**

I read a number of books about the financial crisis, including *Too Big to Fail* by Andrew Ross Sorkin and *The Big Short: In-*

side the Doomsday Machine by Michael Lewis, to name two. I worked as a money markets broker for two years in my first job out of college. I also have many friends and acquaintances who work in sales and trading in New York. Many of my friends sat with me to help create a credible backdrop for the novel.

I picked 2005 because the ensuing financial crisis allowed me to address the themes of greed and hypocrisy that I was so interested in. It also let me examine the ignorance of and disregard for the catastrophes that people with little apparent power can create.

How did you come to the title *Ghosts of Manhattan*? Were there any other titles you considered?

It came to me while I was sitting on an airplane writing the second chapter, though at that time I had a vision for the complete novel. So, I knew the message I wanted to convey with the title. It was the only title I considered.

How closely are characters—like Jerry Cavanagh, Dale Brown, and Jack Wilson—modeled or inspired by people you've encountered in the financial world?

The characters are amalgamations of people I know, have read about, or have heard stories about from friends. Fortunately, or by subconscious design, none of my friends is a match for these characters, though every sales and trading floor has them.

The novel ends before the financial meltdown that Freddie predicts actually occurs. What do you think Nick's reaction would have been?

When Bear collapsed, he may have briefly considered that karma exists.

You evoke New York City vividly in this novel and the particular time in which this book is set. How did writing about such a controversial, hot-button current event influence your writing? Was it difficult to develop this fictional story within that accurate historical context?

Living in New York is a great advantage for a writer. For a person who naturally makes observations, there is no richer place. The financial crisis is also a great source of material to work with. Taken together, I had plenty of places to go.

Do you see any part of yourself in Nick's character?

Had I continued to work in sales and trading as a career, I may have resembled Nick in some way. That's all I'll admit to.

What kind of conversations do you hope *Ghosts of Manhattan* will spark?

Primarily I hope it will spark a conversation about the choices we make with our lives. Happiness is one of those choices. Understanding what makes us happy, or unhappy, requires significant self-reflection.

What are you working on now? Do you think you'll write more about the volatile world of Wall Street?

I'm working on a novel that is set in the world of politics. I may return to Wall Street some day.